Fall Flip

Fall Flip

For Colleen—
Hope this renovation romance
brings a dash of fall fun!

Great to see you
at Durham
Apothecary,
Denise
Weimer

Denise Weimer

FALL FLIP BY DENISE WEIMER
Published by Candlelight Fiction
an imprint of Lighthouse Publishing of the Carolinas
2333 Barton Oaks Dr., Raleigh, NC 27614

ISBN: 978-1-64526-188-9

Cover design by Elaina Lee
Interior design by AtriTeX Technologies P Ltd.

Available in print from your local bookstore, online, or from the publisher at:
ShopLPC.com

For more information on this book and the author, visit:
https://deniseweimerbooks.webs.com/

Brought to you by the creative team at Lighthouse Publishing of the Carolinas (ShopLPC.com):

Eddie Jones, Shonda Savage, Jessica Nelson, Nancy J. Farrier.

Library of Congress Cataloging-in-Publication Data

Weimer, Denise.

Fall Flip / Denise Weimer 1st ed.

Printed in the United States of America

Praise for *Fall Flip*

With amazing, realistic dialogue, vivid word pictures, and brilliant storytelling ability, Denise Weimer has the ability to captivate readers and not let go until the end. After I read *Fall Flip*, this author is now on my must-read list.

~Debby Mayne
author of *High Cotton*, *Fit to Be Tied*,
and *Out of Pocket*

Denise Weimer's latest will have readers "flipping" pages faster than ever! *Fall Flip* brings a unique blend of romance and mystery as a former Home Network TV star helps remodel a home, and in the process, gets a few unexpected renovations to her heart. *Fall Flip* is the perfect novel to cozy up with for a satisfying Autumn read.

~Betsy St. Amant Haddox
author of *All's Fair in Love and Cupcakes, Love Arrives in Pieces,*
and *To Have and To Hold*

Acknowledgments

Any story begins as a seed of an idea in the author's mind. I'm thankful to God the Creator for that idea and its development into a story that strives to communicate love and truth.

The sacrifices of our families enable us authors to transfer that idea into a manuscript. I'm thankful to my parents, husband, and two daughters for their ongoing support.

That manuscript is then beta read by members of an author's launch team. I'm thankful to the behind-the-scenes ladies who volunteer their time as readers and social media influencers.

The author's agent shops the manuscript to publishing houses. I'm thankful to Linda S. Glaz of Hartline Literary for all she has taught me and accomplished on my behalf.

Finally, the right managing editor offers the manuscript a publishing home. Thank you, Jessica Nelson, for inviting *Fall Flip* to join Candlelight.

A general editor then labors alongside the author to polish the story for publication. Nancy Farrier, thank you for applying your amazing editorial expertise. And to all the proofreaders, interior design team, and cover artist. The staff of Lighthouse Publishing couldn't be more inspirational and professional.

Reader, thank you for investing your time in this story. All reviews are deeply appreciated, and I would love to connect with you on social media. I hope you enjoy *Fall Flip*.

Chapter One

The moment Scott Matthews strolled into the overgrown back yard of the Wentworth bungalow, life changed. If only he'd whistled a tune, or if the rusted metal gate creaked, he might not have startled the blonde woman sitting with her knees drawn to her chest on the stucco stoop. Her head snapped up. She shot to her feet, fumbling in a large, expensive-looking purse, and pulled out—

"Whoa!" Scott held up a hand, bracing for pepper spray.

Shelby Dodson clutched a cell phone. "Who—who are you?"

Everyone recognized the local queen of television's Home Network, but—big surprise—she didn't remember him. "Nobody dangerous, I promise." As Shelby's index finger jabbed toward the screen, Scott added, "Please don't dial 911."

Judging from the rapid shouldering of her purse as she backed away, she remained unconvinced. "Why are you here?"

Scott hooked a thumb over his leather satchel in a purposeful, nonchalant gesture. "I'm looking over the house for my clients."

"There are no sale signs. The house is off the market."

She thought he was a real estate agent? Well, appearances could be deceiving. He eyed her bright, sleeveless shirt, shorts, and flat sandals. If he didn't know the woman before him to be a respected interior designer, he'd think her a sorority girl. "Right. My clients are the couple who bought it."

"I'm not sure I believe you, seeing as how I'm involved in plans to renovate this place. I'm Shelby Dodson."

Scott's pride rankled at the entitled way she announced her name. "I know." The answer popped out in a tone much more sarcastic than he intended.

"Then who are your clients?" Raising her chin, she took a swipe at one wide blue eye, smearing mascara, and Scott's heart stuttered.

She'd been crying? All the bravado left him.

The Wentworths told him they'd found this 1920s bungalow—paint faded to a horrible mauve-burgundy with peeling white trim—in Augusta's Summerville district because of Chet and Shelby Dodson. Had tragedy not altered the plan, the house would have been the next featured flip on "Dodson's Do-Overs." At first, he'd feared the older couple lured Shelby back onto the job. But simple nostalgia probably drew her here, and he'd barged in at a sensitive moment.

Shelby tapped her toe. "What? Cat got your tongue?"

How could he tell her he kept silent because he felt sorry for her, not because he wanted to somehow trick her?

At that second, the phone in her hand rang. Her eyebrows flew up. "Aha! Your *client* is calling me back. We'll get this straightened out right now." A look of satisfaction settled over her flawless features. As Shelby swiped a long layer of golden hair back with a manicured hand, she answered with Southern charm. "Mrs. Wentworth—Ruby. Yes, hello! Thank you for calling me back so fast. … Right, as I said in the message, I could never get you and your husband off my mind. … Yes, I'm still here at the house, but a man showed up saying he's checking out the property for a client. I did hear correctly that you and Lester closed escrow, didn't I?"

Scott slacked a hip. Through the phone, he could hear Ruby Wentworth provide some information, then ask for a description. Shelby's impersonal gaze scanned him head to toe, making him feel like a scrawny ninth grader again. "Um, blond-brown hair, needs a shave …"

Scott frowned and rubbed his chin. He thought the slightly scruffy look worked.

"Green eyes. Medium build and height. About my age, mid-twenties, maybe?"

"Oh yes, that's Scott!" Ruby's perky affirmation carried from Shelby's cell phone. "Our new general contractor."

"Your new … contractor?"

Scott raised his eyebrows at the dismay in Shelby's voice.

After a moment of Ruby talking, Shelby looked at him again. "She wants me to put her on speakerphone." Shelby gestured to the stoop behind them. He edged closer, and they sank onto the steps. She laid the cell phone between them and pressed a button.

"Hi, Scott," Ruby said.

"Hello, Mrs. Wentworth."

"Ruby. It's Ruby, dear. Listen, I knew you were going over there today, so when I missed Shelby's call, I phoned her back as fast as I could. You know, some people would call this serendipity, but I call it God. It's positively providential that you both ended up at the bungalow. Shelby, when I got your message that you wanted to renew your offer to act as our designer, I did a happy dance."

Scott stiffened. No. Oh no. He absolutely couldn't work with Shelby Dodson.

Ruby's sing-song voice floated from the phone. "Lester and I hired Scott to oversee the physical renovations, but I have to admit, I wasn't looking forward to trying to design and decorate the place myself. Frankly, I could never have your special touch, my dear."

"Thank you."

So sweet … *now*.

"I've talked to Lester, and we don't see why you two can't work together."

Scott looked into the blue eyes that had looked right through him a decade before. He swallowed.

Shelby voiced what he could not. "Who would act as project manager?"

"Well, I understand that was your role, to make sure everything conforms to the overall design plan. We showed Scott your original renovation plan. We're proceeding with most of it, although there have been a few changes. And there will also be changes to the budget now, but how about if both of you come to our final walk-through tomorrow and discuss it then?"

Everything had just rocketed from simple to massively complicated. If Ruby Wentworth could witness the trepidation he and Shelby eyed each other with, her voice wouldn't sound so cheerily confident. In the beat of silence, their gazes asked questions, measured, assessed. Scott had already promised his crew this job right up to the Christmas season. Unlike him, they had families to feed.

"No film crews, right?" Scott asked Shelby.

She shook her head. "The crews are gone. Home Network didn't want to continue the show after … after we lost Chet. It was his big personality that drew the audience."

"I see." Scott looked away, partly to diffuse the sensitive moment, but partly to avoid revealing the very thing audiences liked had been the main reason he'd never watched "Dodson's Do-Overs."

A sparkle of moisture appeared in Shelby's eyes. "This is a private investment I want to make in Lester's fiftieth wedding anniversary present for Ruby."

Scott nodded. He respected the reason for Shelby's commitment because he respected the Wentworths. "Okay."

At the gesture of conciliation, Shelby said into the phone, "What time, Ruby?"

"Nine a.m."

"Thank you, Ruby, for this second chance."

It was the thickness in Shelby's voice that made Scott remain silent as she hung up. That and the fact that an adolescent awkwardness swamped him.

Shelby extended her hand. "Looks like we'll be working together. I'm sorry, I thought you were an agent."

He gave a faint smile. "Yeah."

Shelby's brows drew together. "I guess this does save me interviewing a bunch of contractors. You are licensed and insured, right?"

Scott nodded. "My liability and worker's comp are up to date. Would you like to see a copy?" He attempted to infuse a teasing note into the question. Didn't she realize she came across as condescending?

She sat up straighter and draped a hand across her folded legs. Long, tan legs. "Actually, yes. And could you bring a copy of the contract you signed with the Wentworths tomorrow for my file?"

Scott rose, then offered Shelby a hand. His mama taught him to treat women like ladies even when they didn't deserve it, but he couldn't quite avoid a deadpan tone when he said, "Sure. See you tomorrow." He started to turn away.

She let out a little gust of air. "Uh—wait. Aren't you going into the house?"

"No."

"Then what were you here for?"

Scott nodded across the knee-high grass to a white-washed storage shed squatting among thick-leaved hydrangea bushes. "Going to see if that's salvageable."

"Salvageable for what?"

"An outdoor dining spot."

Shelby raised her chin. "My plan calls for a pergola beside the stoop here with access from French doors off the master bedroom. And the white blooms of these paniculata hydrangeas would be better appreciated in the front."

"We'll see what Ruby thinks."

"She loved the pergola idea."

Scott furrowed his brow, preferring to avoid a full-blown argument before they even met with the Wentworths. Scott had seen Shelby on her show once or twice, probably at his parents' house since they liked to watch it. While the episodes framed Chet as being in charge, Scott began to suspect Chet had given Shelby free rein in her design sphere. She clearly wasn't accustomed to being challenged. "Well, a lot can change in a year."

Shelby's mouth thinned. "Yeah. It can."

Realization that the prior year had decimated Shelby's life hit Scott with instant regret. "I'm sorry, Shelby." He tried to touch her arm, but she jerked away, swatting at a mosquito.

"Never mind." She pulled her cell phone out of her pocket. "We should exchange numbers before I go."

Scott wasn't sure that would last past tomorrow, but after his blunder, he wasn't about to offend her again. He grunted in agreement.

Shelby caught his gaze. "What did you say your last name was?"

"I didn't. It's Matthews." He turned to look at her so he could witness the exact moment that Shelby Dodson reverted to Shelby Holloway … and recalled his identity. Yep. There it was. The mouth falling open.

"Wait. Scott Matthews, from Richmond County High?"

"The same."

Yes. The same guy who cowered behind her in high school algebra, too afraid to speak to the perfect girl who balanced running track, cheerleading, and As in AP classes. And now he got to fill the shoes of Shelby's brawny, outgoing, TV-star husband on her next house flip.

Chapter Two

Shelby didn't know why she felt like she should apologize again for not remembering Scott. They'd hardly known each other in school. He'd been so quiet she'd probably not have recalled her sandy-haired, scrawny classmate at all except for his frequent tardiness in algebra, as it possessed the unfortunate distinction of following shop class. She could still hear the other boys goading Scott—"Forgot to blow off the sawdust, shop boy." She remembered glaring at them, but back then, coupling the As her dad had expected with the athletics that guaranteed social acceptance had absorbed all her energy.

Shelby spoke over her shoulder as Scott followed her to the side of the house. "Wow. What are the chances we'd meet up again? Can't say I'm surprised that you became a contractor."

"Yep."

"And you live close by?"

"Near downtown."

"Your family doesn't mind urban living?"

He glanced at her. "I'm not married."

"Oh, okay." As Scott held the gate for her, Shelby studied the man. "You're still not a big talker, are you?" Granted, she had to admit quiet masculinity hung on his lanky frame a lot better than adolescent insecurity.

Hazel eyes, flecked gold in the sun, met hers a moment before something made her step through quickly. "My dad taught me you only talk if you've got something important to say."

Shelby widened her eyes. "Duly noted." As he smiled and latched the gate, she entered the rest of his number in her phone. "I'm sending you a text."

"Thanks." After checking his cell, he shoved it in his pocket. "What about you? Live close by?"

"Yes, in the four-square over on Meigs. Right after I moved in, Chet renovated the house as his first televised project. That was how we met. After we got married, it was our home. We wanted to move out to West Lake, but we stayed so busy that being in town was more convenient."

Scott nodded. "You can't top a house on 'The Hill' as an investment. And it's probably best now ..."

Now that she was all alone? "Yeah."

Scott cleared his throat. "What about your parents? They still on Carpenter Street?"

Shelby tugged oversized sunglasses out of her purse and slid them on. She'd never quite gotten used to strangers feeling like they knew her from a TV show, but now she wished Scott knew a little more so she wouldn't have to answer his politely intended but painful questions.

"Uh, no. My dad's in Atlanta now, and my mom just moved to Columbia, South Carolina, last year." She flashed a smile. "She went back to school, got her RN. She hated to leave Augusta, especially during my little sister's freshman year at Augusta State, but the hospital in Columbia offered her a dream job in obstetrics."

"Cool." Scott smiled, lightening the tension. "At least she's only an hour away."

"Right."

"And your sister's here. My stepbrother, Austin, is too."

At the mental image of the big, handsome football player Austin had been in high school, a smile quirked up the corners of Shelby's mouth. "I remember Austin." In fact, at one point, she'd thought he might like her, even though he was a good deal older.

"Everybody remembers Austin. Catch you tomorrow?"

"Yes. Tomorrow." Shelby waved.

As Scott Matthews gave her a backwards salute, Shelby headed to her Honda CRV. She'd parked at the end of the lot so it wouldn't be obvious someone was at the vacant house. She snorted. That had worked out well.

As Scott's black Chevy truck roared to life across the road, a teeny octogenarian enrobed in a flowered house dress watered a flourishing stand of knockout roses steps away from Shelby's driver's side door. The woman glared at Scott as he drove away, as though the mere noise of the motor disturbed her peace.

Shelby nibbled her lip as she approached. Sour-spirited senior citizens set her on edge. She never seemed to know what to say to make them happy—something she never had to worry about with the Wentworths because their joyful zest for life made Shelby forget almost half a century separated her birthdate from theirs. The neighbor stood too close to her car to ignore, so she decided to keep things short and sweet.

"Hello."

The lady gave a curt nod. "You and that young man buying the house?"

"Oh. No." Unlocking her door, Shelby smiled. "But we will be helping the new owners renovate."

"I hope the first thing you do is clean up the yard."

Laughing, Shelby recalled her first impression of the property, which a flipper was always supposed to remember. Yucky stucco trim, cracked and dirty driveway, and overgrown yard. The fact that all three represented simple fixes promised future curb appeal. "That's definitely on the to-do list, and I can promise you'll love the final result." Glancing back at the bungalow, she could already envision how fresh it would look painted gray with stone over the stucco. "But we have to tear up before we can fix up."

Giving the water stream a jiggle, neighbor lady pursed her thin lips.

Deciding extra diplomacy would be required, Shelby slung her purse into the car. "I'm Shelby Dodson, from 'Dodson's—'"

The woman gave her a half quizzical, half irritated frown that said she didn't watch Home Network, despite her immaculately tended front yard. Shelby pinched her lips together. Didn't matter, anyway. She needed to stop introducing herself like that.

"Betsy Lou Clark."

"Nice to meet you, Ms. Clark."

"What'd they pay for it?" Betsy swung toward her, frowning into the setting sun.

"Oh … I don't know if they'd want me to disclose that, although you can look it up online."

"Do I look like I go surfing online? I heard at church that they got it for $85,000, on account of the weeds and the roof needing replacing."

At the mention of the roof, the pit in Shelby's stomach that she was mostly able to ignore until bedtime opened up. In her mind, she heard the yelling again and saw the sun slanting over the empty gable, blinding her. In fact, the accident had happened right about this time of day. She blinked, willing herself back to the present. "Well, there's also a rotted subfloor in the bathroom, '70s paneling, and a dated kitchen."

Betsy Lou sniffed. "Hoity-toity. Folks throwing away stuff they'll go bonkers over in fifty years. Well, if they got it for under ninety, they did all right for themselves. Nod if I'm warm. As you can see, I try to keep my house up nice." She waved a hand toward her brick Tudor cottage.

Shelby smiled. "It's very nice. And you're probably in the ball park." Another cardinal rule for renovators danced through Shelby's mind. She needed to find out about the neighborhood. "So you've lived here a long time?"

"Ever since I married my late husband."

"You knew who the previous neighbors were, then?"

"Well, yes, don't you?"

The way Betsy Lou delivered the question jangled alarm bells in Shelby's mind. "No, should I?"

"You mean to say the new owners don't know the history of this house?"

Shelby glanced back at the bungalow, half expecting to glimpse a ghostly shape in the upstairs side gable window. "Um … I'm sorry, but what history?"

Betsy Lou shuffled over to baptize the phlox, Shelby following.

"All I know from when I first inquired about the house was that a middle-aged man put it on the market when his father went to an assisted living home."

The silver bun on top of Betsy Lou's head wobbled as she nodded. "David Barnes grew up next door. I remember him riding his red Radio Flyer down this very sidewalk. Can't say as he had a happy life, poor child."

The skin on Shelby's arms tingled despite the heat. "Why was that?"

"Well, when one's parents don't get along, that's generally the way of it. Charles Barnes had quite the temper, and Sharon bore the brunt of it. We could hear 'em arguing from our own bedroom, seemed like every other night there at the end. Come to think on it, that was right at forty years ago." Betsy Lou paused and gazed at the high-pressure sky for a moment, the flowers forgotten. Then she nodded. "Yep, autumn, forty years ago."

"What happened then?"

"Sharon disappeared. And never was found."

When Scott pulled into the driveway of the ranch he and his stepbrother renovated for Austin's bride four years earlier, he grinned at the sight of Austin's F150 beside Kaleigh's crossover. His older brother waved from the garage, his bulky frame hidden in the shadows as he unloaded equipment.

"Hey, man, thanks for coming over." Muscles popping out of his T-shirt sleeves, Austin ambled forward to meet Scott.

"Are you kidding? I never pass up a dinner invite. Or a chance to see my niece."

Austin gave him a hand clasp and half hug. "Glad you were free. I couldn't wait to tell you about the salvage from the Quillen house today. You'll be stoked. And Alexis has been asking for you. 'Scotty, Scotty! Where's Scotty?'" Austin imitated his daughter's high-pitched, pleading tone.

Scott couldn't mask his pleasure. Fifteen years ago, Austin and Austin's father filled a void in Scott's life he never expected them to, but the addition of his three-year-old niece, who adored him for some reason, warmed his heart like nothing else.

"So you got some good stuff?"

Austin ran the deconstruction company his father, Mike Culpepper, had started before Mike married Scott's mom, reclaiming old wood and architectural elements before it was considered cool. In fact, neighborhood kids had called Mike "the junk man," since he'd stored old doors and window frames in his back yard before purchasing his warehouse at Ninth Street and Broad. Now, the company worked alongside demolition crews at houses and commercial buildings slated for razing.

"Yeah, check out these pictures." Austin took out his phone and swiped through several shots of ornate mantels, spindles, and baseboards. "And look at this heart pine flooring. I mean, pristine. No telling what you could make out of it for the shop."

"Uh-huh." Scott rubbed his jaw and nodded, his mind whirring with possibilities. He put on the mental brakes before he could get too inspired. "But it might be a little while until I get free time."

"The Wentworth job's a sure thing?" Austin glanced up, brown eyes shining with the same interest in others that got him voted homecoming king and "most likely to succeed" in high school.

"Yes, but with an … addendum. It seems I have a new project manager."

"What? You don't need a project manager."

"The original project manager who pitched the renovation to Lester and Ruby in the first place."

Austin's jaw went slack. "You mean Shelby Dodson?"

"What about Shelby Dodson?" Kaleigh asked from the door to the house, amazing smells and a tiny person escaping from the culinary domain behind her.

"Scotty! Scotty!"

Scott could hear the voice before he could see the toddler as Alexis ran around her mother's vehicle. Picking up the little body encased in a bright, ruffled sundress, he buried his face in the child's honey-colored curls.

Alexis drew back and smashed both of his cheeks with the palms of her chubby hands.

When she let go, Scott grinned. "I missed you, pumpkin."

"I'm not a pumpkin!" She ducked her head and wriggled away as Scott blew on her neck. He lowered her to the ground and gave her a pat to send her back to her mother.

Austin cocked his head. "Dude, Shelby Dodson! Didn't you have a crush on her in high school?"

"When she had no idea I was alive?"

Austin made a face. "Sure, she did. She made the varsity cheer squad as a freshman when I was a senior. She talked to me every time I passed her in the hall."

Petite, attractive Kaleigh laughed. "Every girl talked to the star of the football team who was going on to play for the university."

"She didn't even remember me until I told her my last name." Scott ran a hand over his hair and quirked up a corner of his mouth.

"But she did remember you then, right? Man, she's gorgeous!"

Hands on her hips, Kaleigh exploded. "Austin Culpepper!"

He waved in her direction with the confidence of the happily married and addressed Scott. "Look how much you've got in common now. This could be your second chance."

"Now that she's lost her husband, you mean?" Scott scoffed.

"Yeah." Austin sobered and put a hand on his shoulder. "That was a tragedy. But it could be a perfect time to move in."

"'Move in?' I can hardly form a sentence in her presence. And I'm not sure I want to. She's really uptight. Before tomorrow's walk-through, she expects me to go home and make copies of all the paperwork I gave the Wentworths. I probably need a color photo booklet documenting every house renovation I've ever done. And I bet she's on the phone right now, checking to see if anyone's filed complaints against my crew."

Austin laughed. "Did you tell her you still live at home?"

"What? No! And I'm not going to. Shelby Dodson's walking perfection. It's disgusting."

Kaleigh helped Alexis up the steps. The toddler carried a big pink ball in her chubby hands. His sister-in-law called back. "A lot has changed since high school, Scott. Things probably aren't as perfect as they appear. Now, y'all quit talking about hot women and get in here, or you'll get *cold* homemade baked ziti!"

"Yeah, Daddy, come on." Alexis peered over the top of her ball.

Even though she was looking at Austin when she said it, Scott's stomach clenched. Was it his imagination, or did she look an awful lot like a miniature Shelby Dodson?

He cringed. Definitely his imagination.

Chapter Three

The first day of her new job, Shelby welcomed her cell phone's cheerful ringing. The silence in her house could almost make her miss even her fights with Chet. Almost.

"Sorry I was working last night when you texted."

Shelby almost dropped her mom's call as she let her white, ten-pound Malt-Tzu into the fenced back yard. She tightened her grip on the phone. Maltie's tan ears bounced as she trotted out to do her business.

Shelby blinked in the bright light. Coffee. She needed it soon, but today called for something more special than her Keurig could produce. "It's okay. I figured you were on second shift. How's it going?"

"Great! But I'm calling about you. I'm so excited that you decided to contact the Wentworths. Wasn't he that high school football coach?"

"Yes, from Schofield County. He retired, then opened a Southern-style restaurant. They sold the business, but they've still got their house on the market. I really admire him wanting to renovate this bungalow for his wife even though he has some sort of medical condition."

Concern filled her mother's voice. "What kind of condition, honey?"

Shelby ought to have known her nurse-mom would only be satisfied with a full diagnosis. "I'm not sure. His hands shake sometimes." Shelby perched on her patio chair, opened a compact, and applied mascara.

"Does it happen while he's using his hands?"

"Yes. I heard Ruby say something about essence … essential—"

"Essential tremor?"

"That sounds like it."

"Oh dear. That would be frustrating if he likes to cook."

"Is there a treatment?"

"Um, some medications, I think, and some try Botox, but it's not curable. I'm glad you can help them. And yourself too."

"Well, I need the money. Living here's about drained all the savings Chet and I put back. I was feeling pretty good about the job until I left last night.

Get this. They already hired a contractor who has his own crew. Funny, I went to high school with him."

"Is he that bad?"

"No, although he's so serious it will be nothing like working with Chet." Shelby wanted to hurry on to the next subject for some reason. "There's something else, something the neighbor lady told me."

"What?"

"Apparently, a young mom went missing from the house back in the '70s. The police and folks in the area thought the husband had something to do with it. They never found anything to incriminate him, but the case was never solved either. And had I been in charge of the escrow process, the Wentworths would have known about this long before the final walk-through."

"Oh, my goodness. Are you going to tell them?"

"Yes, this morning." She gave a slow blink in her mirror to assess the spread of her mascara-encrusted lashes. Yep. Perfect.

"Wow. Well, I'll pray it all comes out like it's meant to."

"I just don't want to be relocating a pipe under the house and find a body." Shelby shuddered.

Her mother gave a gentle laugh. "I doubt it will be anything that dramatic."

"That's what the people said who bought the 'watcher' house." Shelby wanted no part of that kind of real estate nightmare. "I did some Googling last night, but I want to make sure I understand Georgia disclosure law. You remember my real estate agent friend, Tasha Clausen?"

"Yes."

Shelby ignored the disapproval in her mother's voice. After Tasha had a fling with another man, her husband had divorced her. But that had been years ago, and Shelby employed Tasha for her business sense, not her morality. "I tried to call her last night. I'm going to try again today."

"Hopefully, she'll have answers. Listen, I don't want to hold you up."

"You're not holding me up." Hearing from someone who cared about her more than made up for the delay. "It's good to hear your voice."

Her mom's tone softened. "Yours too. I've been worried about you. I can't tell you how many times I've reconsidered my decision to move here. If only I had known what was about to happen."

"Mom, don't. You did what you needed to do for yourself."

Her mother released a sigh. "Well, I'm hoping that your little sister moving in will help."

Shelby rolled her eyes and snapped her compact shut. "Me, too, although I doubt she's gotten any neater after a year in the dorm and a summer with dad's flighty artist wife."

Mom surprised her by murmuring her name in a slightly scolding tone. Last Shelby recalled, her mother resented Tom Holloway's second wife … and with good reason. The grad student he'd had an affair with, ten years his junior, destroyed their marriage. But her mother now thrived in a new church in Columbia, and while she'd always been a Christian, God peppered her conversation more and more these days.

"What?" Shelby smoothed her hair. "You know what she's like. Aubrey's filled her head with talk of displaying Angelina's art in her new Atlanta gallery."

"Well, as much as I don't want Angelina moving there after school, if your sister has bad habits, it's probably due more to me than anyone. I'm afraid I overindulged her after your father left, and even more when I thought I had to compete with Aubrey."

"There's no competition, Mom." Shelby stood up and called Maltie, who sniffed around a tree. "Anyway, I guess she's still coming Saturday?"

"Last I heard."

"I'll batten down for the hurricane."

Although Shelby made a joke of it, Angelina's boundless energy might come as a welcome addition. They were so far apart in age Shelby hardly knew her little sister, but the idea of having family close again felt comforting. After the Wentworth renovation, she'd have to make some tough decisions. The businesses of two other designers flourished in her absence. One of them had opened a store at Broad and Tenth.

Shelby hung up and called for the dog in a firmer tone accompanied by claps. Maltie complied—until she caught sight of a squirrel and whizzed across the yard, trampling Shelby's flowers.

"*Now* you see the squirrel." Shelby stomped across the grass to take the errant canine in hand. "Ugh, your paws are soaking!"

When Maltie huffed happily into her face, the tan mask making the toy breed look like a miniature bandit, Shelby's heart melted. "Bad girl." Her voice almost cracked on a laugh as she kissed the fluffy head. After all, Maltie was all she had to curl up with now.

Settled on the living room settee with a view of the yard, Maltie watched as Shelby checked her belted, royal-blue dress and pearl pendant necklace in the mirror by the front door. A cursory glance around the room assured her everything was in place. She loved the modern art and black furniture she'd chosen against gray paint and white historic trim. The room popped with silver accent pieces and pillows, a fuzzy throw, and flowers in sunny yellow.

Swinging the strap of her black leather briefcase over her shoulder, she let herself out and checked her watch. Just enough time for a cinnamon latte from Buona Caffee Artisan Roasted Coffee on Central Avenue. She always marked important days with the frothy beverage made with the shop's homemade syrup.

Double-punch Mondays and three-dollar-latte Tuesdays drew a crowd to the converted bungalow, today being no exception. When she opened the door into the line, Shelby groaned and almost turned around. But then she smelled the coffee and realized Tasha Clausen stood right in front of her.

"Oh, my goodness. Shelby Dodson!"

Tasha grabbed her hand. The white linen suit that graced the Eastern European woman's model-esque figure made Shelby feel like a pledging sorority girl. Funny, when she considered herself professional and attractive around anyone else.

Shelby pumped enthusiasm into her voice. "What amazing timing. I tried to call you last night."

Tasha slid a strand of platinum hair behind her diamond-studded ear. "I was going to call you back when I got to the office. I went out with some girlfriends. You should come along next time."

They sidled forward in line. "Maybe." Shelby pressed her lips together, then admitted, "I don't go out much."

Tasha showed her white, even teeth. "That should change."

"Probably. I was actually calling you about work."

A blink, then a glow infused the cat-like eyes. "You're working again? Is that why you called, to ask me to show some houses?" Tasha had enjoyed her role as real estate star at the height of "Dodson's Do-Overs" success, arranging several potential flip houses for each set of clients to choose from.

"Oh no, I offered to help the couple who bought the bungalow we showed them last year." Shelby touched Tasha's arm. "Of course, you'd be the first real estate agent I'd call if I ever assembled a team again."

"Are you considering that?" Tasha slid out her wallet, inclining her head back to Shelby.

Shelby shrugged. "Not at the moment, but who knows what the future might hold." No need to burn one's bridges. As quietly as she could over the hiss of steaming milk, she went on to explain how she'd be working with a contractor the Wentworths hired, but how the unsolved missing person case related by the neighbor concerned her. "I read online that Georgia law doesn't require sellers to disclose any crime, unsolved cases, or paranormal activity for a property, but if the Wentworths don't want to move ahead when they hear about the Barnes case, is there anything to be done?"

Tasha got out a tiny notebook and jotted down a set of numbers and dashes. "Find out if they asked the seller anything about the house history, and I don't mean water damage. If they asked about crimes in the area or anything like that and the seller did not answer honestly, they may have grounds to annul the contract or ask for further price reduction. Maybe more. Here's the Georgia code number."

Shelby took the paper. "Thank you, Tasha."

"Here to help." Her blue-eyed gaze speared Shelby. "A perfect example of why you need to keep realtors in the loop."

Feeling chided, Shelby molded her lips into a smile. "I will."

"Skinny mocha latte, single pump." Tasha rattled off her order to the barista, then twirled around to jab her manicured fingernail at Shelby. "Keep me updated. I'm curious. Do I know the contractor?"

"Scott Matthews."

"Umm, nope. He anything special?" Tasha sounded skeptical that anyone of importance in Augusta could fly under her radar, and the admiring gaze of the college student behind the register reminded Shelby that Tasha moved in influential circles, as Shelby once had.

The girl offered Shelby a shy smile as she cleared the register to take the new order.

Shelby stepped forward. "Hi, Kara."

Kara's rounded face turned a pleasant pink. "Good morning, Mrs. Dodson. Will it be your regular today?"

"You know me too well. And it's Shelby. Please."

As Kara rang up the order, Tasha slid an elbow into Shelby's side, signaling her impatience for an end to Shelby's exchange with the employee. "You were saying? About Scott Matthews?"

"I don't know. He seems like a nice, normal guy, I guess." She shrugged, shoving aside her memory of the moment at the gate when she'd looked into Scott's eyes. She'd spent her whole life trying to be a lot better than normal.

Tasha summed Shelby's fears up pretty well. "Huh. Sounds boring. Of course, anyone would seem boring next to Chet."

The comment reminded Shelby to keep her defenses up. Working with someone new would be anything but easy, and she couldn't seem weak on her first day on the job.

Chapter Four

Scott had already been standing on the bungalow porch with the Wentworths for fifteen minutes when Shelby parked her navy CRV by the curb. Not that the wait had been awkward—because he liked the couple. Lester's hulking form and booming voice made him think of an older Austin, while petite, energetic Ruby, with her white hair cut in a spunky style and her stylish clothes, embodied the classic Southern lady. But the Wentworths were getting up in years, and there was no place to sit down.

"Good morning. Sorry I'm a little late." Shelby's black boots clicked a hurried cadence up the broken sidewalk.

"Oh, you weren't late. We were early." Ruby clutched her big purse in front of her. "We were just so excited to see the house."

When Shelby reached the steps, the effort to balance her coffee with her purse, remote, and a clipboard resulted in the loss of a few papers. "Sorry." She bent to retrieve the documents.

Softened by her clumsiness, Scott swooped down before she could reach them. As he handed the papers back to her, he caught a distinct whiff of cinnamon from Shelby's Buona cup—accompanied by a fresh, intoxicating shampoo scent.

"Actually, those are for you." Shelby pressed the paperwork back into Scott's hands.

The per-room checklist for every item and fixture, with columns for "good," "repair," and "add or replace" canceled out any endearing relatability. She actually expected him to check everything off today? Scott wanted to ask if she had brought a #2 pencil for his assignment.

"And do you have some paperwork for me?" Shelby didn't wait for him to answer, greeting the Wentworths with smiles and hugs. As Ruby cooed over Shelby's painful past nine months, Scott dug out copies of the line item estimates for each fix-it project, an overall budget, and the contract he'd already provided the Wentworths, then handed them to her with a flat smile.

"Oh. Thank you." She thumbed through, looking surprised.

"You'll find the contract specifies the start and finish dates and states I'll supply warranties for appliances, take responsibility for permits and zoning, and run change orders by all parties."

She nodded. "Good. I see on this fix-it list that you determined the water heater, HVAC, and fuse box all need upgrades. I'm not surprised. Most older homes we worked on had similar problems."

Pleased by her agreement, Scott provided a brief explanation. He wanted to get the Wentworths off the porch as soon as possible. While their expressions remained patient, Ruby kept shifting her weight.

Shelby studied the papers he'd given her. "Sounds reasonable. Just one more quick question. Do the prices quoted for each of the projects include all the necessary materials and labor?"

He paused a minute to make sure he'd heard her correctly, then replied with emphasis. "Of course."

Shelby fished a pen out of her purse and wrote a statement to that effect at the bottom of his estimate. She held it out toward him. "Would you mind signing that?"

With a glance at the Wentworths—who concealed their smiles as they looked away—Scott scratched off his signature.

"Thank you." Shelby tucked the list into her briefcase. "I'll run this by my Marshall & Swift after I get home."

Really? Not only did she question his word, she planned to check his renovation costs against a home repair manual? Scott opened his mouth to assure her his estimates were fair, but something checked him. Something about the way Shelby squared her shoulders and shot an anxious glance at Ruby. Like she was gauging if she came off as competent. Scott rubbed his jaw, glad he'd held his tongue. Shelby had been flipping houses forever, but Chet had probably handled the labor and construction issues.

Visibly softening as she addressed their clients, Shelby touched Ruby's sleeve. "I'm sorry for another delay, but before we get to the fun part, there's something I should share with you. I only wish I had known sooner."

"What's that, dear?"

Shelby proceeded to relate a conversation she'd had with the neighbor after Scott left the day before. She told about a young mother who had disappeared from the house some forty years prior and the suspicion cast on her husband, the previous homeowner. Ruby listened with a gentle frown and exclamations of dismay while Lester stood with his arms crossed.

"Did you ask the seller about the history of the occupants or any crime in the area?"

"Well, we did ask if there was anything important about the house we should know, and they said 'no,'" Lester said.

Shelby's eyebrows went up.

Ruby extended her hand toward her husband. "To be fair, we did not specify whether we meant the physical or social history of the house."

"Well, I did mean social history, but if I didn't specify that, they couldn't have known." Lester took Ruby's hand, and Scott noticed the tremor that often shook the older man's limbs. "Does this make you uncomfortable, Ruby?"

Scott frowned. This latest development could steal the older couple's dream before they even walked in the door. "And that's probably all it is, a story. I'm sure there's a reasonable explanation."

Before Ruby could react, Shelby turned to him in a huff. "Are you suggesting I keep such pertinent information from the Wentworths?"

He sighed, acknowledging her predicament. "I guess not."

"Good, because I couldn't live with myself." She turned back to their clients. "Miss Ruby, like your husband asked, does this make you uncomfortable? Because I can pursue legal action through my real estate friend."

Ruby studied the paneled front door. "When I was in the house, I did get this sense of sadness, but I felt with your remodeling ideas, and dedicating our house to God, we could make it a happy place again."

"I like that." Shelby smiled.

"And let's be practical." Lester held his big, wrinkled hands out, a gold watch glinting on his wrist. "The house has a crawl space, and the shed is on a more recent slab. It's unlikely we're going to dig up bones. If that lady was harmed, I can't see that she'd be here."

Ruby shuddered. "Poor thing. Maybe she was kidnapped—or fell victim to an accident."

"I can do more investigating for your peace of mind." Shelby quirked up a corner of her mouth. "And mine."

Scott thought it the perfect moment to unlock the front door. "Sounds to me like the Wentworths want to move forward. They liked your idea of rocking the stucco and painting the outside medium gray with white trim, Shelby, with the window muntins and front door a red-brown. I agree, since contrasting trim was common to Craftsman houses."

They walked into a foyer in front of a staircase, a bedroom to the left and the living room to the right. Someone had painted the coffered ceiling beams and fireplace built-ins white, but Scott knew most 1920s homes showcased natural oak and pine tones. "In my line of business, it's a crime to cover good wood."

"Oh no." Shelby walked into the living room and placed a hand on the colonnade—with columns balanced on glass-fronted book cases—that separated the living room from the dining room. "Dark wood would interrupt the flow of the house. Miss Ruby was going for airy and welcoming, weren't you?"

"I do plan to entertain a lot, and I like the clean look. I want to stick with Shelby's recommendation for white trim, and for opening the wall on the other side of the stairway and installing iron railing."

Scott's heart sank. *Tally one for Shelby.* "What you want is most important, Miss Ruby."

Smiling her satisfaction, Shelby came back into the foyer.

Ruby turned to her. "I do prefer rustic to contemporary. Sort of shabby chic. Can you go for that?"

Shelby swallowed and lifted her chin. "Of course."

Scott suppressed a chuckle. Miss Ruby would whip them both into shape.

He diverted the women's attention by patting a hand on the wall near the front door. "That brings up another thing we should discuss. As you can see, this isn't one of the fancy bungalows with plaster. The builders added sheathing, or what most folks today call shiplap, to the exterior walls. That was covered in cheesecloth, then wallpaper. Around 1970, the owners installed one-fourth-inch sheetrock in the main living areas and that wood paneling in all the bedrooms."

"Can't wait for that to be gone." Ruby rolled her eyes.

Scott chuckled in agreement. "We agreed to paint the sheetrock, but when we tear out the wood paneling, did you decide whether to hang drywall or expose the shiplap?"

"The shiplap." Ruby and Lester spoke in unison.

Scott made a note. "Good. It will save money and be easy to remove the top board for any rewiring and blowing in insulation. Not to mention, it will enhance the trim work."

Shelby came and stood close to him, looking over his arm at what he was writing. "Painting the shiplap, of course."

"Whatever you decide, Shelby."

Her face lit up. "We can even do wallpaper on accent walls, Miss Ruby."

As the women discussed color options, Lester wandered into the front bedroom. Scott followed. Shelby's plan suggested they make the room Lester's den.

They would convert the closet in this front room into a half bath so guests could use it rather than the master bath.

Shelby appeared in the doorway, frowning at him. "You need to stay with us."

"Sorry."

The way she pressed her lips together said she saw right through his false penitence. "I want upgrades to make this house feel luxurious, things like a digital HVAC display, a hot water recycler, wiring for under-counter lighting in the kitchen. I need to know we're on the same page as we go through each room."

"I'll get out my sheet."

Shelby spun on her heel and marched away.

Lester winked at him. "Best do as we're told."

They trailed the women through the living room into the dining room, with its bay window seat.

"Once this floral wallpaper is gone, I'm picturing a stencil above the plate rail." Shelby waved her hand. "I read that geometric or natural-styled stencils were popular during the 1920s."

The pointed look she gave Scott let him know she did her homework. Where it agreed with her style notions, he'd dare say.

"Oh, that will be beautiful," Ruby said. "And we're still good with taking out this wall between dining and kitchen."

"Yes, and putting an island here, painted gray with Carrera marble."

To Scott's surprise, the dimensions Shelby gave him were perfect. He nodded as he jotted them down.

"Can you order that early?"

"I can build that."

She blinked. "Cool. I want all the cabinets gone. The new ones will have distressed white finish with dark-gray granite countertops. Glass uppers in this section. Farm sink, gooseneck faucet, pendant lighting over the island."

"Wait, why are we replacing the cabinets?" Scott asked.

Already gesturing to the back door, Shelby frowned. "I always like to start fresh with cabinets. Old cabinets are yucky. Who wants someone else's gross stuff?"

He almost laughed. "But if you're not adding any cabinets in here except for the island, which is a different color, why not just replace the fronts and hardware? After a light sanding and my spray paint guy, they'll look brand new, and you'll save a lot of money."

"I like this guy." Lester touched his wife's back with a gentle hand. "What do you think, love?"

"I'm happy with that." The brief but tender glance she gave Lester fanned Scott's faltering hope that lasting love was worth waiting for.

"Fine. That's what we'll do." Shelby moved the check on her sheet.

Mike Culpepper, his stepdad, had engrained certain work principles into Scott like veins in a board. Preservation, practicality, and savings came first, trumping even Shelby Dodson's whims.

"Let's go to the master." Sliding a strand of hair behind her ear, Shelby led the way.

As in the front bedroom, the Barnes family had "updated" the back bedroom with gloomy brown paneling and brownish-orange carpet. All that would go in favor of bluish-gray paint and hardwoods. Ruby praised Shelby's plan of adding French doors onto the back patio and expanding the existing closet into the linen closet.

Scott measured off the section of wall involved. "That's going to make a long opening. What about if we used a sliding barn door? I have access to the right type of wood."

Pursing her lips, Ruby stood back with a hand on her hip. "Yes. That would warm up the room."

That seemed to spur an idea for Shelby, who rushed into the bathroom.

He followed her. "You're keeping the bead board trim in here, right?"

"Yes, I love it. What you said gave me an idea. I wasn't sure if we could fit a double vanity in here, but if I found an old dresser and painted it the color of the kitchen island, it would complement the barn door."

Ruby peered past Scott. "Now you're talking my language."

"*Yesss.*" Enthused that Shelby "got it," Scott extended his fist toward her, and she gave it a lame bump. But why was Shelby looking at him that way? Not angry, but pained. Almost sad. As if someone twisted a knife in her side. As his brows knit in a silent question, she made a weak effort to smile and walked out of the room.

By the time they caught up with her on the back stoop, she acted normal again, discussing the fountain and pergola. She didn't mention his idea about making the storage shed an outdoor dining space, so he suggested Ruby place lounge chairs under the pergola and allow him to supply a long, rustic table and benches for the backyard slab. Ruby loved the idea, but Shelby's frown told him he'd invaded her design sphere.

The upstairs bedrooms required only simple updates with the expansion of the shared half bath into a full. By Scott's standards, an easy renovation should produce a chic cottage for the Wentworths' extensive family. What would *not* be easy was working with the complicated Shelby Dodson.

As he drove away, he pictured the tears in Shelby's eyes yesterday and that look she gave him today. Annoying how those glimpses of vulnerability taunted him with the possibility of a connection. But unlike his overconfident brother, he recognized the impossible.

Chapter Five

"I hope you're pleased."

Shelby stood with a hand on her husband's tombstone and the damp grass soaking her sneakers. Until now, her commitment to redesign the Wentworth bungalow had felt like a memorial to Chet, a final project that might bring closure. But today, on demo day, Chet's favorite day in the flip process, Shelby felt she had to ask Chet's permission to go to the work site. If she could get peace, she could get strength.

Ripping out appliances and smashing down walls had best showcased her husband's strength and zany personality. Hyping it up for the film crew, he pulled pranks and staged daring feats. Sometimes, they captured an exciting discovery behind old walls—or, heaven forbid, an actual injury.

Shelby had no idea what a demo day with Scott Matthews' crew would be like, but there would be no laughter, no lunch break when Chet downed two subs and three cookies, and no sweaty hugs. But she'd promised Scott a check for another ten percent of materials cost and a labor payment, and she needed measurements. She'd pop in and out, then maybe she could salve her smarting emotions with an afternoon at the antique mall. The Wentworth project did call for a different style than most of the furnishings and decorations she'd accrued at their—her—storage building.

She left the cemetery, gloomy under the heavy, dark clouds lingering after overnight storms, and drove to the work site. Two vans and Scott's truck were already parked behind a metal dumpster. Grabbing her phone and her wallet containing the checks from Ruby, Shelby locked her purse in the car. Two men carrying a 1950s, raised-burner gas stove nearly reamed her as she stepped onto the porch.

"Oh sorry!" She and one of the men spoke at the same time.

Scott appeared in the doorway. "There she is! Guys, take a load off."

The workers, one tall and one short, but both dressed in scruffy jeans and faded T-shirts, lowered their heavy burden.

"Shelby, meet Hector, electrician." With his hammer, Scott indicated the shorter, Hispanic man, who nodded. "And Ronnie, plumber. They've already got everything disconnected in the kitchen. Guys, this is Shelby Dodson ... but you probably knew that."

Ronnie removed his ball cap and swiped at a hank of sandy hair with a grease-smeared forefinger, then held out his hand to Shelby. "Ma'am. A real fan."

"Thank you. Nice to meet you, Hector Electrician and Ronnie Plumber." Smiling, Shelby shook their hands.

"You too," Hector said. "Now we'll just get this stove out of the way."

Shelby stepped aside so the men could maneuver the heavy appliance down the steps.

Scott offered a grin and held the door open. "I see you're dressed to work. Sort of." He gave her a brief once-over, taking in her careless bun, flowing rust-colored T-shirt, and khaki shorts, before settling back on her face. Well, if he thought her makeup was too fancy, too bad. She didn't leave the house without it.

Shelby waved her hand as she walked ahead of him toward the kitchen. "Demo day isn't my thing. I'd get in the way. Besides, I'm not licensed and insured like you guys."

"What do you mean? There's a ton you can do without being insured. Demo, remove wallpaper, scrape paint, switch faceplates, spot paint. Didn't you help Chet with some of that?"

"Sort of." Shelby raised a shoulder as she moved around another man working in the empty space left by the range. With a pry bar, he lifted the Formica off a small section of cabinet. The refrigerator had also been removed, allowing her to envision the kitchen with stainless appliances and a custom vent hood. "I told everyone where I wanted everything, but to be honest, I only helped with demo and construction stuff if the producers wanted to include me in a few shots. Pretty much stuff they staged."

Scott stared at her blankly. "You mean you missed out on most of the project?"

She stared back. What was with this guy? "Trust me, I do plenty of work. There's a lot of shopping and planning in design—some of it on computer programs the construction crew never sees—and when it's time to decorate, it's all me." Sliding her phone and wallet onto the remaining counter, Shelby broke eye contact in hopes of alleviating the tension.

Scott shifted. "Uh, Shelby, this is Todd, my handyman."

The round, middle-aged worker with a balding pate turned to her with a smile. "Nice to meet ya."

"You too."

"Pretty much anything you want done, Todd can do, but we'd actually thought these kitchen cabinets would be a good job for you."

"Eh … how so?" Shelby turned with trepidation to inspect the hundred-year-old shelving behind her.

As Scott walked over and rubbed his finger into the groove of an antique hinge, Shelby couldn't help but notice how his T-shirt outlined a fit, if not bulky, physique, while the bill of a worn ball cap framed his long-lashed green eyes. "We agreed to remove all the doors and keep this section in place, but the paint needs dug out so you can get at it with a screwdriver, see?"

"Well, yeah, but I just stopped by with the checks, and because I need some measurements before I furniture shop." Save for a few favorite pieces of the clients', Shelby's remodels included full new furnishings. Otherwise, she couldn't accomplish the needed sense of unity and flow throughout the house.

"Aw, Ms. Shelby, you're missing all the fun. Check this out." Wood splintered with a familiar crack as Todd swung his hammer into the front panel of the cabinet section that would make way for an island. He palmed a sledgehammer and turned, offering her the tool. "You want to help?"

"Oh … no."

"Come on. In memory of Chet, take a swing."

Shelby blinked sudden moisture from her eyes. "No. Thanks." Right now, she just wanted out of here, away from the eyes of two strange men. This house should have been Chet's and her project, done *their* way. She turned away, searching for the checks in her wallet.

"Hey, man, I think Hector and Ronnie were waiting on you to help load the fridge," Scott said.

"Oh, okay. No prob."

As Todd trotted outside, Shelby handed Scott his payment. "These should reflect the adjusted amounts we discussed."

"Thanks." Scott refolded the checks and stuck them in his pocket without looking at them. "Hey, I'm sorry about that. Todd had the best intentions. Like Ronnie, he was a big fan of your show."

Shelby mustered a smile, but her face felt like she'd applied one of those green seaweed masks. "It's fine."

He rested a hand on the counter and ducked his head as if struggling with something.

With a tinge of dread, Shelby prompted him. "What is it?"

Scott let out a sigh. "Well, it sounds like you and Chet had a different way of doing things, and I realize this can't be easy on you. But you need to know something about my crew. *Your* crew for this project." He paused, seeking her gaze before continuing. "They're honest, hard-working guys who will stand on their heads to please you, but only if they think you're invested. If you want to get the most out of them, earn their respect, you have to be part of what's going on, not just give orders. Does that make sense?"

Embarrassment heated her face at the unexpected criticism his comments, even more than his question, implied. Her words hissed out terser than intended. "I'm not five."

Expecting the smart retort Chet would have given, Shelby's brain remained blank when Scott placed the handle of a knife in her hand. She stared for a second at the potential weapon before her eyebrows went up. "So I get to use this?"

A hint of a smile danced around Scott's lips. "On the hinges, not on me. Because I know you're not five."

"I'm telling you, handiwork is not my gifting."

"You don't have to be good at it. You just have to be willing to put in some elbow grease, and I'll help you. Please, Shelby?"

Why did he care? And why did she soften? "Fine. I'll do the cabinet doors. That's it."

Multiple cabinet and drawer doors later, Shelby sat on the floor of the upstairs bathroom, scouring the old linoleum in twelve-inch strips with a utility knife. How had she gotten into this? She paused to rub her back. As she looked up, Hector appeared in the doorway with a cell in his hand. He tilted it back and forth.

"Is this your phone? Because if so, it's about to blow up. *Bzt, bzt, bzt.* Even though it's on vibrate, it's really distracting. That under-counter kitchen wiring takes a lot of concentration, you know."

Shelby raised an eyebrow at Hector's petulant tone. "I thought you and Todd were taking down the breakfast room divider." They planned to turn a smaller portion of that area into a Craftsman-appropriate, corner breakfast nook.

"Finished with that. Todd's pulling up carpet, and I moved on to electrical."

Shelby's grin faded when she took her cell and looked at her screen, then swiped to open her messages. "Oh no. Oh no!"

"What? Did somebody get in a wreck or something?"

"No, but this is just as bad." Shelby struggled to stand. "My family's been texting and calling all day to tell me my crazy sister decided to drive up a day early!"

"You have a sister?" Scott appeared behind Hector, heat gun in hand.

Shelby ran shaking fingers over her bun, feeling one too many long locks trailing down her sticky back. "Yeah, Angelina."

"How did I not know this?"

Hector frowned over his shoulder at his employer. "Why *would* you know this?"

Shelby tried to edge around the small rock of an electrician. "She's—like—six years younger than me."

"She's up from Atlanta for a weekend visit? That's nice." Stepping into the small space she'd vacated, Scott plugged the heat gun in above the bathroom counter.

Shelby shoved the utility knife at him and started typing a reply to the last text while answering. "No, she's moving in. I've got to go. Now!"

Scott quirked a brow at her panic. "Sure. See you Monday."

Monday? Who said she was laboring here on Monday? Throwing Scott a perturbed glance, Shelby hurried down the steps. Already flustered with the man for coercing her from one task into another in front of the crew, she fought nausea at the thought of her father and sister sitting on her front porch since lunch.

But when Shelby pulled up in front of her tidy four-square, only a single, petite figure in a flowered romper perched on the top step, corkscrew ginger curls spilling over arms crossed on knees. A lidded Starbucks cup sat a few feet away while behind Angelina, it appeared someone had unloaded the contents of an entire U-Haul trailer.

"Oh. My. Stars." Shelby forced herself out of the CRV.

The slam of the car door brought Angelina's head up. She bounced off the step. "What kind of person doesn't answer their phone for four hours and doesn't hide a key under the planter?" Angelina compensated for her mild rebuke by throwing her arms around Shelby.

"I'm so sorry, I expected you tomorrow. As you know."

"Right, well, can't a girl change her mind? And get a bathroom?" Angelina clasped her hands in front of her and jumped up and down. "I downed a venti latte half an hour ago!"

"Yes, of course, if I can make it to my front door. You do realize my house is already furnished and decorated?" Fishing out her key, Shelby pushed her way past stacks of clear storage bins and crates holding small lamps, clocks, and photo frames.

"Ha, ha. It's mostly clothes and art supplies, but I did bring a few things that were *me*. That's okay, right?"

Gaze gravitating to a round lounge chair covered in a fuzzy, puce-green material, Shelby tried not to cringe. "Sure, but we'll need Dad's help. Where did he go?"

Maltie tumbled out the door, barking. Angelina darted in, glancing from the curve of the stairs on her right to the living room on her left. "Where is it? Sorry, I can't remember."

Shelby sighed. "Straight ahead through that door, into my bedroom." The four-square shared the same original problem as the Wentworth bungalow—only one bathroom downstairs.

Invigorated by the appearance of an intruder, Maltie chased Angelina into the master, where her sister lost the yapping canine with the slam of a door.

Shelby picked up the dog. "Shh," she whispered over Maltie's growling head, trying to also quiet the churning sense of impending hurt. She repeated, "What about Dad?"

"Oh, he left."

"What?"

"Yeah, I mean, he took me out for coffee, but when you still didn't answer, he unloaded and hit the road." Angelina turned on the water, then opened the door. Catching Shelby's expression in the mirror, she added, "Oh, don't take it like that, Shel. He wanted to see you. He really did. But he had an important dinner tonight."

"Sure." Shelby buried her face in Maltie's fur as the truth punched her gut. The dog let out a whimper. "Let's take you out to potty, then start clearing off the porch." Though gracious knew how any of the four small rooms upstairs could hold all that stuff.

Before Shelby could open the door, voices came from the porch. "Now who could that be?"

Coming alongside her, Angelina wiped her hands on her shorts and tossed Shelby a bright smile. "That would be Casey, my roommate from last year, and Lin, my best art buddy, here to help me get settled. See? No worries. It's gonna be a great year!"

Chapter Six

After a day spent squatting and kneeling, Shelby's leg muscles protested her fourth trip up the stairs in her four-square. She tried to hurry because she wanted to help strike a balance between Angelina's eclectic style and her home's modern chic. But when she reached the bedroom door, she could hardly get inside. The girls had strewn bubble wrap and newspapers over every square inch of carpet as they dove into boxes to unpack decorations and pictures.

Shoving aside a blanket, she lowered the hamper she carried to the floor. "Just try to keep it all up here, okay?" Shelby offered a lame grin as she backed away.

"We will, big sis." Angelina turned to her with her arms stretched around a bright bedspread in a plastic zipper bag. "Is it okay if I put my own comforter on the bed? I like to lie on top when I'm studying and don't want to mess yours up."

Shelby glanced at the muted print, elegant Pine Cone Hill comforter that tied everything together. How could anyone not be delighted with it? She and Chet had shopped for each decoration together, and it seemed disloyal to move anything, even for her sister. But she wanted Angelina to feel at home. If she didn't, she might not stay. "Sure."

As Angelina folded up the comforter, Shelby held her arms out.

"You can probably store this too." Casey nestled a Mary Jurek hammered silver bowl atop the bed linens. "Doesn't really go with Ang's look."

"Okay. I might use this in the renovation. About dinner …"

"Oh, I'm starving!" Angelina cried.

Shelby smiled. "I thought I'd run out and pick something up. Do y'all like Mexican?" In truth, she needed to soothe her flustered emotions with a stroll along River Walk to her favorite Mexican restaurant at Eighth Street. Scott's and Angelina's changes were in a single day sweeping away any remaining evidence of Shelby's old life.

"Sure." Lin looked up from testing Angelina's bulletin board against the far wall. "We like Mexican. Thanks!"

No one offered any money.

Shelby nodded and backed out. Boxing up the decorations, Shelby wondered if this was her life now. The big sister who provided a laundry and meal stop for college students. Maybe she should just go ahead and hang some Greek letters on the porch. She giggled. That could be funny.

In the shower, hot water washed away the grime of Shelby's first real demo day. Scott had been right, she'd felt a sense of accomplishment when she'd finished the cabinets. So what if Ang showed up early? And her dad left? Like that was something new. Why did she feel so off-kilter?

Maybe because today reminded her how little control she had over her life. One second, you could have everything. The next, it all could disappear. No more marriage. No more admiring friends. No more plan for a family of your own. No more career. She was no one now.

Shelby scrunched into her fluffy bath towel, trying to shake the feeling of wanting to disappear, that same feeling she'd get when Chet was mad at her, not talking to her. Small and alone … but worse, because even though they'd fought a lot, she'd known someone stronger stood between her and the world. Now, she had to face reality. Other people were changing the course of her life. Everything Shelby once thought she could count on had faded.

I'm still here, a voice whispered in her head. *I will never leave you nor forsake you.*

A sense of comfort stirred, a remnant of the faith that had been strong when her family remained intact, before she went out on her own and married Chet. And with it, the sense that God might want more control of her future than she'd granted Him in the past.

A walk by the river would help. She needed fresh air and the chance to think. She couldn't let the Wentworth project consume all her focus. She had to start planning for the future.

After a quick blow dry, Shelby changed into athletic clothes. From the sounds of laughter and quiet talking, the girls were taking a break from the unpacking, no doubt clustered on that gaudy bedspread. Shelby shoved aside a twinge of jealousy and grabbed her purse, calling upstairs that she was heading out.

She parked near the head of the River Walk at Tenth Street and descended to the lower level. As usual, the brick walkways, mature trees, and breeze off the Savannah River soothed her. Sparkling like diamonds in the sun, water sluiced off the oars of a college rowing crew, while a tug boat belched a short blast from the South Carolina side.

Some of her business owner friends might know of good lease options downtown. She could start her own interior design firm, capitalizing on her success from "Dodson's Do-Overs" before the market grew cold. Perhaps she could even open a shop like her main competitor, Julian Etier, who, on the few occasions she'd met him, behaved as though the TV show cheapened her talent. But now, no one could fault her for returning to her original plan before she met Chet and they started flipping—and filming.

By the time she reached the restaurant, she'd decided dinner provided a good opportunity to get to know her sister's friends. Shelby ordered two family packs and felt in her purse for her wallet. Compact, cell phone, gum, pen, but no wallet. The dark-haired owner stared at her. She snatched the purse open and pawed around inside. A memory formed of laying her wallet and phone down in the Wentworths' kitchen before Scott put her to work. Later, Todd had brought the cell phone but not the wallet, and she'd run out to meet Angelina. She closed her eyes. "I'm sorry. I left my wallet at work."

"Then I'm sorry, but I have to clear the order."

"I understand." Murmuring apologies to the couple behind her, Shelby moved away from the register.

As the sun dipped on the horizon, tinging the river with orange, the walk back to her car seemed to take forever. Shelby's stomach rumbled. She was half surprised her CRV started. She'd go back to the house and see if Angelina and her friends wanted to order a pizza or ride with her to retrieve her wallet, then go out to eat.

But when Shelby pulled up at home, she had to park on the curb because not only the Civic belonging to one of the girls but a black Chevy truck occupied her short driveway. Scott Matthews? What was he doing here?

Voices and laughter competed with the volume on the TV. The scene through the front window revealed Scott, Angelina, Casey, and Lin seated with their feet on the glass coffee table, eating tortilla chips and salsa out of a big pottery bowl. A white-and-tan ball of fur curled on Scott's leg.

Outside the door, Shelby froze when she recognized a voice she hadn't heard in nine months. Chet. She identified an episode of "Dodson's Do-Overs," not a regular renovation, but the bloopers show from the end of season two. Chet's bloopers had been intentional. Hers had showcased her lack of fix-it know-how or pranks played on her by Chet and his crew.

One such prank repeated on the screen in vivid color as Shelby let herself into the foyer. With a finger over his lips, Chet placed a mouse flattened into a trap on the other side of a paneling wall. Shelby entered and agreed to help remove the wall. When she reached down for a fallen piece of paneling and instead touched the dead rodent, she screamed and ran out into the front yard of the 1950s ranch. Chet followed her, hugging her and laughing while she pummeled his chest.

Shelby was still remembering the feel of those muscular arms around her when Angelina hit the fast forward button. "Check this one out," she said to Scott. "She's trying to nail two boards together and hammers her own thumb. This is why I can't believe you had her working all day without hurting herself. I mean, she can hang pictures, but that's about where handy ends with my sister."

The DVD zoomed to Shelby's pouty face. Everything was perfect, the outfit, the make-up, even on demo day. All except for a strand of hair making a wild loop, courtesy of Chet's rough-housing. On the playback she said, "I'm really mad at him this time." She held up a bandaged thumb. "Almost as mad that I ruined a fresh manicure."

The girls laughed while Scott said, "Wow."

At that moment, they noticed Shelby standing there. Angelina sat up straight and hit the pause button, leaving the tousle-headed TV Shelby in a grimace. "Oh hey, Shelby! We didn't know you were home. Scott couldn't believe you didn't work at all on 'Dodson's Do-Overs.' Well, you know, '*work*' as in physical labor. Can you believe he never watched a single episode before now?"

"That wasn't a regular episode. And you know Chet planned stuff with the production crew just to get entertaining footage." Her voice sounded tight. She'd thought people found Chet clowning around at her expense endearing, but the perspective gained with time and distance made her wonder if she'd always looked just as foolish as she felt right now.

As Scott leaned forward, Maltie jumped down and trotted over. Bending down to scoop her up, Shelby addressed Scott. "What are you doing here?"

He lifted her wallet from the coffee table. "Brought this from the site." Before she could pose her next question, he said, "Your address is on your driver's license."

"Oh. Of course."

"And he helped us move some stuff around." Lin's almond eyes glowed with approval as she glanced at the contractor.

Shelby caught sight of the puce-green chair as Scott stood up. "*What* is that doing in my living room?"

"You don't have a single place in this room to just relax," Angelina said. "I mean, half of these white, fussy chairs don't even have cushy backs. And see? My wildflower watercolor ties it all together. Just two little things down here, that's all."

"We took the adjoining bedroom to be Angelina's art studio." Lin tilted her head, clasping her hands under her chin. "We hope you don't mind. She just had too much stuff."

"You aren't using it for anything, anyway, right?" Angelina fluttered her ginger lashes and shot Shelby a hopeful grin.

Shelby took a deep breath. Then another. "That's fine." She bared her teeth in a smile. "Thank you for bringing my wallet, Scott. And now, I am going into the kitchen to order a pizza, and then I am going to bed. After which time you girls can watch any number of embarrassing out-takes you desire, as long as you refrain from laughing too loud. And I will see *you* Monday, Mr. Matthews."

"Ew, you went from 'Scott' to 'Mr. Matthews' in one paragraph." Casey's neat brown bob framed her perfectly rounded eyes.

"And I think she stopped using contractions." Lin shook her head. "That could be a bad sign."

Scott made his way past the girls. "I noticed that too."

Angelina waved a tortilla chip, then dunked it into salsa. "Oh, don't mind her. She's always that way." She leaned over the bowl, crunching a bite. "When I was growing up, she had all these U.S. Girl dolls in her room, only she kept them on this high shelf. She was too old to play with them anymore, but of course, she wouldn't let me touch them."

Shelby flashed Angelina an accusing glare. "You drew lipstick on Alabama Mollie with a red Sharpie!"

The girls hooted, but Scott approached Shelby with his head lowered. Once she snatched her wallet, he slipped his hand into his pocket. "I'm sorry." His low tone didn't soothe her frazzled nerves. "I thought you'd okayed what your sister wanted to do. I can move things back if you want."

Shelby pulled Maltie back when the wagging dog tried to lick him. "It's fine. I realize, I'm going to have to compromise."

Scott grimaced. "Eh, but maybe not on the chair."

"Agreed." She cocked an eyebrow at Scott and opened the door. "I might trip as I carry it upstairs. Maybe you should stay for that. It could be entertaining."

"Shelby, I wasn't laughing at you."

"It's okay. It was supposed to be funny, right?"

Scott studied her a minute. "I didn't find it funny at all."

Just like that, like tossing a warped board onto the "damaged" pile, another piece of her married life got stripped away.

Chapter Seven

As the next week started, Scott rehearsed ways to request Shelby's help at the bungalow when she stopped by—ostensibly for other reasons than to join in the grunt work. She wasn't talking much to him. He realized he'd messed up on Friday, but something told him she needed jobs to do. Needed to feel needed. And he hoped if she stuck around, she'd open up.

"If you have the time, think you could run the shop vac upstairs?" he asked. And, "You know, that dining room wallpaper needs a lot of TLC to get it off without damaging the drywall. More TLC than me or Todd are capable of."

Shelby would check out the problem. A few minutes later, he'd hear her at work.

By Wednesday, he questioned his approach. Shelby wiped walls with hot water and white vinegar and scraped stubborn adhesive with a putty knife, still avoiding any real conversation. From the kitchen, where he and Todd were framing out the breakfast nook, Scott heard her speak with more enthusiasm than she had all week.

"Lester, what are you doing here? This is supposed to be a surprise."

Lester. No wonder her tone held more teasing than scolding. Scott fired another nail to secure the frame, then ambled into the dining room in time to see their client reach around to pat Shelby's back in a half hug.

"Aw, sweetie, I couldn't stay away. And it's just me, not the wife—and she's the one who needs to be surprised, right? I had to see the house with the walls moved. I promise I won't poke my nose in."

"Oh, okay." Shelby relented, taking off her gloves to reciprocate Lester's hug.

Lester's fly-away brows jerked upwards. "I didn't expect to see you either. Ruby said you handled design and decorating—not physical labor. Hey, Scott! Did you put Shelby to work?"

Shelby smirked as Scott pumped Lester's hand—not a conspiratorial smirk, but one that couldn't wait to tell on him.

She didn't wait for Scott to respond but answered Lester's question herself.

"Typically, I'm not on construction, but Scott must not have enough crew. He keeps guilting me into work. You have to see what he has planned for me next, the wallpaper on cheesecloth we found under the paneling in all the bedrooms." Her face glowing with a sheen of perspiration, Shelby put a hand on the hip of her expensive-looking jeans.

"Guilting you?" Was that really what she thought? "I offered to walk you through some stuff your husband's crew always took care of, so you'd feel more invested in the project."

"And be less of a laughingstock?" Shelby's blue eyes sliced into him.

He felt color to match his red T-shirt seep up his neck. Really? She was using Lester's presence as leverage against him? Scott shot a glance to the older man—who watched with mouth slightly agape—then back to Shelby. He lowered his voice. "I told you I wasn't laughing at you."

"No, but you're definitely doing a good job of correcting my deficiencies." Shelby turned to Lester with a lame smile and gave a weak flap with her elbows. "I can hardly raise my arms above my head, I'm so sore. But come see, it's going to look great. Imagine the gray-blue paint we picked out."

Scott bit the inside of his jaw, following as Shelby drew Lester into the next room. As much as he wanted to avoid any further barbs from her, neither could he afford to miss what she might say to their client next.

"What a difference with the wall gone," Lester exclaimed. "I can see why you wanted to use iron railing on the stairs now." He wandered into the kitchen, nodding to Todd. "Oh yeah! This eating nook is so much better than that tiny breakfast room."

"We'll reuse the beadboard on the booth area." Shelby indicated the proper trim height on the wall before turning back to them. "And you should check out your den, Lester. When you walk in, try to look past the disintegrated wallpaper and picture the far accent wall with rustic shiplap."

Scott blinked. This was the first he'd heard of such a plan.

Shelby intercepted his expression. "What? I thought it would be masculine. Ruby said they wanted rustic touches. Right, Lester?"

"Sounds good to me."

"No, it's dead on. I'm just glad to know about it before we started painting." Scott shrugged to try to alleviate any sting from his statement.

"Good. Glad we're all on the same page." Shelby slid her gloves back on and walked over to her bucket, bending down to squeeze out her rag. "Sorry, guys, but I need to get back to work if I'm going to finish this wall before my afternoon appointment. Scott, maybe you should show Lester the den. Then how you framed out the new shower upstairs. See if he'd prefer a pocket door where you turn that corner and it gets kind of tight."

Scott knew when he'd been dismissed, the same as in high school when he'd held the door open for her but she'd been too busy talking to her group of friends to notice.

Lester tilted his head and lowered his voice in a conspiratorial manner when they reached the foyer. "Butting heads a little bit?"

"Yeah, just a difference on the way we do things, but we'll work it out."

"Oh, wow." Lester paused in the middle of the den and gaped at the sight of the front room covered in the 1940s, leaf-print wallpaper that had hidden behind the wood paneling.

"Don't worry." Scott patted his shoulder in an exaggerated gesture of sympathy. "It will all be gone. We'll make it a man cave."

"That's going to be a lot of work." Lester put his hands in the pockets of his jeans and rocked back on his heels. "You know, I thought Ruby was being too idealistic about bringing Shelby in on this so soon after she lost her husband, but seeing as how we wouldn't even be in this house if it weren't for her …"

"Of course. As it should be. Shelby needs this, but she seems to resent it if I suggest anything."

Lester punctuated the air with a gnarled index finger. "But are you suggesting, or are you manipulating? Women like to be asked, son. Not told. Not tricked." When Scott let out a frustrated breath and grinned, Lester asked, "You ever been married?"

"No."

"Engaged?"

"No, but I don't see what that has to do with anything. This is a work thing."

"Is it?"

"Mr. Wentworth—"

Lester lowered his voice to a raspy whisper. "Now don't you 'Mr. Wentworth' me. I see the way you look at her. And can't quit looking. She's a pretty thing but vulnerable now. You got to handle things right."

"I'm trying to focus on business."

"Which is why you care what she *needs*? Pulls your heart strings, doesn't she? Yep, I get it. I remember. You knew Shelby in high school, didn't you?"

"Yes, but she was way too good for me. Still is."

"Who are you kidding? Are you still in high school?"

Taken aback, Scott withdrew when Lester tapped on Scott's forehead. He was quickly learning this man had zero respect for professional boundaries.

"For what it's worth, I think you're right—that young woman needs this project. And I get your point. How can you enjoy icing the cake as much if you don't help bake it? But she needs more than that, even though she doesn't know it yet. She's still raw, son. You've got to anticipate her needs."

Scott let out another soft scoffing sound, raising his ball cap to ruffle his sweaty hair. "Uh, Lester … can we just look at the bathroom upstairs?"

The older man stepped into his line of vision. Even though age had diminished his once-bulky stature, he still had to hunker down to meet Scott's eyes. "Let me tell you something, Scott. Ruby was once too good for me, but I won her heart. And you can do the same with Shelby. You want to know how? Come out to my place after work today."

Scott had no idea why he went. Maybe curiosity. His mom and stepdad were about the happiest couple he knew, bonded by shared faith and interests in life. But before they met, both of them had learned the hard way how *not* to go about a marriage. So maybe he just wanted to know if Lester possessed some secret to matrimonial longevity. That must be it because he definitely did not believe Shelby Dodson would ever look on him with romantic desire.

As Augusta rush hour traffic gave way to outlying subdivisions, then stretches of pine woods, he started to feel foolish. By the time Scott turned down the sand driveway of a twelve-acre plot near the outlying town of Sonoria, he considered backing the truck around and heading east. Then he saw the man waving to him from the front porch swing of the sprawling ranch house.

When Scott's truck rumbled to a stop, Lester met him at the vehicle's door. "Hey, I'm glad you came. Ruby's at Bible study. Come on in."

A little uneasy at this overtone of secrecy, Scott stretched as he got out of the vehicle. "Nice piece of property."

Lester glanced over the fields studded by mature trees. "Yeah, it was great when the boys were at home, but I can't keep up with the mowing now, and the house is too big for us. Ruby spends all her time cleaning empty rooms. At least with the bungalow, we can close off the upstairs until company's coming."

"Right."

"Come on. We only have an hour. I've got everything laid out."

Frowning, Scott followed the older man's halting gait. "An hour for what? Lessons in courtship?" He expected a shared laugh but got the second pointing finger under his nose that day, coupled with an intense glance.

"Yes, exactly that." Lester held the door for him, and they stepped into a tile foyer overlooking a carpeted, sunken den with stone fireplace. The house possessed an '80s feel but an open layout and quality fixtures. Not a bad potential flip project in itself.

Lester directed Scott's attention to a framed montage of photos on the wall depicting various decades of his life with Ruby. He pointed to one in particular, a youthful Ruby in a voluminous 1950s skirt and sweater set, standing beside a two-tone Chevy with an older man and woman—presumably her parents.

"Ruby came from a much wealthier and better educated family than mine, the only child, no less. She was a member of the Junior League and class president. Her father was a lawyer. My daddy was with the railroad, and not its management. Not even a conductor. Ruby thought I was just like all the ruffians from my neighborhood. But I had aspirations. And football was my way out of the boon docks."

"Like Austin."

"Who?"

"My stepbrother. Football was his ticket to the good life until an injury sidelined him his freshman year in college."

"Austin Matthews?"

"Austin Culpepper."

"Oh, right." Lester's gaze narrowed on him, and for a second, Scott glimpsed the fiery Coach Wentworth. "I remember Austin Culpepper. Big sensation a few years back for Richmond County. My team always dreaded when we played you guys."

Scott laughed. "Well, they never played *me*."

Lester clapped his shoulder. "That was a lot to compare to."

"I didn't even try. I was a runt back then. What I did have was a talent with wood. Thankfully, so did Austin's dad. When he married my mom, he also became my mentor."

"And now you work in the family business. I'm glad it ended up well for you, son. For many, it doesn't. Divorce and remarriage are painful under the best of circumstances. I'm guessing you don't want that. One shot deal, right? That's why you haven't married yet?"

Scott grinned and rubbed his neck. "Actually, I'm probably not married because I'm too slow to speak up."

Lester grinned back like a co-conspirator in some diabolical plot. "Come with me."

Scott followed him into a spacious kitchen with a massive island and updated, expensive appliances. "Nice reno."

Lester tapped the granite counter. "About six years ago, Ruby wanted these, so I gave her what she wanted, see? I got the new stainless. I was still cooking then. Even though I'd retired from coaching, it was a tradition for us to have the football team over every Friday before the game. Can you imagine how many carbs twenty male athletes can consume?"

Scott nodded. He'd forgotten about Lester's culinary background.

"That was before this dratted tremor. It got worse fast. I hadn't thought about closing the restaurant up. But God has His plans. He knew my wife needed me as the kids left the nest and she retired from teaching. But I do miss cooking for her. And although she won't say so, she does too. You see, my offer isn't totally selfless. I need your help."

"My help?"

Lester nodded. Only then did Scott notice that his host stood behind an array of ingredients, from spices and nuts to oatmeal, brown sugar, and raisins. "Wait. We're going to … bake?"

"It's time to make the hermits. A little early, I admit, but your problem gives me an excuse to push the timeframe."

"Hermits? What is a hermit, besides a reclusive person? And what does it have to do with my … problem?"

Lester smiled and pushed a worn cookbook toward him. "Hermits are the cookies of the season. The cinnamon and nutmeg say 'welcome, fall!' The nuts and raisins can get you through an afternoon better than any granola bar. I grew up baking these with my mother every September. She was the one who taught me something every woman knows, including what Miss Goody Two-Shoes Ruby Scottsdale learned really fast. If a man can cook, he can do anything. And with his cooking, he can say anything. Can you cook, Scott Matthews?"

Chapter Eight

"*She left her purse?"*

"Shh." Shelby jabbed an elbow into her sister's side when Angelina's strident hiss earned a stare of rebuke from the librarian.

The middle-aged employee glared at them from behind the desk of the Georgia Heritage Room. Angelina responded with her own stare, eyebrows raised, before turning back to Shelby.

Angelina moderated her tone if not her enthusiasm. "Aren't you glad we loaded the *Herald* as well as the *Chronicle* onto microfilm? Otherwise, we'd never know that Sharon Barnes left everything! Clothes. Keys. Money. Purse. I mean, leaving my purse somewhere might not be a big deal, but for most people like you, it would. Think what that means."

Shelby pondered for a moment. "It probably means she was taken."

"Or killed." Angelina met her eyes, then jabbed a finger at the screen of the humming microfilm machine. "It said 'with no trace.' Who better to accomplish that than the husband?"

"He said she walked out after an argument." Shelby glanced at the sepia photo of a lovely brunette. Coupled with the emotionally embellished write-up, the likeness presented the sweet young mother as the victim of foul play.

"Of course, he did. The article also reports the police were investigating Charles Barnes."

Shelby shot her sister a skeptical sideways grimace. "They probably had it out for him from the start."

"For good reason. She'd called the police the week prior during one of their arguments. The question is, do you want your clients moving into a house that has a good chance of having hosted a murder?" Angelina shivered, then pressed the button to forward the tape.

"Wait. I wanted to see if there were later reports."

"You know he wasn't arrested. The only way you're going to learn more is if you talk to him yourself."

"Ugh." Shelby opened the case for her sister to place the 1976 newspaper reel inside.

"So? Shouldn't the Wentworths be told?"

"Of course, but they don't seem as concerned as I am."

"Because this reflects on your career, right?"

Shelby scoffed. "What career?"

After paying the austere librarian, they made their way through scanners into the main section of the library, allowing them to raise their voices a notch.

"Scott was right. I'd be better off to drop this obsession I have with the Barnes case." Shelby slung her purse strap over her shoulder and gave herself a little shake as if to shed the unpleasant news they'd just learned.

"Me, I like a good mystery. You, it drives crazy." Angelina winked. Her mischievous grin made her appear more pixie than ever.

"Maybe I shouldn't have told you about all of this." Shelby rolled her eyes. "I don't know why I can't just put it out of my mind."

"I do. You don't want folks saying it was your bright idea to help a sweet, older couple create a retirement nest out of a murder house."

Shelby cringed. "That would definitely be the worst-case outcome."

"I can tell it keeps eating at you." Angelina squeezed her arm as they pushed through the exit doors. "That's why I suggested we come here today. I know you won't rest until you get answers."

"Thanks, Ang."

"Sure thing. Nancy Drew did her best work with a trusty sidekick."

Shelby smiled, but Angelina's earlier statement left her uneasy. Had her sister unwittingly hit on something? Deep down, if Sharon Barnes had been murdered, which worried Shelby more—how the Wentworths would feel about their new home, or what people would say about Shelby?

Exiting the atrium of the three-story building onto Telfair Street, she shoved that concern aside. Did it matter, when proving Sharon wasn't murdered would bring everyone peace? And if she *had* been murdered—well, better the PR nightmare uncovered early and controlled than one that reared up and bit you unexpectedly.

A lingering wisp of morning cool promised an end to the tropic heat and prompted Shelby to release a sigh of satisfaction. "Ah, the first day of September, the start of my favorite season."

Angelina glanced at her watch. "Girl, this sleuthing is gonna make me late to class. But it was fun." She reached out and grabbed Shelby for a hug, smacking a kiss on her hair.

The gesture warmed Shelby's insides, filling something that had been lacking since their mother moved to Columbia. She was glad they'd reached an understanding over the weekend, moving the green chair upstairs and setting up the second bedroom together as Angelina's art studio.

Shelby didn't want to go to the bungalow today, but one wall of stubborn floral paper remained in the dining room. Scott probably realized a job unfinished would taunt her. Why did she care if he thought her prissy and unskilled? He sure couldn't decorate a room like she could!

But she found herself driving down Heard Avenue. Shelby might not have recognized the bungalow had it not been for Scott's truck parked in the driveway. And well, the faded burgundy house exterior. But they'd removed the overgrown wax myrtles planted along the porch, as well as the privet and a diseased willow in the side yard, making the lot look twice as wide. The grass had been cut, and a chain saw roared in the back yard.

Inside, hammering drew her to the gutted master bath, where Todd greeted her as he replaced the subfloor. Todd's son, Seth, applied a dissolving solution that smelled of strong soap and vinegar to the old wallpaper adhesive in Lester's den. The number of tacking nails still jutting out of the wall promised hours of frustrating labor, but Shelby could glimpse the sturdy-looking shiplap.

The empty palate of the house now whispered potential. As Shelby walked toward the dining room, mental flashes of design vignettes caused her to smile. She paused, disturbed to realize that she didn't find decorating a turnkey house near as exciting as one that had been gutted and renovated. That did not bode well for her future, when decorating alone appeared to be her only option. Why was Scott teaching her all this renovating stuff, anyway? And was she wasting her time cooperating?

A lidded Buona cup and a plate displaying homemade cookies with mounded clusters of mouth-watering raisins, dates, nuts, and oatmeal waited on a TV tray. Frowning, Shelby picked up the cup. Room temp now, but a sniff revealed the scent of cinnamon. Twirling it around, she beheld her name scribbled in Sharpie.

"You're late."

She whirled at the sound of Scott's voice.

"I mean, it's okay. I'm glad you're here." He spread his hands—dirt-encrusted, as were his jeans, and his T-shirt already stuck to him despite the mid-morning hour.

Shelby refocused her attention from her co-worker's physique back to the snack. "Are these for me?"

"Yeah. Sorry the coffee got cold. But obviously that's because … I thought you'd be here earlier."

"Is this a cinnamon latte?"

Scott nodded. "I noticed you had one the first day on the job."

"It's my favorite. And the cookies?" Shelby didn't try to hide her astonishment.

"Made them with Lester last night." Grinning, Scott approached, uncovered the plate, and reached for one of the clusters. "They're called hermits. From his mom's cookbook."

As he took a bite, Shelby lifted a cookie and sniffed it. More cinnamon and other spices. "Why did you make cookies with Lester? I'm sorry, but that's a little strange."

"He told me he misses cooking for Ruby. I guess it's a tradition he started when he was dating her. She was so high-class he was scared to talk to her, so he started watching for occasions to make her something. As we know, he became an awesome cook. He baked her right into getting engaged."

"That's sweet." Overcoming the strange sensation that couldn't be butterflies in her stomach, Shelby nibbled the edge of her hermit. Fall exploded onto her tongue. "Oh my."

Scott grinned at her, reminding her in a bittersweet moment of the way her dad once watched her tear into her Christmas stocking. "To be honest, Lester kind of tricked me into helping, but he's a hard man to say 'no' to. He wants me to come again. He has several family dishes in mind leading up to their fiftieth. The way his hands shake now, he can't do it alone."

Shelby swallowed, unsettled. Why had Scott brought her cookies and coffee? The cookies could be a lucky offshoot of Lester's plan for Ruby, but the coffee showed intentionality. She couldn't believe he'd absorbed such a small detail as her favorite brew so early in their acquaintance. Or re-acquaintance. Maybe he felt guilty for twisting her arm about the work projects.

To break the moment, she raised the cup.

Scott's hand shot out. "Don't drink it cold. I'll take it to Betsy Lou's and ask her to microwave it."

Shelby spluttered in laughter. "You've met Betsy Lou, and you really think she owns a microwave? She'd probably heat it in a saucepan on the stove … if you offered her money." She used the excuse of brushing crumbs from her lips to cover her smile.

Scott chuckled, hooking a thumb in the belt loop of his jeans. "She paid me a visit this morning and instructed me to trim rather than remove the hedges."

"Oh no."

"Now she thinks it looks too bare, too much view into her yard. I assured her that while we need easier access for the roofers and the stonemasons to rock over the porch stucco, we'll re-plant something that looks better—and grows more slowly. Which reminds me …" Scott frowned, lowering his head. "You might not want to come the rest of this week."

"Why? You running out of projects for me?"

"No. Next week you can help Seth with the wallpaper upstairs and removing tacking nails. But tomorrow they're coming to replace the roof."

"Oh." As lead settled in Shelby's stomach, she lowered the coffee. He knew. Of course he did. Everybody knew. News reports of Chet's tragic fall on his last flip job had spread all over the state, the nation. Her grief was no private thing. At least the network possessed the sensitivity not to televise those agonizing moments when she knelt by her husband's broken body, screaming. As a shudder moved through Shelby, Scott's hand contacted her elbow.

"Let me heat up your coffee."

Again, with that intensity, that touch offering quiet support after he tried to spare her a painful situation with his advance warning. Shelby couldn't remember the last time someone had paid such close attention to her. She took a step back, into herself. "You'll do no such thing."

The hurt flashed across Scott's face faster than he could mask it. "Kind of ruins the point to drink it cold."

Shelby cleared her throat. Rephrased. "I mean, I actually like flavored coffee any temperature. It's great just the way it is." When he looked doubtful, she took another sip and smiled to reassure him. "You already went out of your way, although I'm not sure why. But I won't have you interrupting what you're doing again. Certainly not to face Betsy Lou."

"Okay, if you're sure." A smile faltered across Scott's lips.

Funny, his slight sprinkling of whiskers had kept her from noticing how well-shaped they were.

"I'm sure. It was … incredibly kind."

"It was a peace offering. Lester said I've been too bossy with the boss."

Shelby burst into a laugh, then clasped a hand over her mouth. How could he have her laughing a few seconds after she wanted to cry? She nodded. "Lester would be right, and he found the proper language to beg for my forgiveness."

When Scott brightened, so eager to please, he resembled his high school self. It crossed her mind that maybe he'd wanted more of her attention back then. The possibility that she'd shunned someone roused the familiar guilt of perfectionism. Maybe after all her effort, she'd failed where it counted most.

"I'll try to be less opinionated in the future, but I think you can do more than you've given yourself credit for."

Shelby's lips twisted into a thoughtful smile. "I'm starting to see that. Does that mean you're going to swallow your own medicine and help me decorate this place?"

"I'm willing to learn."

"I'll keep that in mind." Suddenly uncomfortable, Shelby bent down for her bucket and vinegar. "Well, I'd better get this project finished up."

"One wall shouldn't take you that long. Wanna trim the liriope after you're done?"

She whirled around, pointing a finger at him before she saw his teasing smirk.

Chapter Nine

The first Saturday of September, Shelby woke with a sense of anticipation. She cracked open her bedroom window, ready to inhale autumn. A somewhat balmy, peaceful day greeted her. She made a face and shoved the heavy pane down. Well, at least the morning breeze off the Savannah would feel invigorating during Augusta's Market on the River. Local shops carried much of the pottery, art, jewelry, and baked goods one could purchase at the weekly seasonal event, but Shelby always enjoyed an extra degree of satisfaction, making that personal connection as she bought directly from the crafter.

She checked her phone. Last night, she'd texted three friends from the Sunday school class of the large, non-denominational church she and Chet had attended. Never mind that it was a couples' class. Over the years, Shelby and the ladies frequently met for coffee, movies, or shopping trips, sans husbands. After the funeral, they'd kept her stocked with salads and casseroles. Returning empty dishes with thank-you cards, she never revealed that most of their labors of love ended up in the trash.

Now, a string of texts offered excuses. No, good reasons, Shelby told herself. Christy had family coming into town. Wendy an aerobics class. And Nicole's morning sickness kept her a few feet from the toilet with a handy box of Saltines.

It felt like forever since she'd had a girls' day out. Well. Never mind. She had a sister, and sisters were upgraded BFFs. At least, down the road they were supposed to be, after they matured a little. Today would be a good bonding experience.

After taking Maltie to do her business, the two tiptoed up the stairs, and Shelby flung open Angelina's bedroom door. "Morning, sunshine!"

A groan and a pillow over red curls resulted from Shelby's outburst. Maltie jumped onto the bed and began a frantic attempt to rescue the suffocating girl.

"How about going to the riverfront market with me?"

Flailing an arm at the dog, Angelina muttered something that sounded like she'd stayed out too late.

Immediately aware of her responsibilities in her mother's absence, Shelby edged a hip onto the mattress and helped Maltie turn back the comforter. "You weren't out drinking, were you?"

Angelina slanted an eye at her. "No, dancing. The only intoxication occurred about midnight when we tackled Renfro's by the River's death by chocolate. I think I gained five pounds. Now can I please sleep? This is my only day to stay in bed."

Shelby took the extra pillow and smashed it into Angelina's head. "Fine, but you're missing a beautiful morning."

"Leave the dog. She's sweet, unlike you."

Half an hour later, wearing a navy sundress and sandals with her hair in a low, side ponytail, Shelby parked at Eighth Street and joined the families and couples making their way to the river walk. Was she the only person alone? As their pedestrian group passed street corner musicians spouting bright jazz notes through brass instruments, a mom pushing a stroller offered Shelby a tentative smile. Did she recognize her?

Shelby pulled her hair farther around her face. She should have worn a hat. The last thing she wanted was the millionth repeat conversation about her tragic loss.

She stopped at the first vendor offering muffins and coffee and bought her breakfast, then perched on a brick wall to share the muffin with a trio of bold pigeons. The squeals of children enjoying the last summery days with a romp in the huge fountain nearby thrust the familiar fist of pain into Shelby's middle. She and Chet had started discussing a family about a month before the accident. Something else that would never be.

Reminding herself of her mission, Shelby noticed a tent across the way where a young brunette artist displayed a professional-looking collection of watercolors. Even from this distance, she distinguished impressive likenesses of the Augusta Canal, Sacred Heart Church, 1794 Meadow Garden, and Imperial Theatre. Tossing her muffin wrapper in a trash can, Shelby started to cross over to investigate when a man coming from the opposite direction delivered a brown paper-wrapped package. The artist jumped up and gave him an enthusiastic hug. The man's stance made Shelby pause. Masculine. Casual. But non-threatening, stopping just short of self-effacing. One hand on his hip as he talked to the artist. And that ball cap. Scott.

A musical burst of laughter issued from the vendor. Curious, Shelby edged up to the nearest booth with handmade leather, metal, and beaded jewelry. The earthy tones drew her, especially one delicate bracelet featuring a hammered bronze cross, though she hardly knew why. Looking at all that shabby chic stuff for Ruby must be getting to her. Regardless, she tried it on while cutting her gaze to Scott and the girl.

The artist touched Scott's arm. "You're so sweet. I knew I could count on you."

Through the mesh wire displaying paintings, Shelby made out long mahogany layers framing hazel eyes, bow lips, and a heart-shaped face. The girl wore a softly draping, forest-green shirt and jeans that flattered petite curves.

The young jewelry vendor appeared at Shelby's elbow. Her auburn hair swung forward as she gestured to the bracelet. "That's one of my favorite pieces. Do you like it?"

"Oh, um, yes."

"Hey, aren't you Shelby Dodson?"

The enthusiastic question drew the attention of the two standing in front of the next booth. They turned. Scott beamed.

"Well, hi, Shelby!"

She responded with a sheepish grin. "Hi."

"I knew it!" The jewelry crafter shook her finger at Shelby. "I loved your show. Recorded every episode. I watch all the other fix-it shows, but none of them are as good as yours. Gee, I miss it."

"Thank you." Shelby attempted to secure her slipping smile. "I do too."

Scott admired the bracelet on her wrist. "That's nice. Are you going to get it?"

"Oh." She undid the clasp and slid the item back onto the display rack. "I'm going to think about it. Thank you." She made eye contact with the disappointed seller, who gave a polite nod and encouraged her to return.

"Just shopping around?" Scott asked as Shelby stepped out of the jewelry booth.

"Actually, I'm looking for decorative pieces for the Wentworths."

"Oh, then come meet my old friend, Caitlyn Curtis, and check out her art."

"I do like to include the work of local artists, especially when they depict local scenes. And these are very good." Shelby gave the paintings an admiring glance as Caitlyn approached and shook her hand. If she recognized Shelby from the TV show, she gave no indication.

Scott didn't go into elaborate introductions as he came up behind her either. In fact, he seemed to assume Caitlyn knew who Shelby was. He nudged Caitlyn's arm. "Shelby needs some artwork for the Wentworth renovation I told you about."

Caitlyn stirred at the prospect of a sale—or maybe at Scott's touch. "Oh, what are you looking for?"

Shelby examined a collection of neighborhood prints at the back of the booth. "I like these, especially this streetscape of antique shops and restaurants on Broad, and … is this Heard Avenue?"

"Yes."

Scott beamed. "The Wentworths would love a print of their own neighborhood."

"I agree. I'll take these two, but I'm just getting started with my shopping."

Caitlyn stepped forward, her hand resting on her hip. "Oh, no problem. I can wrap them for you and hold them here. You can stop back by later to pick them up." Her gaze shifted to Scott. "Or—better yet—I'll drop them by to your folks' business on my way home. I've been meaning to take a peek at the space for lease next door that you told me about, anyway."

Glancing at Scott for his reaction, Shelby knit her brow. Sounded to her like Caitlyn was more interested in arranging extra time alone with Scott than sparing Shelby inconvenience.

Scott didn't seem to find anything wrong with the plan. His face brightened, and he shrugged. "Sure. I can bring them to the bungalow on Monday."

Shelby smiled at him. "Perfect. Thanks, Scott." Anything from her but agreement would have sounded argumentative.

"Scott doesn't disappoint." Caitlyn removed the bottom print from the wire frame. Before she could ask him, Scott did likewise with the top print. Caitlyn grinned. "See what I mean? He's a perfect gentleman. I would've been in real trouble when my advance sale lady came by for the print I set aside for her—and left at the store—if Scott hadn't gotten my SOS."

Which meant they had each other's phone numbers, something Shelby found strangely annoying.

Scott leaned the second picture against Caitlyn's check-out table. "Gave me an excuse to get out for a while."

"Well, I appreciate it." Caitlyn gave Scott's bicep a squeeze.

Shelby cleared her throat. "Do you take a check?"

A few minutes later, while Caitlyn wrapped the first print in brown paper, Scott asked Shelby, "So, what else are you looking for today?"

"Anything that strikes me with the right look. I'll hit up antique stores later on for some furniture, Oriental vases, Tiffany lamps, and old kitchen appliances and fixtures that Lester might enjoy, but I hoped for prints today, and maybe baskets and pottery. Both were popular in the Craftsman home. See? I do my research."

"I know you do."

"But I always have to keep my overall palate in mind."

"I'm beginning to get that. Any chance you could use a sidekick?"

The burst of pleasure that someone initiated spending time with her surprised Shelby. Her days of turning others down due to her busy schedule were now a memory. "Well … sure!"

A frown flitted across Caitlyn's adorable face. "Didn't you tell me you interrupted a project to come down here, Scott? Will your stepdad be upset?"

He shrugged. "It can wait. Dad knows when I'm renovating a house, work takes priority over anything at the warehouse."

Shelby assumed Scott's stepfather still stockpiled salvage finds and resold them. She remembered how Scott used to get teased about the family business. Not wanting to embarrass him, she merely smiled. Caitlyn pressed her lips together.

"Nice to meet you, Caitlyn." Shelby waved as she walked away. "Those prints are going to look great."

A raised hand supplied her only answer.

"You know her from owning a business close to your stepdad's?" Attempting to sound casual, Shelby ran her fingers over a crowing rooster fronting a display of painted metal yard art.

"College, actually."

"She seems to think highly of you."

If she hoped Scott would offer his opinion of Caitlyn, she was disappointed.

"Oh, I love these." He gravitated toward a farm vendor's display of flavored honey sticks.

As he paid for a handful, Shelby pondered what about the young artist set her on edge. Maybe because Caitlyn was one of those people who seemed very satisfied with herself. Maybe because she was an artist. Given the history behind her father's infidelity, that was quite enough.

"Here, try one." Scott shuffled his treasure trove of liquid-filled straws in a paper bag. "Wildflower, cinnamon or—check this out—root beer. Wait, I know the answer." With a smile, he ripped open the top of the cinnamon stick.

Just to see what he would do, Shelby sucked honey out of the top, made a face, and shoved it back toward him. "Actually, I want root beer."

"Really? Okay." Without missing a beat, Scott pulled out the flavor she demanded. He almost succeeded in not looking disappointed.

"I'm just kidding!" Shelby burst into laughter. "The cinnamon is great."

Scott frowned, totally perplexed. Shelby didn't know what to make of such an eager-to-please guy. She made a conciliatory move of touching his arm. The unexpected warmth and firmness of it, along with the smile he gave her, reminded Shelby of how affirming it felt to have a steady guy at her side. Relieved to spot a quality pottery booth, she hurried over to inspect the wares.

Ten minutes later, Scott half joked, half complained as they left the riverfront loaded down with purchases. "Remind me again why you had to buy so much of one thing?"

"Because this salt-glazed pottery is top quality, and to get pieces in both ivory and the light blue-gray was totally lucky. And because the scale and trim of the bungalow calls for decorating on a bigger scale. One piece would get lost. A collection of pieces will make a statement in any number of rooms. I can even hang those platters and dishes."

"Well, you sure made the potter happy. Wait." Scott nudged her with his elbow as they passed the jewelry booth. "Did you want to buy that bracelet?"

Thankful that both Caitlyn and the jeweler appeared busy with customers, Shelby kept walking. "No, I don't think so."

Scott caught up with her. "I thought you liked it."

"I did. It just wasn't me."

"Okay, but it seems to me if you liked it, it was you."

Shelby sighed as they waited at the crosswalk, feeling defensive at being forced to explain. "It won't match anything I have. My entire wardrobe is preppy and professional. Chet always said jewelry that wasn't gold, silver, or precious stones wasn't worth the money."

Scott remained silent as they crossed the street to Shelby's CRV. But she could hear him thinking. After they deposited their boxes in the hatchback, he caught her gaze. "I don't mean to disrespect the guy after he's gone, but isn't it time now you can decide what *you* like?"

Shelby blinked. "It's just a bracelet, Scott."

"Right." He shifted his weight and focused on a candy bar wrapper lying on the street drain. "Well, this has been fun."

She blew out an exasperated breath. "*What?*"

"You really want to know?" He squinted up at her.

"Yes. Yes, I really want to know." Too late, Shelby realized her somewhat sarcastic tone and crossed arms contradicted her statement, but thankfully, Scott nodded.

"All right. Sometimes, it seems your style, even your lifestyle, doesn't really fit you. You'll see a vision for something different at the Wentworths' house, or an item you like yourself, but you keep going back to what you're used to."

Shelby put a hand on her hip. "And how do you come by this special knowledge, pray tell? Do you have a psychology degree I don't know about?"

"No." He shrugged. "Just by watching. I mean, you were kind of like that in high school too. You looked perfect but not very happy. And now, you do what you think you have to, or what others expect of you, but not what you want to."

"Don't we all?"

Scott stubbed the toe of his work boot against the curb. "To some extent."

"Have you been testing me?" As this unsettling notion took root, Shelby slammed the hatch and faced him. "Seeing if I'll do stuff at the house because I think you expect it? Seeing if you can manipulate me into extra labor?"

"No! Manipulating you is the last thing I want. Just the opposite. I thought if you learned some renovation basics, you'd discover that not only could you do more than you thought, you'd take satisfaction in it. And acquire more skills for your future."

Shelby twisted her lips to one side, annoyed he'd been right. But then, maybe this conversation presented an opportunity for a little manipulating of her own. "Fine, I'll make you a bet."

Scott glanced up, eyebrows raised.

"I can prove you don't know me as well as you think. I'll ask you questions about what I'd do in certain situations. Say, three. If you get two or more right, I'll … let's see, what's a yucky job you said I should do … scrape the paint off the window frames."

"Each and every one?"

She nodded.

Like a plotting mad scientist, Scott drummed his fingers against his chin. "And if I get only one, or none, right?"

Shelby dipped her head in an attempt to detract from the blush that spread over her cheeks. "You go spy out Julian's for me."

"What?"

"Julian Etier's new shop at Broad and Tenth. I can see some of what he stocks online, but I've been dying to know how he's marketing it."

"Who is Julian Etier?"

A puff of disgust escaped Shelby's lips. "This wealthy dude who was supposed to have retired from a career in Atlanta interior design. He moved back home to help care for his elderly father and at first, just did a few decorating jobs for friends. But then, since my show stopped airing and his dad passed away, he's gone public and opened a shop—for those who can afford him, anyway. I need to know if I start my own design business how much competition he's going to be. Augusta and surrounding regions can only sustain so much style panache."

"And you can't just go in there and say, 'Hi, Julian, I came to see what you've been up to in my absence'?"

"Good gracious, no. That would be humiliating. And stalkerish." As Shelby pressed the lock button on her remote, a reassuring beeping sang out. "Well? Are you up for it?"

The calculating gleam that lit Scott's green eyes tightened the muscles in Shelby's stomach. "I'll make the time." He gave a slow nod. "With one alteration to the bet."

Chapter Ten

Shelby looked so cute in her navy sundress and big, movie-star sunglasses. Scott had already searched for an excuse to spend more time with her before she proposed her crazy bet. Under Shelby's terms, he didn't care if he won or lost. Didn't she get it that he wasn't trying to entice her to do things for him—he was dying to do things for her? Just walking down the street next to her filled him with pleasure. But with this opportunity to get to know her better, fear of how she'd take his suggestion almost froze him.

His blonde companion tapped the toe of her sandal. "Well?"

He had to sound convincing. And selfish, even if it went against his grain. "I'm starving. You're taking all my morning, so you can buy me lunch."

She blew air through her rounded lips and put her hands on her hips again. "Okay, fine. If you win, we'll walk by the front of Julian's, then we'll go to lunch."

Scott relaxed and nodded. She didn't suspect his motives.

"So question one." Shelby peeked at him over her shoulder and over the top of her sunglasses as they set out walking. "Would I choose as a flip project a 1980s ranch or a Victorian cottage?"

"Easy. The ranch."

"But I live in a historic house."

"Because of convenience, not love. You'd choose the ranch because its open floor plan and clean lines would lend itself to your contemporary design style."

"Hmm." Shelby frowned, and Scott chuckled. She had to stump him on both of the other questions. She remained deep in thought as they bypassed a line of tourists boarding a red-and-green tour trolley stopped along the divided historic business corridor. Finally, she asked, "Back in high school, I didn't talk to you because I was stressed out, or because I didn't notice you?"

What kind of question was that? She could have asked any number of remote personal things about herself. Scott went with his gut. "Because you didn't notice me?"

"No!" Shelby did a two-step to get in front of him, pointing her finger in obvious delight. "Man, I thought that was a dead giveaway, but I felt like I should clarify after you seemed bummed I didn't recognize you. Did you really think I was such a snob?"

No secret, insecurity from those days remained his biggest weakness. "Um … yeah?"

"Scott Matthews!"

"Oh, come on. You're just trying to make yourself feel better for not noticing us little people. You had everything going for you. What did you have to be stressed out about?"

"Only being the oldest child of a highly successful, type A, workaholic lawyer. I'd do anything to get his attention, not to mention his approval."

"Surely you already had it just because you belonged to him."

"Try telling that to my mom when he left her for his artist girlfriend, ten years her junior." Shelby clamped her mouth shut as if the confession had popped out without her permission.

A couple of college guys hogging the sidewalk forced Shelby to circle a Chinese elm. As Scott caught a low branch for her, he shot them a dirty look. "Shelby, I'm sorry. You know my parents are divorced too."

"Yes, but your mom's remarriage turned out well."

"It did, but that didn't mean it wasn't painful."

"Of course. My mom's really struggled since the divorce. She never remarried. She's only now getting her footing and identity back."

The surprisingly intimate nature of the conversation made Scott lean forward so they could keep their voices low, even though he still walked slightly behind her. "What changed? The job you mentioned?"

"Yes, and finding God. I mean, she was always a Christian, but just the go-to-church-and-be-moral kind, you know. Now she's really into it." Shelby moved her big purse, cradling it more in front of her to make room for Scott at her side.

"That's good. My mom used to read us the Scriptures about God being a father to the fatherless and a husband to the widow. She said that counted for those whose husbands left them."

Shelby flashed him a surprised expression. "Your dad left too? I thought he died."

Pressing the crosswalk button at Tenth Street, Scott offered her a tight smile. "He's dead now. But after my mom put him through grad school, he decided he married too young and wasn't ready for the responsibility of a family.

Convenient timing, right? He went off to Atlanta to start his career in banking and left her behind. But at least he paid child support."

"Oh, my gracious. Did you make up with him before he died?"

"When I was a junior, remorse got the better of him, and he started inviting me for visits. Yeah, we made up. Slowly. With the encouragement of my mom. I was thankful later ... and even more thankful that my stepfather cared enough to show me how to be a man. So see? We have more in common than you thought."

Staring at the flashing countdown sign, Shelby murmured, "I don't talk to my dad much."

Scott's chest tightened at her vulnerability. "You might want to rethink that."

"Oh, I've forgiven him." Shelby sent him a quick glance, almost as if seeking his approval. "But I don't like his wife."

He laughed at her candor and, without thinking, grabbed her hand to pull her onto the street as the signal for "walk" appeared. When they reached the other side, he didn't want to let go, but Shelby pulled away and pressed her palm against her skirt like he'd burned her. Scott shoved his hands in his pockets. Stupid. She was using him, not dating him. That's what entitled girls like Shelby were bred to do.

"The new store is just down there."

It wasn't hard to spot. In an area still plagued by empty storefronts, an unusual bevy of activity signaled the trendy addition. Shelby gave a nod in that direction as if expecting him to do her bidding even before losing her contest.

He possessed more self-respect than that. Scott raised his chin. "You have yet to ask your third question. Better make it a good one."

Drawing a deep breath, Shelby froze, statue-like, and searched heavenward. The sunlight created a halo on the crown of her golden head. "Yep. Here it is. If I had a choice on a Saturday night of staying in and reading a book or going out to dinner with friends, what would I want to do?"

Scott tried not to look smug. "You really are handing this to me. In your heart of hearts, you want to scrape those windows, don't you? You'd go out, because that would suit the public persona of Shelby Dodson."

Her shoulders sagged. "I would go out. At least, I used to." She straightened to her full height. "But I didn't ask what I would do. I asked what I'd *want* to do."

"I wasn't finished. You'd go, but the whole time, you'd be looking forward to that moment you could get home, kick off your shoes, and run a hot bath."

Shelby's mouth fell open, then she frowned. "I totally clued you in. But I have to admit, now that I get to stay home and read all the time, it isn't as appealing as it used to seem when I had to keep up with an exhausting social calendar." She gave a wistful sigh. Wait, could she actually be lonely? She brightened suddenly and raised a manicured hand to her purse strap. "Come on, let's go window shopping."

They strolled down the street until the storefront under a snazzy sign stating "Julian's" offered design eye candy: a full bedroom layout, complete with fluffy robe, breakfast tray with flowers, and a stack of hardcover books. Shelby moaned. "Oh no. He's not just selling. He's staging."

"What?"

"Before the TV show, this is what we used for an open house if we flipped a property before we had a buyer. And on the big reveal day for the TV show, you create cozy vignettes that arouse emotion. The books, the slippers, candles burning. Everything that says 'home' to people. The buyers come in and fall in love. It looks fabulous. He's going to sell not only his merchandise, but his services. He's done exactly what I would do." Shelby's shoulders sagged.

Scott pointed out the obvious. "But if you did this, you wouldn't be decorating renovated houses anymore."

"Right. I don't see how that's going to be possible in the future, do you?"

Scott bit his tongue to keep from blurting, "We could work together again." He knew she wasn't ready to hear such a thing. Might never be.

He was so opposite of Chet, the Wentworth project probably proved painful for her in ways he could never imagine. Not even from his distinguished position of twenty-six years of lonely. "Well, if this is what you want, you should know exactly what you're up against. And you can't tell that from the window display." Without waiting for a response, he entered the store.

"Scott." Shelby hissed his name, darting in behind him.

The bell jangled. A tall, dark-haired woman swathed in an expensive-looking ivory dress, big gold jewelry, and the scent of floral perfume stepped forward. "Good morning. Can I help you?"

"No, we heard about the new store and thought we'd check it out." On impulse, Scott snaked an arm around Shelby's waist and smiled down at her. "Didn't we, honey?"

"Oh. Hee, hee." Shelby's laugh came out high-pitched. "We sure did. We've got a big new house to decorate." She wiggled her fingers as if she couldn't wait to dig into Julian's fancies.

Well, that much was true.

"Wonderful. Have a look around and let me know if I can help you. Julian is at the consulting area in the back." Gazing down a patrician nose, the woman smiled. Didn't she recognize Shelby? If she did, she was probably too condescending to let on. "We have wine and cheese laid out."

"Of course, you do." Scott snorted back a laugh at Shelby's muttered comment and the theatrical glare she fixed on the woman's back as the sales associate glided away on stealthy heels. Then Shelby jerked Scott around a partition wall simulating an entryway and snatched his Augusta GreenJackets cap off his head.

"Whoa!" He put a hand to his head. "I have hat hair!"

"Well, fluff it up. You're the one who decided to come in here. I can't let him see me." Loosening her own hair to fall over her ears, Shelby shoved her sunglasses back on, then added his hat.

"That looks very natural."

"Shhh. Now, what am I going to owe you to video the back of the store even though you won the bet?" Shelby perused the display, causing her to miss the sly grin that turned up Scott's mouth. She muttered about Dash & Albert rugs and Christy towels, then turned around and caught sight of his expression. She snapped, "Fine, I'll pay for lunch *and* scrape the windows. Just go. Circulate. Video."

"I'm beginning to see how stress affects you."

Shelby gave him a little shove. "Go. See what he's doing back there while I drift through the front, close to the exit."

He pulled out his phone. "Yes, ma'am. I must say, though, I feel not only lunch but a massive slice of Boll Weevil's hummingbird cake coming on."

Moseying away, he rubbed his stomach. Shelby growled. He was enjoying this way too much. Just like he enjoyed being around Shelby too much.

He pretended to check out fine soaps and linens while making his way to where he could see a tall, bald man in a tailored Herringbone suit, deep in conversation with a puffy-haired Southern matron. They reposed on a leather sofa amid a living room suite, the finger foods spread on silver trays atop the coffee table. The woman flipped through a style book and asked questions.

Scott lurked around the corner and held his phone out to take a surreptitious video, then switched the setting to allow a photograph of a shelf filled with bedspreads. He figured Shelby would want to read the labels. As he stepped back to include the entire selection, he bumped into a display, and with a clatter and multiple thumps, a half-dozen candles slid to the floor.

Before he could get to his knees, Shelby crouched beside him, picking up the boxes and frantically sliding them back on the glass table. "What are you doing?"

Scott tried to keep his answer to a whisper, but it came out more like a growl. "Taking the secret footage you requested."

"Hello." At the sound of a deep, cultured voice above them, they looked up like wide-eyed schoolchildren caught in mischief. "Is that Shelby Dodson?"

After yesterday's downtown debacle, Shelby couldn't wait to get back to the comfort of her church friends. Angelina, however, didn't seem to share her anticipation. She dallied so long in the bathroom she almost made them late. Then she stopped in the door of the Sunday school class, scanning the chattering twenty- and thirty-somethings with a quirked brow.

"Remind me again why we're going to a couples' class when we're both *single*?"

As faces turned toward them, Shelby smiled and adjusted the skirt of her tailored dress. Was it too short? Funny, she'd never have worried about that on Chet's arm. He would have assured her it possessed the right label and boldness to outshine the other wives' outfits. "Because this is the class I've attended since we joined this church. These are my friends, and I want you to meet them."

The teacher, Tim Stafford, a man around forty, approached to shake their hands and welcome Angelina. After he walked off, Shelby turned to her sister with an encouraging smile. "Let's get coffee."

As Shelby slid her cup under the pump spout, a breezy voice said, "Hey, there. Did you make it to the market?"

Shelby glanced up into her friend Wendy's glowing face. "Yes, I had a great outing." *No thanks to you.* She pulled the tab, allowing fragrant, steaming coffee to spill into Styrofoam. "How was your class?"

"Oh. Terrible. They all are. It's exercise. But it's the price I pay for a slowing metabolism. Not like you, obviously. Have you been eating? Do we need to start bringing you dinner again?"

Angelina cleared her throat and nudged Shelby, prompting Shelby to say, "Wendy, meet my sister, Angelina."

Wendy extended her hand to Angelina. "So good to have you. Are you married? Oh, never mind, you're still in college. I hope you're not married." She dumped a liberal amount of artificial sweetener into her brew. "I'm so glad you're keeping Shelby company. We've been worried about her. Now we can all relax, knowing she's not alone."

Did Wendy have no idea her statement sounded like they were relieved to be unburdened? Apparently not, for she offered what appeared to be a genuine smile as she stirred her coffee. Shelby aimed for bright rather than defensive with the tone of her reply. "Actually, I'm staying quite busy now, overseeing renovations on a historic house for an older couple."

"Oh, that's so sweet." Wendy slid the tip of her stirring stick into her mouth, passing her gaze over the rows of chairs. "There he is! Brad never stays where I left him." Wendy squeezed Shelby's hand and said to Angelina, "Enjoy the class."

"Thanks."

The seats were filling up fast. Shelby spied Christy occupying a row with her visitors and drew Angelina over to meet them. After a few seconds of chit-chat with Christy's South Carolina family, Shelby indicated two empty chairs on the end. "Are these open?"

Christy laid her hand on the back of the nearest seat. "Oh no. Sorry. My sister-in-law had to take her son to the bathroom."

"Of course. So good to see you." Shelby smiled and stepped to the periphery of the classroom.

Tim arranged his materials at the podium, and stragglers doctoring coffee darted wary glances over their shoulders and exaggerated their hurried movements.

"Do you see what I see?" Angelina whispered.

"Yep. Front row." Biting her lip, Shelby led the way to the ignominious area.

Tim decided to make sport of Shelby's hesitant approach. "Come on up. Make yourself comfortable up here with me. Visitor's section!"

Everyone laughed as Shelby and Angelina sat down and Tim started taking prayer requests.

"I don't see Nicole," Shelby murmured to Angelina. "She's expecting and feels terrible in the mornings. She'll need a place to sit when she slips in." Taking a sip of her coffee, which tasted sterilized without liquid creamer or syrup, Shelby directed her eyes forward.

Halfway through the praise reports, the door opened and, to the tune of whispers and snickers, a gray-faced, petite brunette sneaked in ahead of her well-built husband. Cal gave a sheepish shrug and pointed at the back of Nicole's empire-waist jumper. Nicole smiled, and while waving to the room, caught sight of Shelby and waved faster. Shelby beamed in welcome and slid her purse off the chair next to her.

Nicole didn't seem to notice. Hand clasped in her spouse's, she filed to the very back, where Cal fetched a chair from the storage closet so he could join Nicole next to a platinum blonde with an unmistakably rounded belly. The two women put their heads together to murmur something sympathetic and patted each other's hands.

Shelby swallowed. Yesterday, she'd been caught eavesdropping on Scott and Julian Etier both. Yet in the ten minutes she had been in this room, she felt far smaller and more out of place than she had during yesterday's embarrassing moments—combined. And completely opposite of how Scott wanting to spend the morning with her had made her feel. Like it or not, her world had changed. It might be time to let some things go.

Feeling Angelina's eyes on her, she glanced to the side. Her twenty-year-old sibling lifted one corner of her mouth in a surprisingly sensitive smile.

Chapter Eleven

By Monday night, Shelby hated her phone. Well, that wasn't exactly true. She hated its silence.

Sunday afternoon and evening, when Angelina headed to the library to write a paper, Shelby snagged Maltie and a bowl of popcorn and lost herself in a Hallmark movie marathon, trying to forget the humiliation of the weekend.

Monday, she had to face it—work on the bungalow represented the only thing moving forward in her life.

Workers had replaced the roof at the end of last week. But where plumbing, HVAC, and electrical work were concerned, even Scott agreed she was a liability. So donning old jeans and a T-shirt, she made a trip to her storage building and separated a pile of wall art, light fixtures, and knick-knacks to decorate the Wentworth house.

When a text dinged around dinner time, she jumped, then scanned Scott's offer to pick her up in the morning for an outing to Savannah River Tile and Stone. They could swing by the builder's supply for the new front and French doors. Yes! Shelby loved this stage, the first step in making her visions come to life. And the first step back into her element.

Shelby pulled her iPad from her purse on Tuesday as she and Scott approached the showroom entrance. "I already know how I want everything to look, so this shouldn't take long."

"Let me guess." Holding open the door for her, Scott whisked off his sunglasses—the ones that made him look annoyingly like a Top Gun pilot—and hung them on his shirt collar. "You've got a checklist."

"Why, yes." Shelby booted up the page that came as part of her design program and showed Scott the room-by-room columns. "I want the same tile in both bathrooms, with a nice, geometric mosaic design. Kitchen island and bathroom countertops in white Carrera marble. For the other kitchen counters topping the antique white cabinets, I'm more open. Maybe black or dark gray."

"But we can't give them specifications on the master bath counter because you haven't found the dresser yet."

Shelby gravitated toward the "glam tile" wall, running her fingers over the samples. "True, but we can reserve a section that will be pretty close. No need to cut anything yet. Oh my. Isn't this Hirsch glass silhouette tile amazing? The glass tile we did a couple of flips ago sure turned out great." Shelby's voice trailed off as it hit her that the man standing behind her wasn't Chet. Her world tilted on its axis, blurred, and rearranged all in the space of a heartbeat. The initial shard of pain left a fallout of regret and sadness.

"I bet it did." The softness of Scott's voice revealed his awareness of her near-lapse. "But don't you think it would be at odds with the bungalow? Remember, we're keeping the white beadboard waist-high in the bathrooms, like the breakfast area nook."

Shelby lowered her hand. "Right. But my goal isn't period correctness. It's to give Lester and Ruby the beauty and comfort fifty years of marriage deserve."

"I think we can do that with a nod to the architecture. They like rustic, right? What about this wood-inspired tile? It's got a gray tone." Scott tapped the display board.

"No. It's great for … a lodge or something … but doesn't have that elegant feel."

"Hexagons were popular in bungalow bathrooms." He drew her to a neighboring display, pointing out a small tile in shades of gray. She noticed he positioned his body between her and the glam tile. "What about this?"

"Oh, my goodness, no."

"Not on the shower walls, or the bathroom floor, but on the floor of the shower. With white subway tile shower walls—like the tile we're using in the kitchen—and the gray-blue painted walls. Glass framing on the shower."

Shelby stood silent a moment, annoyed that Scott interrupted her original vision, replacing it with one that … "Just might work."

"Clean, right? Uh, and I don't mean to push you, but over there is a wide hexagon in white-and-gray marble that would look just *fabulous*." Baring his teeth and rubbing his jaw, Scott tilted his head toward the ceiling. "I'll pretend to let you see it first."

She followed the direction she'd seen him look. "Mm, too light."

"Not if we set it off with a thin, double border in dark gray or black, a common treatment in"—he faked a cough—"period bathrooms."

Shelby stared at the man in amazement. "How do you know all this?"

"If you noticed from my resume you requested, I've done a few Edwardian and Craftsman flips. My stepdad was into preservation before starting his business. They live on Milledge Road."

"They do?" Shelby's eyes opened wide. Intersecting Walton Way, Milledge offered the entrance to the in-town country club. Augusta's most established, historic homes clustered in the Walton and Milledge area, along with beautiful churches and prestigious private schools. The "junk man" must have come up in the world.

"Let's just say I've been steeped in historic architecture."

"Okay." Shelby pursed her lips and crossed her arms. "I'd consider forgoing my tried and proven, modern mosaic treatment, except I don't believe we budgeted in marble on the floor."

"I like a woman who considers the budget."

Shrugging, Shelby dismissed the moment of satisfaction Scott's statement gave her. "I always consider the budget, though if you watched 'Dodson's Do-Overs,' you'd never know it. They always made me appear to pick expensive stuff and Chet protest, then eventually give in. Of course, it had all been figured out in advance … by me."

Scott had the grace not to point out that such an arrangement had forced her into yet another compromise of her true self. Instead, he observed, "The bathrooms are small, and we'll offset the cost by using the cheaper subway tile with no mosaic on the shower walls."

To show her reluctant agreement, Shelby rolled her eyes and held out her hand for a high five. The pleasure of working out an even better plan than she'd anticipated—and the approval in Scott's grin—took her by surprise.

"Excuse me." They turned to see a college-aged guy with heavy-framed glasses and gelled, dark hair. "I'm Max." He pointed a faltering finger. "Are you … are you …"

"Shelby Dodson." Scott supplied the answer when the clerk's voice failed. He stuck out his hand. "And I'm Scott Matthews, Mrs. Dodson's humble assistant for the renovation of a bungalow over on Heard Avenue."

Max shook Scott's hand but directed his eyes and words to Shelby. "Pleased to meet you. How can I help? Will I be on TV?"

"Sorry, Max, no cameras this go-round," Scott said.

Smiling, Shelby couldn't help but respond to the man's obvious admiration. He clasped the hand she extended longer than necessary between two thick, damp palms. "I'm afraid Scott is right, although who knows what the future may hold. But I do have a very large work order to fill."

Once he got himself together, Max proved quite helpful. The morning fled as they selected marble and granite and visited the stone yard outside to inspect veneer pallets for covering the porch and chimney stucco. The paint swatches Shelby had brought along kept them focused, while Scott continued the game of guessing what Shelby would prefer before she made every selection. Four out of five times, he was right.

Walking to the truck, Scott pointed a finger in her direction. "Hamburger or sub? Let's see, sub, because a hamburger would be too greasy."

Shelby laughed and nodded. "I'd take a sub, but I do occasionally enjoy an old-fashioned burger too."

"I know a great place on the way to the builder's supply."

Shelby couldn't believe how comfortable she felt eating in front of Scott, maybe because they took the order to-go, rather than facing each other across a table. When she and Chet first met, she couldn't drink a milkshake in his presence, much less eat with her hands. She finished her Italian sub as Scott loaded the doors onto the back and secured them with bungee cord. Well, of course she felt comfortable. Theirs was nothing more than a friendly, temporary business partnership. No comparison to dating, even though it felt familiar, and rather affirming, being out with a man.

Her eye fell on Scott's sandwich, still wrapped on the dash, mostly uneaten. Well, he had to drive, right?

When Scott returned to the cab, Shelby asked, "Can we paint the door as soon as we get there?"

"Yes, ma'am." He flashed her a grin. "*You* can paint the door."

"Oh goody." Shelby clasped her hands under her chin in delight, earning a disbelieving glance.

"This is strange. You're noticeably excited."

"Because the color is going to be so cool."

Scott laughed. Warmed by his approving glance, Shelby devoted herself to finishing her chips and Coke. When they turned on Gordon Highway, he spoke again. "I need to get started on the island. Why don't you tell me what you have in mind in terms of design?"

Shelby patted her lips with her napkin, then fished in her purse for lipstick. "Okay. Picture this." She waved the tube in her hand. "I'm going to find three tall, gray padded chairs. They'll pull under on the dining room side, so I want leg room offered by columns. Smaller columns for balance on the other side, but no major overhang. We'll need pull-out cabinets on the width of the island and shallow shelving for storage on the ends. Does that make sense?"

"Yeah."

After checking her teeth—which earned her an even more skeptical look than her enthusiasm over the front door color—Shelby got out her phone. "Let me see if I can find a picture."

"No need. You got some paper?"

"Yes." She located a small, jeweled notebook and removed a sheet.

When Scott pulled into the driveway on Heard, he put the truck in park, reached for a pencil from his glove compartment, and bore down on a code book. As he sketched the island, she watched his deft movements in amazement. "Raised panels here, where the stools go, Craftsman-style. A little arch over the shelving like this? Is that close?"

"Uh. Yeah." Shelby blinked. "That's ... *better* than I imagined. Where did you learn to draw like that?"

He made a deprecating face and turned the ignition off. "Been doing it my whole life."

"You're really talented."

Thinking of what Scott said earlier about his experience with renovating vintage houses, Shelby's eyes narrowed as the seed of an idea dropped into her mind. Maybe Scott lacked Chet's charisma, but his skills and passion could satisfy a niche market. Anything vintage was hot right now. If she pitched a new angle for her flipping show and the producers recognized potential, she'd never have to worry again about what Julian Etier was up to. "You could make something of that, you know."

"Thanks. But Shelby, do you not realize that I make—"

Caught up in her idea, Shelby forged ahead despite Scott's effort to speak. "Numbers on our show always shot up when we renovated a historic house. Have you ever thought of capitalizing on that interest?"

Before Scott could answer, the rev of a powerful engine stole their attention. A yellow Chevy corvette whipped around the corner and into the driveway, nosing alarmingly close to Scott's bumper.

Beneath the ball cap, his eyebrows descended. "What the blazes?"

"Oh." Looking in her side mirror, Shelby laughed. "It's Tasha."

"Who?" Scott croaked as three-inch, black heels touched the pavement. With the slam of a door, Tasha strode toward them on her long, bare legs.

"My real estate friend, the one who always worked on the show. She's the agent who advised me about Georgia disclosure laws."

"I see."

They got out of the truck and walked back to meet Tasha. Shelby had barely introduced Scott when, after giving him a cursory glance, Tasha slapped a newspaper against Shelby's slacks. "Glad you're here. You're going to want to read this."

Shelby unfolded the newspaper. "*The Augusta Star*?"

Scott spoke into a fake cough. "Fire-starter."

"It does amount to little more than a local tabloid." Shelby raised her brows as she scanned over-sized pictures with sensational captions. "What's in here that's so important?"

"Even if that's true, people read it voraciously." Tasha opened to the local section and stabbed a headline with her finger. "'Infamous Barnes Bungalow Dodson's New Project.'"

Shelby gasped at a photo of the property they now stood on, taken after the trees had been cleared with the dumpster sitting in front. "Oh no."

She read aloud. "'With the demise of Home Network house flipper Chet Dodson, known for his zany antics, daring ideas, and stunning renovation skills, viewers expected an end to the popular series Dodson hosted with his wife, Shelby, "Dodson's Do-Overs." Now, sources confirm that Shelby's going it solo, albeit sans cameras, on a Heard Avenue property.

"Long-time locals may recall the dark history of the 1920s bungalow, now owned by a retired couple. In 1976, Sharon Barnes disappeared from her home, leaving behind all her belongings including her purse, keys, and a young son. Investigations by local police considered all possible scenarios, including accident, abandonment, and kidnapping. However, due to the couple's history of arguments, authorities suspected the husband, Charles Barnes, of foul play. Police found no evidence against him. The Barnes bungalow history, and not just the death of "Do-Overs" star Chet Dodson, may explain why cameras are not rolling on Heard Avenue.'"

Shelby flapped the paper down and speared Scott with wide eyes. "This is the work of Julian Etier."

"You don't know that."

"Who else would have the knowledge and the motivation to get this scrap trash printed?"

"Wait, you told Julian Etier about this renovation?" Tasha wanted to know.

Shelby nibbled her lip. "Not exactly. We were kind of checking out his shop when he, uh, came upon us. He asked if I was working. What was I supposed to do, lie?" And, of course, she'd had to buy a candle. Three of them. And hope the posh older man hadn't heard her little espionage exchange with Scott, although his amused smile told her otherwise.

"Uh, yes. In this case, I'd say it would be advisable." Tasha fixed a hand on her slender hip, wrapped in a belted, knit dress.

"She didn't tell him where, or for whom." Scott stepped forward as he spoke up.

Tasha brushed that off with a disgusted look. Obviously, that was no trouble to find out."

"I'm just saying, innocent until proven guilty. It could have been one of the neighbors."

"Well, regardless, we're in a fix now," Shelby said. "The other day you talked me into not telling the Wentworths what I learned at the library, Scott. You said just to let it blow over. Yep, it's really blown over!"

Tasha touched Shelby's arm. "You know we have a lawyer on staff at our firm. I'll contact the seller, set up a meeting. I'm sure I can pin him to the wall."

The bold-faced, black-and-white claims of the newspaper left Shelby feeling vulnerable, exposed. She could already imagine the text messages flying and social media posts popping up even as they stood there debating. "Maybe it would be good to speak with them."

"No." Scott's firm response made both women jump. "Not without permission from Lester and Ruby."

Tasha frowned at him as if he was a random bum interjecting unwanted opinions.

Tilting her head, Shelby appealed to Scott's desire for a positive outcome. "But consider if a simple conversation with Charles' son reveals there's nothing to these suspicions, it will give everyone peace of mind. Don't you think this article will stir up the Barnes family too?"

"I think if you go poking and threatening on the tails of it, it will only make things worse. And I think you're not going to discover some magic answer the police failed to find forty years ago. Sometimes, if you ignore things, they go away."

Tasha typed something on her phone. "This is not going away."

Scott ignored her and pled with Shelby. "All I'm asking is that we discuss it with our clients."

"Of course." This day-wrecking conversation needed to end. She smiled at Tasha. "Thank you for bringing this to our attention. I'll be in touch."

"Fine. But don't be surprised if reporters and psychics start popping out of the bushes with cameras and energy sensors."

"Please." Scott rolled his eyes.

Shelby gave him a disbelieving stare. She'd never seen him so sarcastic with anyone.

She pressed the newspaper back into Tasha's hand. "Take this awful rag with you. The thing that makes me most mad is how this article, if you can call it that, sours the memory of Chet and the work we did together."

"I know, honey. I hated to show it to you, but you had to know."

The frown that flitted across Scott's face offset the comfort of Tasha's gentle squeeze to Shelby's arm. She couldn't let this latest sign of Scott's displeasure go unchallenged. "What?"

"Nothing. I just … think this stands to hurt the Barnes family more than you, or even the Wentworths." Almost apologetic, Scott's voice trailed off.

The fact that he thought her selfish for wanting to maintain the good reputation she and Chet had established stung.

As he turned to lower the tailgate of his truck and loosen his bungee cord, Tasha shook her head. She winked at Shelby. "I got you, girl. Call me. Better yet, I'm going to Rudolpho's at the marina Friday night. You should come. There's a snazzy lawyer I want to introduce you to."

Chapter Twelve

Scott didn't like to make the sort of phone call he had to make to Lester on Friday. Further investigation had revealed the house needed more extensive rewiring than anticipated. The work meant greater cost and delay.

He apologized for the third time, although Lester took the news with his usual aplomb. "I'm sorry, man. The good news is, Hector's a pro, and your house's block-n-beam foundation does help us out with the re-plumbing and re-wiring both."

"Okay, but are we still on track for our Thanksgiving finish date?"

"Yes. I always budget an extra margin of both time and money because something always goes wrong." Scott surveyed the front yard from the bungalow's front step. Might as well bring out the jackhammer and reserve the bob cat. They could salvage lost time by breaking up the driveway during the electric repairs.

"Well, I trust you to keep us on course. I'm itching to get in the kitchen again. You got any free time this weekend?"

"Uh ..." Scott thought of the dining room table he'd planned to start making tomorrow, but his client's emotional satisfaction took precedence. "I might."

"Good. Come out tomorrow while Ruby's at garden club. What should we make?"

Scott could practically hear the sandpaper sound of the older man rubbing his hands together.

Seeking a more comfortable position, he removed his tool belt and shifted his tired body. "Whatever you want to."

"Well, how's your girl?"

"My girl?"

"Little Miss Shelby!"

"Oh. Lester, something tells me she'd take exception to being called that."

"Not so good, huh?"

"We're working great together." Scott extended a cramping leg as he hastened to reassure his client. "But I told you earlier this week how she wanted to sit down with David Barnes about the article in the newspaper. She wasn't too happy when I told her y'all agreed with me that we shouldn't pursue a meeting."

"Mm, I'm sorry about that, but be patient with her. I think she's got our best interests at heart."

"I think she's got *her* best interests at heart. She's way too worried about what everyone thinks and listens too much to that *femme fatale* real estate agent of hers." Scott stopped, rubbed his jaw. "I'm sorry. I shouldn't talk about that."

Lester fell silent a moment before replying in a firm tone. "Scott, you're our contractor, but I'd like to believe you're more too. Ruby and I have taken a real interest in both you and Shelby. I hope you can think of us as friends, not just clients."

"I do. I just—don't want to see Shelby trying to fill her husband's absence with the wrong things. Even though she said she didn't come by the house today because she thought she was coming down with a cold, she's going to this fancy dinner with Tasha, the real estate agent, tonight."

"At which there will be eligible men?"

Scott sighed. "It's not like it's my concern."

"It's clear from the frustration in your voice that you like Shelby. A cold, hmm? And a cold front coming in tonight with rain too. I know what we're making. Be here at ten."

After the double beep, Scott found himself staring at the "call ended" screen.

Scott told himself as he drove to Lester's the next morning that he'd maintain professionalism, not talk about his dratted attraction to Shelby, and simply provide the hands to make what Lester's couldn't. This was a God thing.

But like before, Scott found he was the one receiving a blessing. And he did talk about Shelby. A lot.

"We're making chicken soup from scratch."

Amazing, savory smells gave credence to Lester's announcement as he led Scott into the kitchen.

He had Scott take the meat off the carcass he'd simmered in his Dutch oven, then begin the time-consuming process of dicing onion, celery, garlic, bay leaves, sage, thyme, rosemary, and marjoram. The tiny, flaky herbs kept escaping Scott's thick fingers. As he chopped and Lester asked questions, Scott shared how he feared Shelby entertained the notion of rebooting "Dodson's Do-Overs" with an emphasis on historical renovations.

Lester seemed amused at the idea. "And with you as the male lead?"

"I guess. With a name change, of course. Maybe Dodson and Matthews, in that order."

"And would that be so bad?" With slow and careful movements, waiting it out when a tremor took control of his hands, Lester added Scott's ingredients to the chicken broth.

"Yes!"

"But you said you like working with her."

"Yeah, but not with a bunch of cameras pointed at us. When it's just us, she can be herself. She doesn't even know what that is yet. I think that show changed her. I don't want it changing me. I don't want to be some second-rate Chet Dodson. Call me old-fashioned, but I want her to want me around for me, not for some show." The intensity of his own response surprised Scott.

Lester's wizened smile accepted his feelings without criticism. "Now that we've got the broth back to a boil, just keep it simmering, son. Some things can't be rushed. While we're waiting, we'll make the noodles."

"*Make* the noodles?"

"You want authentic flavor, you don't use store bought." Lester shoved a medium-sized mixing bowl in front of him. "Two cups of flour, half a teaspoon of salt. Make a well in the center, and add your egg in. Three yolks, and one whole egg. I'm afraid you'll have to do those. I've cleaned one too many eggs off the floor in the last six months."

Watching Scott mix, Lester's brow knit in concentration, and he indicated the exact moment to start adding water.

"You in the kitchen reminds me of myself in the workshop." Scott paused to glance at Lester. "I can see why you love this. It's therapeutic."

"Have you told Shelby about your family's business yet?"

"I was about to earlier this week—"

"Now, knead it. Every time you add water."

Scott plunged both hands into the bowl as he finished his sentence. "But now I'm afraid to. You should've seen her face when I told her my family lives on Milledge Road. If she knows the extent of my family's success, it could fuel this ridiculous notion she has about re-starting the show."

"No, no, only a few tablespoons. Too much, too quick, and it won't come out right. You just keep plugging away, son. She'll soon be taking notice. But don't be afraid to show her your assets when the time is right."

Waiting on the porch of Shelby's four-square, Scott feared this wasn't the type of "taking notice" he and Lester had counted on. Shelby's red-nosed, make-up-free face looked far from happy that he stood there with a container of chicken noodle soup in his hand.

"I'm a mess," she said. "I wasn't expecting anybody."

Her fluffy robe over PJ pants, tank top, and messy bun made her adorable, although Scott doubted Shelby would see it that way. She might not accept the food, much less invite him in. Scott tried not to sound desperate. "We made it from scratch. Lester knew you were sick and will be disappointed if you don't try some." As he awaited the verdict, he reached down to pet Maltie, who scrambled at his leg.

A hand flecked with dried paint jerked the door open, and Angelina's sunny face appeared behind her sister. "Oh, stop being such a grumpy pot and let him in, Shelby. Who turns down chicken noodle soup? Not me, and I'm not even sick."

"Hey, Angelina." Scott took the opportunity to push past his frowning co-worker and follow her younger sister to the kitchen.

"It smells marvelous," Angelina said. "Have you eaten?"

Shelby muttered as she trailed them through the living room. "Not sure this is professionally appropriate."

While Scott appreciated Shelby's obvious taste and creative decorating touches, he found her proclivity to turn historic homes into show places for trendy furnishings and modern art a disappointing use of her talent. Ignoring that as well as Shelby's comment, he responded to Angelina. "Not unless sampling the broth counts. But it should be great, at least if rolling out homemade egg noodles counts for anything."

"You went to that much trouble for Lester?" Shelby asked from behind him.

Scott paused and looked at her, wondering if she could really be that dense. "And for you." Now what made him admit that? Maybe the lingering effect of the emotional honesty oozing out of Lester's kitchen.

Shelby's puffy blue eyes widened, then blinked.

Scott cleared his throat as though to diffuse the warmth creeping up from his collar. "You *are* sick, right?"

"Right. I just think it's super nice … what you're doing for Lester."

If Shelby could admire kindness to Lester rather than accept interest in herself, he'd have to take that for now. Scott smiled. "It's my pleasure."

Shelby looked embarrassed as Angelina rummaged for bowls and crackers, but since she kept righting her drooping bun, maybe that was due to insecurity over her appearance. She sniffed and blotted her nose with a crumpled tissue.

"I guess you were too sick to go to the party last night, then?" As he and Shelby took seats at the breakfast room table, Scott couldn't keep from feeling hopeful. In any case, the need for a report on Tasha's country club crowd event was one of the main reasons he'd shouldered his way inside rather than allowing Shelby to dismiss him. He was not impressed by Tasha's posturing. Even though his parents had become successful, apart from church and business involvement in the community, they chose to lead quiet lives rather than getting caught up in the need to compare and compete.

Shelby placed Maltie on the floor. "No, I made it, although I left a little early."

"Oh? Did you have fun?" Scott thanked Angelina as she set a napkin and spoon in front of him.

"Yes. I caught up with a lot of my old friends."

"Did the Barnes case come up?"

Shelby wrapped her fingers around the bowl Angelina slid in front of her as if to soak up the warmth. "Some of the people had read the article, but I got the opportunity to clarify that the reason I took the job was to honor the Wentworths' long-standing commitment as a couple, and in turn, to honor Chet."

With that exalted sentiment, Scott wouldn't be surprised if confetti fell from the ceiling. So she'd been lauded as the noble young widow.

She sniffed and dabbed her nose with a tissue. "And of course, the spirit of that private endeavor, and not some unsolved case, calls for no cameras. I think they got it." Shelby inhaled the aromatic vapors wafting up from her bowl, then dipped her spoon in and sipped as Angelina sat down. "Mm."

Scott grinned when Shelby closed her eyes. "Like it?"

Shelby seemed unable to admit her approval directly to Scott. Instead, she said to Angelina, "Don't tell Mom, but I think this is better than hers."

As Angelina sampled and the girls discussed the merits of the soup, Scott bowed his head to say a quick, silent blessing. Looking up, he realized both sisters watched him. "Sorry. I didn't mean to make that awkward."

"No, it's our fault. I'm afraid I've set a bad example with saying the blessing." Shelby slid a loose strand of hair behind her ear and tucked her chin. "We'll get back to that, won't we, Angelina?"

"Sure, but you'll have to remind me. Dad and Aubrey don't bother to pray before meals."

"Nor attend church either, I dare say." Shelby muttered the comment before blowing on her soup.

"Nope."

"Well, next time we go to my church, we can try a different Sunday school class. And I hope you'll find a good campus ministry to get involved with."

Angelina nodded, cutting her eyes at Scott, giving him the feeling she didn't want to protest in front of him. Had Angelina not liked Shelby's church?

After an awkward beat of everyone eating in silence and trying not to slurp the hot liquid, Shelby spoke again in an overly bright voice. "Julian was there last night. I think it was good for him to see me."

Scott tried not to chuckle at her choice of wording. "Why is that?"

"To realize I wasn't shamed into hiding after your embarrassing debacle at his store, of course. Scrambling about on the floor disguised like a common thief!"

"Hey, it was your idea to wear the hat and glasses."

Angelina pushed back from the table and cackled with laughter, earning Shelby's scolding stare.

"Well, you left me little choice when you barged in there."

"I thought you'd wait outside."

"*Obviously,* you needed my help."

Shelby seemed determined to argue. You'd almost think he'd offended her with his offer of dinner. Why? Crumbling another handful of crackers over his bowl, Scott returned to the subject of the most interest. "And the lawyer, was he at the party too?"

"He was very charming." A smug smile danced over Shelby's lips. "He wanted me to stay for the karaoke and dancing, but I started feeling blah."

Angelina's head popped up. "You said you came home early because he bored you to death talking about real estate law."

As Shelby turned red, Scott stifled a laugh, blessing the little sister's honesty. He decided to save Shelby an explanation by gesturing to Angelina's stained hands. "Shelby said you like to paint. What are you working on?"

Angelina beamed. "A painting of Shelby's house, as a little thank you for putting up with me." She winked at her sister.

"It's so good, I asked her to paint the bungalow for the Wentworths too," Shelby said to him. "Angelina's style is similar to Caitlyn's. I know I'm prejudiced, but I might say she's even better. In any case, I can use both when I decorate."

"Well, that's great." Scott ignored the slight to Caitlyn. When Shelby and Caitlyn had met, he'd sensed they didn't like each other, though he didn't know how that could be on such a short acquaintance. Perhaps a certain tension was to be expected between two attractive, successful women.

"After I finish the house paintings, I've got to get inspired." Angelina waved her spoon in Scott's direction, flinging a tiny drop of liquid onto his arm. He surreptitiously wiped it with his napkin as she kept talking. "If I come up with something cutting edge, my stepmother promised me a spot in her spring showing in Atlanta. She'll invite some very influential people in the art community there. It could be a big break for me."

As the lines of Shelby's body tightened with tension, Scott offered an alternative. "If your work is as good as Shelby says, I can introduce you to Caitlyn. No cutting edge needed, just what you do naturally. She's looking at opening a bigger gallery right here in Augusta."

"Really? That would be awesome!" Slurping down the last of her soup, Angelina sprang up from the table. "Come on, I'll show you what I've got so far."

Rising with hesitation, Scott glanced at Shelby.

She smiled. "Go ahead. I can clean up."

Angelina's art did possess a similar vibe to Caitlyn's but demonstrated just enough less maturity that Caitlyn might view Angelina as a mentorship opportunity rather than a threat. He praised the golden, early autumn light bathing Shelby's four-square in Angelina's painting. A likeness of Maltie even waited on the steps.

"Are you enjoying living here as opposed to the dorm?" Scott asked as Angelina restacked a line of paintings she'd shown him.

"Oh yes, although it has its pros and cons. I don't notice a mess the way Shelby does. One thing can be out of place, and it will drive her crazy. But I'm trying to keep stuff cleaned up. It helps that I'm on the second floor. And I think she's trying to not be hard on me."

"I'm glad you can be here for her."

"She likes you, you know," Angelina said as she led Scott into the hallway. At Scott's shocked expression, she added, "Sorry that she's kind of salty today, but the fact you can ruffle her feathers is a good thing. You're pushing her boundaries. Not like Chet did, not loud and obnoxious. Subtler, but steady. And I like the food idea."

Scott didn't have a chance to respond to Angelina's unexpected observations or the exaggerated wink she gave him because as they descended the stairs, she started chattering loudly about how excited she was to meet Caitlyn.

Shelby waited for them in the living room, Maltie in her arms. "I take it you approved?"

Scott cleared his throat. "So much so that I feel sure Caitlyn could not only show your sister's talent, but might be interested in helping her further develop it. I'll talk with her."

"Okay, well, you've got me inspired! I'm going to paint." Angelina accompanied her announcement with an enthusiastic wave from the bottom step. "Thanks for the soup, Scott."

Before he could say "you're welcome," Angelina disappeared around the landing.

Shelby turned to him and shook her head with a smile. "She's still so young, even though she went through a lot after the divorce. Mom tried hard to shelter her from the worst. I want to see her succeed with her dreams, and to realize she can do that without Aubrey. I don't think she's a good influence."

"I understand. I'm happy to do what I can to help. I know you'd like her to stay close after she graduates, especially since your mom moved."

"Yes, I would. Thank you." Following him to the door, Shelby fell silent for a moment, then she said, "Scott, can I ask you something?"

Scott's heartbeat kicked up a notch, but he tried to keep his voice casual. "Sure."

"Why are you being so nice to me?"

When faced with a potentially awkward conversation with a girl, Austin always advised maintaining the upper ground by countering with more questions. "Aren't you used to people being nice to you?"

"Well, yeah … mostly when they want something. Which was a lot when I had the show. Not so much now."

"Can't somebody just be nice for the sake of being nice?" Scott shoved his hand in his pocket as Shelby reached for the doorknob. "It's not all about getting ahead or using someone. I prefer to look at my business partnerships as friendships."

Swinging the door open, Shelby hid her face in Maltie's fur. "Okay, as long as that's all it is. Because you know … I'm not ready for anything else."

He tried not to react to the punch to his chest. "Of course not. I wanted us to be friends in high school. I'm glad we get the chance now."

"Me too." Moving past the personal declaration with a brevity that revealed how little Shelby had invested, her eyes lit up. "I should mention, Tasha found a phone number online for Sharon Barnes' older sister, who was married and living in Anderson, South Carolina, when Sharon married Charles. Tasha called her this morning."

Scott's control slipped. "Why? This isn't her business."

He just wanted to do this renovation in peace and forget a woman had ever disappeared from the house. Besides, this quest into the past diverted Shelby's attention from meaningful work and relationships in the present.

"Because she's like a pit bull when she gets a hold of something. And she's very protective of her friends."

He closed his eyes for a second. "Or she's one of those hoping for something in the future."

"Scott, that was rude! You don't even know Tasha."

Scott sighed. "You're right." *Just what I surmised in sixty seconds.* "Although I don't think the Wentworths received the best impression of her in the past either."

"What—"

"Doesn't matter." Cutting off any questions or protests, Scott waved his hand to prompt Shelby along. "What did she find out?"

Shelby pressed her lips together and adjusted Maltie's weight. "The sister painted Charles as a controlling workaholic who wasn't into women's lib in the '70s and resented his wife working."

"Enough to make him kill her?"

She tilted her golden head. "Unless it was an accident."

"Look, despite my interest in old houses, I'm all for leaving the past in the past. More often than not, you stir up unwanted memories and skeletons, emotional if not physical."

"And I'm all for believing that you can't move into the future with unsolved problems from the past." Shelby stopped and stared straight ahead. "Probably because that's not gone so well for me."

How did she do that? Draw him back in with sudden transparency a mere moment after pushing him away?

"Yeah, but this isn't about us. It's about an old man sitting in a nursing home—a man who might be falsely suspected of killing his wife—and a son who grew up in the shadow of that. And without a mother. I'm trusting you'll take the wishes of the Wentworths into account and not contact the Barnes family again. Okay?"

"Okay." Shelby smiled, but from the brief way she met his eyes, Scott feared there was something she wasn't telling him.

Chapter Thirteen

"West End Premium Pre-owned." Shelby read the sign aloud as Tasha turned her yellow Corvette into the parking lot a few days later. "A used car dealership? This is the Barnes family business?"

"West End's reputation is well-established in the area as a luxury car dealer. They'd probably take exception to the term 'used car dealership.' Kind of like calling a flight attendant a stewardess these days." Tasha parked and slid a strand of hair behind one ear. "I bought my own car here. That's how I got a quick audience with the owner."

"Well, that was a lucky break."

"Not luck, sweetheart. Leverage." Tasha opened her door and slung her Vuitton handbag over her shoulder.

Quelling a stirring of unease, Shelby followed the taller woman into a glass-framed showroom that smelled of wax, air freshener, and fresh-brewed coffee. She'd told Scott she wouldn't ask any more questions. Well, she hadn't. She'd just not volunteered the information that Tasha was already setting up this meeting. When Tasha called with a date and time, Shelby's curiosity overcame any misgivings.

"Miss Clausen, so good to see you." A short, stocky salesman of middle age hurried to intercept them as Tasha strode toward the reception desk. "I can take you right back to Mr. Barnes. He's expecting you."

Tasha looked down her nose. "Wonderful."

He chuckled and gestured to a Corvette the color of a fire engine in the middle of the showroom. "And as you can see, she's still right there waiting for you."

"You're buying a car?" Shelby frowned at Tasha.

Tasha shot her a threatening moue and followed their escort down a long, paneled hallway with her hair kissing the small of her back and her heels clicking on the linoleum. Keeping her own back straight and matching her friend's confident stride, Shelby repressed that little-girl sensation that often came over her next to Miss European Supermodel. Every tie-wearing male in every office they passed stared as they walked by.

Outside a closed door at the end of the hallway, the salesman pivoted on shiny wingtips and gazed up at Tasha. "Let me apologize again that we lost the note after you called asking us to keep an eye out for red."

Tasha tilted her head and smiled. "It's no problem."

A terrible suspicion came over Shelby as the door swung open and the sales associate introduced David Barnes. A suspicion that almost overshadowed her first impression of the blond, balding man with a slight spare tire who rose from behind a mahogany desk. And what David Barnes said as he shook Tasha's hand only underscored Shelby's dread.

"Miss Clausen, a pleasure to meet you. My manager said you wanted to speak with me about a trade-plus-cash. He said you got tired of yellow! I can't imagine."

Tasha introduced Shelby as her friend. As Shelby shook David's hand, she tried to see the little boy who had waited for days, weeks, months, for his mother to come home. How long had it taken him to give up? Had he ever?

Placing her purse on her lap, the real estate agent settled into her leather-cushioned chair. "I do want to know what type of deal you could offer me, Mr. Barnes, but after we discuss another matter."

"Oh? What's that?" Still wearing a congenial expression slightly tempered with caution, David glanced between the two women. Shelby wondered if he could read her guilt.

Typical to her personality, Tasha went for the jugular. "Why you didn't reveal the particulars of your mother's unsolved case to Shelby's clients when they asked if they needed to know anything else about your house."

Shelby felt her stomach sink, right at the moment the slight natural flush some blond men possessed drained from David's face.

Tasha waited, then spoke again softly, making the threat all the more powerful. "Under Georgia law, I'd consider that non-disclosure."

David fixed on Shelby, making her want to blurt out that this little ambush had not been her idea. "Mrs. Dodson, I assure you no deception was intended. My real estate agent thought your clients were inquiring about the physical condition of the house."

Tasha blew a little air out of her burgundy lips. "Not likely."

"They had just been asking about the roof and the electrical. As for my mother's disappearance, it's merely that. A disappearance. There was no criminal activity to disclose."

Shelby sat forward. "Mr. Barnes, we don't intend to make accusations or to upset you. In fact, I hate to bring all this to light again, but with that recent newspaper article—which you probably saw—it creates a very negative environment for the older couple who purchased the home as their fiftieth anniversary present."

Tasha pressed her lips together. At first, Shelby thought she was annoyed that she'd spoken up, but a sad frown almost immediately settled over her features as she spring-boarded off Shelby's statement. "And what Shelby won't mention is how the selection of such a house on the eve of her own husband's untimely death creates a poor reflection on her professionally."

Shelby weighed the possibility that Tasha's concern might truly fuel her investigations. As nice as it was to feel like someone had her back—an assurance she'd dearly missed—the motivation did not excuse Tasha's methods with David.

"I'd say it creates a negative environment for me too." David pushed away from his desk, elbows on arm rests, fingers steepled. "Since that article, this place has been deserted. I fear a return to the days when my father had to take the family name off the business my grandpa built up from nothing. He almost didn't make it."

"I'm glad he didn't give up on the family legacy," Shelby said.

"Well, that and he didn't want to take me away from his family here in Augusta. At that time, his aging parents relied on him as well."

David swiveled to indicate a grouping of sepia prints behind him, depicting men in fedora hats and ties posed with various models of antique vehicles. When he looked back around, his shoulders slumped.

"Even now, I try to keep a low profile and let my manager be the face of the place, but I'm afraid this will make everyone remember."

Tasha started to speak, but Shelby silenced her with a wave of her hand. Disregarding Tasha's startled frown, she leaned forward, hoping her face communicated her compassion. "We don't want that to happen, either, Mr. Barnes. Perhaps we can work together, help stop the rumor mill. May I ask what *you* think happened to your mother?"

David released a deep sigh and rubbed his face. "This is very personal. It's not something I talk about."

"But now your father's past has impacted a number of other people." Tasha drew her mouth into a flat line.

David sat upright. "But that's just it, it's not his fault! He is the biggest victim of all."

"You're sure he's innocent," Shelby stated.

"That's right. Yes, they argued. He wasn't the most patient man, and maybe he was controlling, but not any more than was typical for his generation. But he would never hit her. He loved her. Maybe a little too much. Maybe she got tired of him up in her business all the time, tired of all the conflict, and hopped a bus to somewhere."

Tasha quirked up a manicured brow. "Without taking her ID, her purse?"

"If she wanted to start a new life, maybe. She could've had money stashed away we didn't know about."

Remembering the first holiday returning home from college after her dad left, Shelby's heart twisted. She asked softly, "But would she leave *you* that way?"

"The alternative is worse."

Shelby offered a sympathetic smile. "For a child, though, is it?"

A shutter came down over the light-hazel eyes. "Mrs. Dodson, with God's help when I was a teenager, I forgave my mother. If I wanted any semblance of a normal life, I had to, because the anger of her abandoning me was eating me up inside. It didn't really matter what happened to her. She left."

Shelby sensed they had pressed too far and sat forward to take their leave. Tasha, however, waved her hand under the overhang of the desk, encouraging Shelby to wait. "Mr. Barnes, we should return to the pressing matter—"

David didn't even seem to notice her. Words rolled off the older man's tongue. "Watching the toll this took on Dad was far worse. In the late '70s, he turned this business over to a friend to manage for a time, then ran it from home after he recovered some mental stability. But he pretty much became a hermit. And he refused to move out of that house. He'd never say it, but I think he held onto some perverse belief that she might show back up there."

"Oh no." Shelby's hand fluttered to her heart. Tasha cut her an impatient glance.

David nodded. Did Tasha not even notice that sympathy, not intimidation, had made him open up? "Getting him into the nursing home was a major feat. Now his health is bad, but he's the most peaceful I've ever seen him. I can't risk this upsetting him again, so I can only ask you to drop this and please, please, leave us in peace. I've been through this a hundred times over the last forty years. I don't have any more answers than I did back then."

As David stood up, so did Shelby, shouldering her purse. In the face of the man's obvious pain, her heart hammered, and she wanted to flee. But Tasha remained seated, legs crossed. "All this is very distressing, I am sure, Mr. Barnes, but still does not satisfy the question of nondisclosure."

The man sighed, his arms hanging heavy at the sides of his pin-striped, short-sleeved shirt. "I guess you'll have to take it up with my lawyer, then, Miss Clausen, because we didn't hide anything a simple Google on the property wouldn't have told you. I won't lie to you about the fact that being rid of that house feels like a fifty-pound weight lifted from my shoulders."

Rising slowly, Tasha replied to David's first statement. "If the situation causes the buyers any further distress, we just might do that."

Shelby hooked a hand through the real estate agent's elbow. "We apologize for taking up your time, Mr. Barnes."

After she pulled Tasha out of the office, she marched straight past the fire-engine-red Corvette they had not discussed at all and out of the showroom.

Later that day, Shelby opened the front door of the bungalow to find Scott and Todd installing the iron rail for the stairs. "Oh wow, that looks good!"

Scott looked up from drilling, undisguised pleasure flashing over his features. The effect couldn't have hit Shelby more squarely in the chest if he'd thrown a hammer. "Hey! You're here!"

"Yep, the guilt of poor Seth removing all the old nails and wallpaper by himself kept eating at me."

"We're touched you thought of us in our sufferings." Todd placed a hand to the front of his flannel shirt before testing the new rail with a gentle shake, while the boss nodded his approval.

Scott winked at Shelby. "I have to admit, I was sore about taking out the old banister, but I like the openness of the iron on both sides."

Shelby stifled a smug smile. "Thank you! Well, I hear Seth upstairs. I'll go see how I can help him." Following Tasha's morning errand, and considering Scott's proclivity to ferret out the truth, she harbored no desire to linger in his presence.

Scott stood and jogged down to where his tool box rested in the foyer. Shifting things around, he lifted out a small, new hammer with sharp tongs. "I'll tell you how you can help him. You can tackle those nails in the master bedroom. After removing the glue and wiping the walls with that first batch of TSP, he hasn't gotten back in there for the nails, and that room's a nightmare." He chuckled when Shelby didn't try to hide her dismay. "I'll come help you in a few minutes."

"Oh, that's okay. I'll do what I can, then leave. Maybe unexpectedly if I can't take it." Forcing a weak smile at her lame joke, Shelby hefted the hammer.

"No running out on us!" Todd's voice followed her. "We'll be listening."

In the back room, Shelby admired the increased light admitted by the new French doors. She couldn't wait to design the patio space on the other side. Then she surveyed the unpleasant labor before her, and her spirits sank. Removing her heels, Shelby placed her purse and water on a folding tray and went to work.

Some of the nails came out easily, while others had been pushed in too far for the hammer prongs to loosen. Threads of the old wallpaper clung under the edges with the stubborn tenacity of age. As she worked, she wondered if this had been Charles and Sharon's bedroom. Had their fights taken place here, muffled from a small child's ears by only a closed door? What tears and hurtful words had these walls witnessed? Remembering with guilt the almost visible weight David Barnes still carried, the unease in her chest deepened.

"You're doing great." Scott stood in the doorway, dressed for the cooler weather in an old Henley with his jeans rather than a T-shirt.

"Some of these nails are impossible."

"Let me see what I can do with them." He disappeared, returning a minute later with needle-nosed pliers. "Leave the stubborn ones to me."

"Thanks, I appreciate that."

Scott flashed her a smile, creating laugh lines around his mouth. "Just trying to get you to stay more than an hour."

They worked in silence for a few minutes before Scott glanced over at her. "You okay?"

"Yeah, why?"

"You're quiet."

"I'm fine. I think maybe I feel some of that sadness Ruby referred to, especially in this room. It's creeping me out a little."

Scott stopped and looked around. "Why, you think something happened in here?"

"I just wondered if it was their bedroom. It makes sense that it would have been."

He peered at her with that discerning look of his. "Did something put you in this mood?"

"No." A swell of guilt rose up from her middle to swamp her at that lie. "Yes. Tasha and I went to see David Barnes this morning."

"You did what?"

"Now don't get all mad. It was her idea, and she set up the meeting."

"But you went!"

"It was set before the Wentworths said not to worry about it."

"You could have refused to go."

Shelby tugged too hard on a tight nail, causing it to fly past her. She bent to pick it up, then dropped it in the box with the others with a metallic *ping*.

"You know what I encountered last night when I was leaving here?" Facing Scott, she put a hand on her hip in a self-righteous stance. "Two teenagers in the bushes, taking pictures for their blog. Just like Tasha predicted! I did my best to set them straight about the privacy of those involved, but I doubt it will do much good. Who knows what they'll publish."

Looking away from her, Scott shook his head, not over the blog, she could tell, but over her actions. Why did his disappointment twist her heart into a knot? She shouldn't care what he thought. Only her career and the future peace of the Wentworths mattered. And now, that added burden for David Barnes.

Shelby jutted her chin out. "I'm glad I went. I mean, it was awful. He was so sad, Scott. Afraid this latest article would harm their family business again. He runs West End Premium Pre-owned—used car sales. But it gave me clarity that he doesn't think his father's guilty."

Unloading felt better. Even if Scott continued pulling nails without much response, she could tell he was listening, weighing her words. Shelby summarized the visit to the Barnes' son, concluding with her own conflicted reaction. "What struck me was when he said he forgave his mother whether she left him by choice or not. I can't imagine being in that situation. But actually ..." Her voice trailed off. "I kind of can."

Scott stopped and studied her. "Then maybe some good can come of this."

Shelby opened a hand on her chest to illustrate her sincerity. "I feel so bad for him. I can't seem to shake it. I wish there was something we could do to make people stop assuming the worst."

"People love a mystery or a scandal more than they love the truth. Trying to tear their fiction away from them is like trying to take a meaty bone from my German shepherd. Or getting this stupid nail out of the wall. It's right here next to the door to the bathroom, so I'd rather not leave it."

"Let me see." Shelby bent and peered over Scott's shoulder. "Maybe if we can get that fabric out from behind, it will loosen it up. I have an idea." As she crossed the room to dig her makeup bag out of her purse, she asked, "You have a German shepherd? Aren't those mean?"

"Luther protects the property, but he's a big puppy where his family is concerned."

"Your house?"

"Uh … yeah." Scott sounded lost in thought, but when she knelt next to him, he asked in surprise, "Tweezers?"

Shelby grinned and started picking at the threads behind the problem nail. "Only wait, and be amazed. A woman's beauty tools serve many purposes."

"I don't even want to know."

"Well? Do you have any ideas for how we can counter the negative publicity?" She flicked her hair out of her way.

"Um …" Again Scott sounded distracted. Maybe she'd hit him with her hair.

When Shelby wobbled, he steadied her with a warm hand on her elbow. She offered a quick smile. "Thanks. I thought of contacting a friend at a local magazine about doing an article. If people read Ruby and Lester's love story, compassion for them could help still wagging tongues."

"I think you're on the right track. Focus on the new and uplifting, not the old and sordid."

"Really?" Encouraged, Shelby glanced over, suddenly aware that without his proverbial ball cap on, Scott seemed much closer. Stomach muscles tightening as his breath fanned her cheek, she focused her attention on the stubborn wallpaper fragments.

"Yeah. You know, the grace David Barnes shows could be a lesson to us all. I think we tend to assume the worst about each other."

"And the remedy for that? Believe the best and be disappointed? Because that's pretty much my track record." Shelby made a face.

Scott lightly touched her back, whether for physical or emotional support, Shelby couldn't tell. "Give a person a chance, and leave the rest in God's hands."

Trying to discern how that applied to her, Shelby remained silent. Chet had never said things she had to ponder like that. Her mom would call Scott "a deep well."

When Scott bent his head close to tug a chunk loose and Shelby got a whiff of aftershave, she held her breath so she wouldn't hyperventilate. She hadn't been this close to a man in almost a year. Apparently, she missed it more than she thought.

"There! Now let me try it." Scott applied the pliers, and the tack slid out. He grinned at her. "Triumph! Amazing what we can do when we work together."

Shelby blinked, smiled, and held up the tweezers for a joking squeeze.

"After that, I need my sweet tea." Scott stood, taking the unwelcome tension of awareness with him. "Can I get you something?"

Shelby sucked in a lungful of man-free air. "Uh, nope, I've got a water right over there, thanks."

After he left, she made a wide-eyed grimace at the wall, gave her head a brisk shake, and returned her attention to a tack right against the thick baseboard. Shifting her weight, her knee bumped the trim piece, and it wobbled against the doorframe. Shelby slid her finger along the edge to determine the size of the crack. Yep, she probably should mention it to Scott. Then she froze, because something with a pointy edge contacted her skin. A piece of paper?

Picking up the tweezers, Shelby fished in the slight opening … and pulled out a faded Polaroid photograph.

Chapter Fourteen

On Friday, Scott startled Shelby with a sudden announcement from the doorway of the bungalow's master bath. "The insulation guys are finished for today, and I've got to go."

Shelby looked up from her sixth row of subway tile in the shower. "Why?" She glanced at her watch. Wasn't it early for him to be cutting out? Did he have a hot date? She frowned at the notion. Not because she felt jealous, of course—but that he'd leave her toiling while he left to have fun.

"Lester called and said Ruby's been working in the yard all day getting ready for their house showing tomorrow, and he wants to make her a good meal."

"Oh, that's nice." She didn't pause to examine the relief that rushed through her.

"That's looking great, Shelby." Scott stepped into the opening behind her and reached down for the level.

She gave an indignant laugh. "Yeah, but you've still got to check me, don't you? I just did that!"

He moved the level along the wall and whistled. "You sure did, girl. Man! I've found my new tile master." When he held out his fist, she tapped hers against it. His eyes sparkled with admiration. "Who would've thought you'd love this?"

Pushing on his leg to get him to move, she dipped her trowel in her bucket of white, thin-set, polymer modified mortar. "I wouldn't say I love it. I'd say once you got me started in here, and then left me by climbing up in the attic with those insulation guys, I had little choice. You know how unfinished projects annoy me."

Scott grinned. "I was counting on it." Then the grin vanished. "But honestly, I don't want to trap you into anything. If you want to go, I can ask Todd to finish this."

"No, I can do it. Todd's got his hands full right now. It helps that these white tiles have built-in spacers."

Scott unbuckled his tool belt. "Right. You've got your reference lines on the backer board. Just keep using the level every few rows so you don't get a bow."

Shelby narrowed her eyes. "I won't mess it up, Scott."

"Okay, okay. Sorry."

Turning back to the wall, Shelby asked, "So Lester won't settle for take-out?"

"Apparently, only his mother's recipe fried chicken will do."

"Oh, that sounds heavenly." Shelby had been so taken up with the tiling that she had only eaten half of her sandwich several hours ago. Amazing how hungry physical labor made a person. No wonder Chet used to eat like a bear every night.

"Why don't you come out in a couple of hours? Uh, you got that?" Scott asked with an undertone of anxiety as Shelby spread mortar.

"I might be clunky and slow, but you can believe I'll get it smooth. You wanted me to learn to do this stuff, right?"

"Yeah, but I really didn't expect you to take to it. I thought I'd end up tiling it all myself." Still hovering annoyingly close, Scott gave her a wink.

Pinching her face into a fake scowl, Shelby whipped around and brandished the goopy trowel in Scott's direction. As he jumped clear of the shower, she cried, "Back, back, out of my domain!"

"Yes, ma'am!" Snatching his tool belt, Scott retreated into the bedroom as she chased him, then whirled and held up his index finger. "But you've got mortar on your face."

She stopped and raised her free hand. "I do? Where?"

Scott grinned. "Right here." Tweaking her nose, Scott displayed the evidence on his thumb.

"Oh, kind of makes me look less fierce, I bet."

The way he smiled made Shelby feel around for other splotches.

"You're good. But seriously, come out tonight. Lester doesn't know how to cook for two."

"Are you sure they'd be okay with it?"

"They'd be delighted."

"All right, but text me if they have other plans." Shelby turned back to work.

She didn't want to give Scott the satisfaction of admitting it, but she did kind of enjoy laying tile. She wished her life possessed the predictable symmetry of the shiny rectangles. Placing them helped organize her thoughts, thoughts that had been whirring ever since she found the photograph of Sharon Barnes.

The young woman pictured wore a little black dress. The center-part of her long tresses just reached shoulder-height of a handsome, dark-haired man. The man who abducted her? Her killer? Her lover? Or perhaps someone who had nothing at all to do with her disappearance.

Scott's advice to content herself and take a life lesson from what she'd learned about the Barnes family fresh in her mind, Shelby had told no one about the Polaroid tucked in her purse. Not even Angelina.

But she *had* pored over the screen of her laptop, searching for old news clippings and even stalking social media for possible relatives of David and Charles. That proved difficult because, for obvious reasons, both men maintained a low profile. But as far as Shelby could tell, the man in the print wasn't a younger Charles, and he didn't resemble anyone Shelby could guess might be related.

In the car, she brushed her hair and applied makeup in the rearview mirror. She opened her sun roof to enjoy the cooling temperature on her drive and turned on the radio to a popular Christian station. Somehow in the midst of this project, while nature faded into winter, life stirred inside her.

A few minutes later, Shelby's CRV bumped down a long, sandy driveway. Ruby waved from the front porch of a brick ranch. Dressed in a rayon blouse printed in autumn shades of rust and gold with coordinated slacks, she stood as Shelby parked. One would never guess the older lady had spent the day trimming hedges and putting out pine straw. Self-conscious of her casual work attire, Shelby brushed off her jeans as she got out of her car. Despite kneeling on a towel and making every effort to putty with care, some white flecks adorned her pants legs.

"I'm so glad you've come!" Ruby leaned down the steps to embrace her.

"I appreciate the invitation. You have a lovely place."

"Yes, it's going to be hard to part with it. Lots of good memories here. This is where I raised my boys, you know." She smirked. "But I know you're going to make that bungalow so snug I'll feel at home the minute I walk through the door."

Shelby laid a comforting hand on Ruby's arm. "That's the plan."

"Speaking of walking through doors, I've been exiled to the front porch. I'm sorry if Lester lured Scott away from important work and left you holding the bag. He can be very persistent when the urge to cook hits."

"Oh, not at all. I'm enjoying work on the bungalow."

"I'm so glad. Scott told us how you've rolled up your sleeves." Ruby extended a hand toward the rockers with gingham cushions grouped by a small table. "Won't you join me? We do have some lemonade and cookies to tide us over."

"Thanks, I'd love a drink, and I'm glad we have this moment to speak alone." Shelby's legs sang in relief as she eased her weight off muscles tight from hours of squatting, bending, and kneeling. "I've been wanting to ask if you have some photos of Lester's coaching days and maybe even some old menus from the restaurant that I could frame for his new office."

"My dear, that's a wonderful idea." Ruby set the pitcher down with an expressive clunk. "You see, that's exactly why I hired you. I do have some things stashed away that I can slip you before you leave tonight."

Shelby clapped her hands. "Wonderful!"

"And what's more, your timing is perfect." Ruby smiled and handed her a glass. "The new owners of the restaurant are refurbishing and having a little sale this weekend. You might want to check it out."

"I will."

After admiring Ruby's roses and flowering crape myrtle, they sipped in silence for a minute, listening to the breeze, the chirp of field crickets, passing traffic, and the faint sound of the men's voices from the kitchen. A tantalizing whiff of the fried chicken slithered past the Plexiglas door, making Shelby's stomach rumble. But not wanting to ruin dinner, she resisted the store-bought chocolate chip cookies. Her mind returned to the Polaroid in her purse.

"There is something else, Miss Ruby."

"What's that, my dear?"

Shelby dug out the evidence and handed it to her client. "I found this stuck behind the baseboard in the back bedroom. From the best I can discern, that's Sharon Barnes, probably in her thirties, but I don't think that's her husband."

Ruby fingered the print, turning it in the light to get the most out of its golden seventies tones. "Their clothing suggests a holiday party. Well, it could be anybody, but the way this man's arm is around her does make you wonder. However, it could be a relative."

"I thought that, too, but there's this light in her eye I hope I don't get when I hug a cousin."

"Oh dear. Maybe a long-lost brother?" Sighing, Ruby lowered the picture to her lap. "What have you done about this, Shelby?"

Shelby leaned back and rocked in her chair. Her legs ached in protest. "Nothing, but I can't quit thinking if this is evidence Sharon Barnes had a significant other, it could be a clue to solving her missing person's case."

"I hadn't thought about the fact that the police might have interest in it."

"That file probably went to the cold case shelf decades ago. What do you think we should do, Ruby?"

Ruby handed the photo back with a frown. "For now, nothing. I'm glad you didn't forge ahead, Shelby. Let's ask the Lord to show us the next step. All right?"

With the sharing of the burden, a sense of peace enfolded Shelby. She nodded, sliding the picture back into the side pouch of her handbag. She'd just gotten it put away when the storm door flew open, and Lester stood there with a goofy grin. "My dear." He bowed over his wife's hand before glancing at Shelby. "Shelby. Dinner is served."

Ruby stood up. "Well, that's wonderful news, but you'd best take off my apron before we sit down at the table."

Shelby burst out laughing.

"Right." Without a touch of embarrassment, Lester looked down at the ruffles silhouetting his slim hips and tugged off the offending garment.

Pursing her lips, Ruby shook her head and snatched her apron, while Lester stole a kiss. The older couple's romantic camaraderie made Shelby recall the antics her parents had once enjoyed … before her dad met Aubrey.

In the traditional dining room, Scott—thankfully, sans apron—placed a steaming basket of chicken onto an autumn-leaf tablecloth. As he smiled at her, Shelby noticed he'd lost the hat, brushed back his hair, and donned a collared cotton shirt over his colored T-shirt. Shelby wished again that she'd had time to run home to change.

After saying a prayer, Lester passed the food with the zest of a young boy. "Scott's strong arms made mashing all those potatoes really fast. And Shelby, these are my mother's secret recipes for fried chicken and biscuits."

Shelby glanced up from serving herself some of the potatoes Scott handed her. "It looks wonderful."

"I can't wait." Ruby selected a large chicken breast before passing the basket to Shelby.

"Yes, my love, it's been far too long. I don't know what I'll do after our house is ready. I'll have to find someone new to finagle into the kitchen." Lester winked at Scott, making one scruffy eyebrow descend like a small, nesting bird.

Scott smiled as he unwrapped the basket of fluffy biscuits. "Our friendship doesn't have to end with the house renovation."

Shelby was starting to feel similarly about the Wentworths. She filled her plate with a chicken breast, a biscuit, creamed corn, square-cut pole beans, and mashed potatoes. As hungry as she was, she had to force herself to slow down and savor the bacon-y sweetness of the beans and the rich buttermilk tang of the chicken crust.

"It doesn't seem like Scott messed anything up too much," Shelby said.

"Not at all. He's a natural." Lester grinned at the young man with grandfatherly approval.

The Wentworths laughed, and Scott pretended to toss his biscuit at her.

Ruby shook her head as she broke open her own bread. "You know, the only thing I can think of to compete with Mama W's biscuits are those the open hearth cook makes at Colonial Days."

Shelby asked, "What's that?"

"The North Augusta Living History Park just across the river in South Carolina has a first person weekend every mid-October. Lester and I always look forward to going."

Scott paused in scooping green beans onto his fork, glancing up. "I know the cabinet maker at the new wood shop there."

"Really?" Ruby raised her eyebrows, then clasped her hands as an idea came to her. "We should all go this year."

As Lester and Scott voiced their enthusiasm, Shelby smiled. She cast her gaze downward and tried to sound as humble as possible as she declined. "Thanks, but I don't really get why people would want to dress up as someone they're not. Like kids playing pretend. It's just … awkward. I guess history's not my thing."

"Exactly why you should go," Scott said. "Even though Colonial is a different period, it would give you a feel for the rustic simplicity the Wentworths enjoy."

"Oh, think about it, Shelby." Ruby's sweet face and pleading tone made it almost impossible to keep up a solid defense.

"Why am I the only one always trying new things?" Shelby fixed Scott with a challenging stare. "I seem to remember a promise to learn some decorating tips."

"You're not decorating yet."

"No, but I'm going antique shopping next Saturday. If you'll come along, I'll consider this Colonial thing." Cupping her mouth in a theatrical aside to Ruby, she whispered loudly, "I really just need someone strong to tote the heavy things I buy."

Ruby laughed in delight. "Scott, I think she's got you there. And may I suggest that your outing include Culpepper's on James Brown Boulevard and Broad? Their reclaimed wooden accent pieces are right up my alley." Patting her lips with her napkin, Ruby directed a wink at Scott.

Why did Ruby look so smug and Scott so blank, almost as if he didn't want to go? Wasn't he the one normally defending their client's preferences?

Uncomfortable over Scott's lack of response, Shelby spoke up. "As crazy as you and your dad are about old wood, you should love it, Scott. Even though we didn't need their style for past renovations, Culpepper's has a great reputation. I met Linda Culpepper once or twice at chamber events. A very nice lady. And the store is right down the street from my favorite antique mall."

"Culpepper's it is, then." Ruby tossed up her hands, her cream-colored napkin waving like a sign of happy surrender. "I'll let you two arrange the details, but I'm so glad to see you working together to create the home of our dreams." Patting her napkin back onto her lap with a quiet smile, she picked up her fork and addressed her homage to Lester's mashed potatoes.

Chapter Fifteen

Shelby didn't have to wait for Colonial Days to step outside her comfort zone. By the time she left their home, the Wentworths talked her into attending Cornerstone Church with them that weekend. Angelina expressed interest in trying out a campus church. Lin and Casey offered her a ride, as they often did for events when the campus bus wasn't running, leaving Shelby no excuse. Besides, she didn't want to use her younger sister as a crutch for her own comfort. So on Sunday, decked out in one of her best, deep-pink suits and the "real" jewelry Chet always liked, Shelby admired beautiful wooden beams overhead, organ pipes behind a raised platform with a choir loft, and a bunch of people who appeared to have their lives perfectly in order.

When a small worship band plugged in on stage, and the congregation started singing with enthusiasm, Shelby relaxed. The people seemed much more engaged than at her old church. The place exuded a warmth and sincerity that continued into the pastor's energetic message. Shelby hung on every word of his Ephesians 2:10-based sermon about finding God's purpose for your life.

After the benediction, Ruby turned to her. "I understand if you're ready to head home, but we'd love for you to try Sunday school. We can help you connect with people your own age, or you can visit in our class."

A lady Ruby's age who had met Shelby before the service leaned up and tapped Shelby's shoulder. "You need to come with us. Granted, we're all old enough to be your grandmas, but we have a lively discussion every week. They'd love all over you in there."

"It's true." Ruby confirmed her friend's statement with a smirk.

"And you can be guaranteed you won't be the only widow. In fact, a lot of us are in a grief support class. It's a revolving, open-door group that meets on Thursday nights."

Thinking that would have been helpful six or eight months ago, Shelby admitted the idea still piqued her interest. "And I'd love to come to your Sunday school today."

As the women seized their purses, Lester expressed pleasure at the prospect of escorting three lovely ladies. Shelby smiled, realizing the older gentleman could easily fill a grandfatherly role in her life.

When Shelby exited the pew, Scott approached down the aisle. An adorable toddler girl with bows in her curly blonde hair snuggled in his arms.

He stopped in front of them, smiling. "Hey, I'm so glad you made it. Did you like the service?"

"Very much."

Ruby patted Shelby's back. "And now she's accompanying us to Sunday school."

"That's great!" Scott's gaze swept Shelby's outfit with something that might be admiration.

Really? She smoothed a hand down her skirt. Judging from Scott's normal work attire and hardcore DIY attitude, she'd figured he liked her best in jeans and a casual shirt. But today, in a tan blazer, button down, and slacks, Scott looked quite different himself. He'd even shaved and lightly gelled his hair, bringing her attention to the clean-cut line of his jaw. She cleared her throat and directed her focus to the little girl gazing shyly at her from the level of Scott's shoulder.

"And who is this adorable person?"

Scott shifted the toddler forward and responded with pride lacing his tone. "This is my niece, Lexie."

The girl aimed a stubby finger at herself and announced in a grave manner, "Alexis."

"Yeah, Uncle Scott, get it right." Ruby laughed, taking the child's plump hand in her own and giving it a kiss. "And where are your mommy and daddy today?"

"Out there." Alexis pointed to the foyer area. "Talking."

Scott laughed. "I'm afraid this is Kaleigh's social time. I left them out there because I didn't want to miss seeing y'all."

"Thanks for introducing us." Shelby touched the child's tights-clad leg.

Lexie ducked her head into Scott's shoulder, mumbling so that Shelby leaned forward to make out her words. "You're pretty. You have princess hair."

Shelby laughed. "Why, thank you! You are too."

Did she imagine that Scott turned a little ruddy? As he said goodbye and headed to what Shelby guessed must be his family's normal spot, she suppressed disappointment that she wouldn't get to meet the mother and stepfather of whom he spoke so highly, or Lexie's parents.

In the busy intersection of hallways outside the Wentworths' classroom, a fancy coffee kiosk with stacking flavor trays caught Shelby's interest.

When Shelby's steps slowed, Ruby looked over her shoulder and smiled. "Go ahead, honey. We'll save your seat."

While fixing her coffee, a strong sense of belonging made Shelby pause in amazement. She'd loved her old church. A Scripture popped into her mind. *To everything there is a season, a time for every purpose under heaven.* Confirmation for moving on?

A cultured Southern voice interrupted her musing. "Why, Shelby Dodson, what a surprise. Are you visiting with the Wentworths?"

Shelby turned, and her stomach sank. Looking like a senior model in a classic ivory pant suit that set off her swirl of salt-and-pepper hair, Julien Etier's mother, Lauren, stood beside her, clasping a steaming cup of coffee.

"Mrs. Etier! Yes, I came with the Wentworths. I didn't realize you attended church here."

"Why, yes, although I go to the second service. Welcome." Lauren reached out to squeeze Shelby's arm. Despite the friendly appearance of the gesture, little warmth accompanied the woman's smile.

"Thank you. I'm enjoying it."

"I'm so glad. I found this church when my Alton passed. I know you'll be able to lean on similar support here."

Nodding, Shelby decided to give Julian's mother the benefit of the doubt.

Lauren's penciled brow arched upward. "Julian has kept me apprised of how hard things have been for you. Of all the things, for good people like the Wentworths to be saddled with a house with that unsettling history. Can they not get out of it?"

"They don't want to." Tilting her chin up, Shelby smiled. "Miss Ruby says we'll renovate the place, pray over it, and dedicate it to God."

"Well. That's admirable for them, but for you … I'm just sorry about how people are talking. I hate to see you end your wonderful renovating career with a debacle."

Lauren did not appear ruffled as churchgoers surged around them, hurrying now to get to the next service. Shelby, however, swallowed a hard knot of anxiety. "People are talking?"

The older woman waved a dismissive hand, still weighted down with a large diamond wedding band. "Oh, nothing malicious. They're people who care for you, old clients who pop into Julian's store. We all know difficulty with your career is the last thing you need after suffering the devastating loss of your husband."

"I don't know if we're behaving any better than Tasha." Shelby lagged behind Angelina as they made their way to the entrance of Magnolia Hills Senior Home in North Augusta, South Carolina, the next week.

"What are you talking about? We're going to visit our childhood neighbor, Veda Smith, who set up tea parties on her porch for us when we were little and gave out the best Halloween candy in the neighborhood."

"Whom we haven't seen in almost a year." The guilt of only showing up now, when they needed something, made Shelby want to sink into one of the sidewalk cracks.

"In our defense, a lot has happened in that year." As Angelina led the way into the building through an automatic door, the slightly overpowering scent of disinfectants and air fresheners whooshed out. "If you happen to see Charles Barnes while we're here, it will be a nice coincidence. He may not even be here."

Shelby shook her head. "This is the biggest and best nursing home in the region, so there's a good chance David referred to Magnolia Hills when he said he took his dad 'over' to the home."

A round little woman parked her walker right in front of Angelina to admire her red curls.

"Yes, it's natural," Angelina said to assure the smiling senior. To her credit, she didn't even attempt to escape the blue-veined hands that purled through her tresses.

"I'll sign us in." Shelby skirted around them before the lady decided she liked blondes.

Stepping over to the desk, she greeted the nurse on duty and picked up the pen by the register book. She entered Veda's name and then hers and Angelina's, scanning the page. No entries for Charles Barnes. As the nurse swiveled in her chair to answer the phone, Shelby flipped one page back. Halfway up the column, David Barnes had signed in to visit his father. Heart pounding, she righted the register and rejoined her sister.

She lowered her voice to a whisper when Angelina escaped her admirer. "He's here."

Her sister's eyes widened. "Did you get a room number?"

"On the men's wing, opposite Veda."

Angelina squeezed her hand. "Maybe we'll run into him in the common area. Shelby, I know you feel bad about snooping, but I see this as a way to get answers that might give you some peace about this case."

"Thanks, Ang. You're right, this mystery's stolen my joy. But I'm afraid Scott won't see it that way."

As they made their way down the hall, Angelina regarded her with a hint of a smirk. "As I recall, you didn't used to care what your employees thought about you."

"Scott isn't an employee. More like a partner."

"*That's* interesting. When the job started, I thought you said you were in charge."

Their arrival at Veda's room removed the possibility of retort as the tiny woman inside greeted them with immediate recognition and joy. Veda still smelled like lavender and vanilla and still possessed full mental faculties, making for a sweet, nostalgic visit recalling childhood antics and holiday traditions.

"How's your mother?" Veda wanted to know. "I miss her coming to see me."

"She moved to Columbia, remember, Miss Veda?" Shelby sat forward, smiling.

"Yes, to be a baby nurse."

"She loves it," Angelina said.

"Oh, I'm glad. I was so concerned for her after the divorce." Veda reached out to squeeze Angelina's hand. "And for you."

Angelina blinked back moisture. "You helped us a lot, Miss Veda. You always seemed to know when Mom wasn't up to cooking and would come knocking on our door with another hot casserole."

"Well, I did what I could, and looks like the good Lord kept you in His hand." Veda smiled. "I'm glad you're staying close to each other. There's no friend like a sister. I sure do miss mine. Say, I have an idea! In memory of old times, why don't we get some fresh air in the courtyard and order a tea tray? It's not my good loose-leaf, flavored variety, but at least they'll bring a body some English breakfast here when we have visitors."

"We'd love that." Glancing at Angelina as she positioned Veda's walker, Shelby asked, "Miss Veda, do you know Charles Barnes?"

Taking a firm hold on the handles, Veda blinked her dark eyes. "Yes. Why?"

"He owned the house the couple I told you about bought. During the renovation, I found something of his wife's."

"Oh dear. I remember the stir when she disappeared. Folks here still talk about it when Charles isn't around. What was it you found?"

Shelby hesitated. "A picture."

They followed Veda down the hallway. "He doesn't speak of her. Doesn't speak much at all, in fact. He's a very sad man. But if you want to talk to him, he always sits under the pergola this time of day when it's nice out. We could invite him to tea."

Seeming pleased with this mission of kindness, Veda forged across an atrium and out another set of sliding glass doors into a shaded courtyard. Shelby followed, weighed down by an increasing sense of dread.

Chapter Sixteen

Due to his strong likeness to his son, Shelby recognized Charles Barnes before Veda pointed him out. The older lady wheeled her walker in front of the man sitting motionless in a sun-slanted rocker, his lap covered with an afghan. A yellow leaf rested on the afghan, which Veda bent down and snatched off.

"Charles Barnes, these girls are my old neighbors. Shelby is helping update the house you sold to that retired couple. She wants to talk to you."

Immediate fear lit the balding man's eyes as they shifted to Shelby. "I don't want to talk."

"It's all right, Charles. Shelby's brought you something." As Veda settled into the chair next to Charles, Shelby cringed, thinking of what the photograph revealed. Veda waved at a passing nurse. "Can we get a tea tray for four, please? With some of those little sugar cookies?"

The woman bent to take Veda's hand, her coffee-colored skin glowing against Veda's paper-white fingers. She whispered back with an exaggerated wink. "Miss Veda, for you, I can make it happen."

"You're the best nurse here, JoJo."

Shelby smiled at Charles. His barrel-chested frame seemed to cave into frailty, shoulders hunched under a thin, brown sweater. Age spots colored his hands and neck, while droopy skin under his eyes exaggerated an appearance of perpetual fatigue. As he stared at her with distrust, he appeared more victim than perpetrator. Just as David described.

Attempting to break the awkwardness, Shelby leaned forward. "I love your house. It has such beautiful historical features. I hope what we do with it would make your father proud."

"What do you want?"

She didn't blame him for being guarded. Shelby took a deep breath. "I want to lay to rest all the suspicions about you. It's ridiculous that people can't let your wife's disappearance go, but until the truth comes out, I'm afraid they won't."

"That's because the police didn't do their job." Charles shook his gnarled index finger at her. "They were so focused on me they didn't look anywhere else."

"You think someone took her?" Angelina asked.

As Charles turned to her, he squeezed both eyes shut in a brief but telling tic. "What else could have happened? She wouldn't leave with nothing, and she wouldn't leave me. Where would she go? And she knew I loved her, even though I didn't approve of her job."

"You didn't want her to work?" Angelina settled onto a nearby wrought-iron chair.

He continued without looking at Angelina as if by staring straight ahead he hoped they'd all go away. "Not the fact that she was working, but that she would do anything for that boss of hers. He called her day and night. Even when she should have been with her family. A woman's place is with her family."

"The man should have respected proper boundaries." Veda reached out to pat his arm. Her gentle spirit seemed to calm him.

Shelby fished in her purse, producing the Polaroid. "I don't want to unsettle you, but this is what I found. I believe this is Sharon, but do you recognize the man?"

Charles took the picture with trembling hands. "Yes, that's my Sharon." He tapped the likeness of the dark-haired man with an emphatic, yellowed nail, his face twisting in another tic. "And that's him!"

"Who?"

"Sharon's boss, Jeff Wilson. I've never seen this photo before. Where did you find this?"

"Behind the baseboard in the back bedroom. Do you think Sharon's boss could have had something to do with her disappearance?"

"The police questioned him and searched Sharon's desk at work, but they should've put half the pressure to him they did to me. She thought I was controlling, but he was so sly, she didn't even realize how he manipulated her. I saw through that snake."

Angelina ventured a guess. "Could Sharon have run away with him?"

"No." Shaking his head, Charles lowered the picture to his lap. "Wilson didn't leave the area. At least not for another two years. He finally moved back to where his family came from—definitely not around here. Somewhere up north, I think."

"What kind of work did he do?" Shelby asked.

"He owned an accounting firm. Thought he was better than a used car salesman. Bah. He had something over her. This false charm. I tried to tell her she needed to quit. I know now that pressuring her made things worse. That's why I feel like in a way, whatever happened to her was my fault."

Even though she didn't want to ask her next question, something told Shelby she had to. "She never talked about leaving you, Mr. Barnes?"

Charles sat back and shook his head. The firmness in his answer left no room for argument, providing a glimpse of the old, authoritative husband. "No. We didn't believe in divorce. We would have worked it out."

"Could it be possible," Angelina asked, "that Jeff wanted Sharon for himself and that led to trouble of some sort?"

"That's what I asked the police forty years ago. They said I was trying to shift suspicion."

"Then do you want me to take this to them as evidence now? It might cause them to reconsider." Shelby pointed to the photograph lying face-down on the afghan.

"No!" The force of Charles Barnes' exclamation made them all—including two gentlemen playing checkers nearby—jump. "I already told you what incompetent fools they were."

"But it would be a whole different staff now." When Angelina looked up after speaking, Shelby followed her gaze. Pushing a cart with their afternoon tea, the nurse, JoJo, had paused just on the other side of the door to speak to another employee. They'd better hurry and come to some sort of understanding with Mr. Barnes.

Charles shook his head. "They'd just put it in the file with everything else."

"Should I … share this with David?" Shelby hesitated. "I don't want to upset him."

"Well, you will. I can't talk to David about Sharon. Anything to do with his mother still makes him angry. It was terrible on the boy, her leaving that way. Whatever happened after she left, she chose to walk out alone, upset, unprotected, late at night. She still made a stupid choice and left us."

Stirred by sympathy, Veda reached out to pat his arm. "Now, Charles, you don't know—"

"No." Charles turned to fix Shelby with watery eyes. "If anyone's going to find out what happened to her, it would have to be you."

Finally, a few days later, she impressed Scott Matthews. He admitted he had no idea how Shelby maintained a vision for each room of the Wentworth bungalow in the midst of the clutter around them. Shelby's favorite antique mall on Broad boasted over a hundred vendor booths on two floors of an old department store with pressed tin ceilings, a skylight, an elevator shaft complete with old ropes, and the still-functioning 1906 cash register.

So far, she'd picked out a black antique fan for Lester's den, a couple of Oriental vases, two large copper lanterns, a Tiffany lamp, and three tall island chairs with torn upholstery. And now she jumped up and down in front of a hideous yellow dresser, causing the uneven wooden boards beneath her feet to screech in protest.

Scott covered his face. "I'm afraid you're going to fall through the floor."

"But do you like it? Of course, you have to picture it the same gray as the kitchen island."

"You're wanting bowl-style sinks?"

"Yes, in white."

Scott shifted, tilting his head in consideration, and nodded. "Yeah, against the white beadboard and the tile we picked, I think that will look great."

Shelby clasped her hands together. "Yea! Let's get it out of here."

Scott quirked his brow at her but smiled in an amused manner as if he was enjoying her joyful mood. Seeing a new side of her as she worked in *her* element.

Little did he realize, part of her enthusiasm stemmed from how attentive he was being, despite the fact that he'd openly admitted antique shopping was not his thing. Just as he had on the scout-out at Julian Etier's, Scott made it clear that he prioritized helping her above his own personal preferences. He'd been *so* helpful, she was getting the shopping done faster than expected. She was also having a lot more fun doing it than she had in the past.

She'd expected drawbacks for the muscles she'd bribed for the day, and not just visiting the history center in return. When she'd shopped with Chet, he'd played with antique toys and donned every hat or pair of spectacles in the room, especially when the camera rolled. In modern stores, he disappeared only to be discovered reclining in vibrating chairs or crossing his legs in a prone position on a new mattress. Shelby could never decide whether she found her husband's antics amusing or annoying. Either way, they'd competed for her concentration.

Now, the joy that shot through her at Scott's partnership brought her up short. His approval of her design plans felt so much more genuine than the staged shopping of the past.

To hide her flustered response, Shelby turned away, removing glass perfume bottles from the top of the dresser. If Scott knew about the little visit she and

Angelina had paid to Charles Barnes, his admiration would dissipate as fast as an August raindrop on the hot pavement.

Somehow, Scott picked up on her inner struggle. He alleviated any tension with a joking tone. "I'm totally in favor of leaving. It's been, what, two hours? After five minutes in here, I wanted to retreat to the corner, close my eyes, and hum 'Kumbaya.' But … how?"

"How?"

"Yeah, remember when we came in, the guy at the register told us he was working alone today, so if we wanted to take any furniture, we'd have to help move it. I can go get him, but it's so crowded in here, I honestly don't know how we're going to get it out."

"No, don't go get him. I can help." She wanted to keep up her impressive streak. Besides, she felt pretty sure she was abler than the senior citizen who'd greeted them downstairs. Shelby straightened and looked around. "I guess down the stairs?"

"The stairs? Do you know how tight that's gonna be?"

"Well, I doubt they'll let us use the hundred-year-old lift. This is why I brought you along, remember?"

"Thanks for reminding me."

In case he might really be offended, Shelby winked. "To be fair, I probably wouldn't have seen that fan sitting up as high as it was if you hadn't spotted it."

Scott grinned. "Thank you for acknowledging that I'm good for more than brute force."

"I admit, you've proved yourself today." Shelby edged up on the dresser and slid her fingers under the edge. "But you're going first."

With shuffling mini-steps, they traversed the crowded aisle to the stairwell. Scott managed the opening with only bumping his head into a brass pineapple sconce and knocking one oval-framed portrait of a severe-looking Victorian widow free from its hanger. Shelby rescued the artwork from hitting the floor by quickly maneuvering her end of the dresser closer to the wall.

Scott sighed in relief. "Good save."

The check-out process involved the write-up of tickets to five different vendors, but finally Shelby paid for their purchases, and they loaded them into the back of Scott's truck. He secured a tarp over the top. "Maybe we should run this stuff on out to your storage building. I hate to leave it unattended."

"No, Culpepper's is right there. We've still got some room in the back, and Ruby would clobber us if we didn't go in there."

"Right." Scott slammed the tailgate and declared in the tone of a man about to charge a military bulwark, "Let's do this."

"I thought you'd be happy about going into Culpepper's. It's right up your alley."

"That's certainly true. Shelby …"

"You really don't like shopping, do you?" Ticking the dresser and the island chairs off her list had put her in a good mood, one which she determined she wouldn't let Scott's strange reserve dampen as she set off down the street.

"Chet and I always took pride in supporting local businesses. I hate that so many storefronts along Broad remain empty when the main streets of smaller towns have boomed in the last ten years or so. Oh, look, someone's checking out the building next to Culpepper's right now!"

As they passed a vacant store, Shelby smiled as a tall leasing agent in a blue suit and tie let a client onto the sidewalk. Too late, she realized the client was Caitlyn Curtis.

"Well, hey, Caitlyn." Scott sounded as surprised as Shelby.

Professional in a fitted golden sweater and brown slacks, the woman adjusted her leather satchel so she could hug Scott. The top of her head slid under his chin like a puzzle piece. "Hi, there. Bet you didn't expect to see me again so soon."

So soon? Caitlyn's hand lingering on Scott's back drew Shelby's gaze.

"Not really. What are you doing?" Scott smiled but stepped back.

"I'm looking at several locations as possibilities to expand as I told you at brunch. And so far, I like this one best."

"Wow. It's big. And close."

"Two positives, in my reckoning … if I can get the price down some." Shelby didn't care for the woman's smug smile as she surveyed Scott. She acted as if Shelby didn't exist. And—brunch? "With two complementary businesses, we could knock out a wall to increase traffic flow. Think on it." Caitlyn lifted a shoulder as if she anticipated some opposition but felt confident the outcome would prove in her favor.

"Uh, you remember Shelby." Scott shifted his weight and—not looking at either of them—lifted his hand in Shelby's direction.

"Yes, as I recall, your reason for our brunch was to discuss her little sister." Caitlyn's teasing wink implied she suspected Scott had possessed another true motive. While the agent locked up, Caitlyn fished in her bag and handed a business card to Shelby.

"Thank you." Shelby stared at it without focusing.

"Scott says Angelina is very talented and could use a local mentor. If Scott says it, I believe it. Tell her to come by and bring some samples of her work. I don't have much space in the front of my current frame shop, but I do small shows there from time to time. I have a growing following. And who knows, maybe next year I'll have a proper gallery right here next to Culpepper's."

Casting Scott a questioning glance, Shelby thanked Caitlyn again. She reminded herself that putting up with Caitlyn would be worth having her sister thrive locally.

"What was all that about moving in next door to Culpepper's?" Shelby asked when Caitlyn and blue suit moved down the sidewalk.

Scott's brow furrowed as he opened the door of the reclaimed wood business, causing the cow bell attached at the top to jangle. "She didn't even mention she was thinking of it when I took her out to coffee ... to ask her about Angelina." The second part of his statement sounded hurried, like the glance he sent her.

"Of course." Shelby made her tone light. Why should she be disturbed even if he'd met Caitlyn for personal reasons?

A long, wooden table with an intricately carved pedestal design arrested her attention. Someone—Linda Culpepper, she assumed—had set it beautifully with linen and dinnerware that looked like it came straight from Julian's. In the center, white pumpkins, autumn berries, and vines clustered on and around a white cake stand flanked by antique silver candelabra. The display's rustic elegance took her breath away.

"Oh, this is it. The Wentworths' dining room table." Shelby ran a hand along the smoothly sanded and finished barn wood.

As she evaluated tasteful chairs, benches, and end tables grouped under wooden chandeliers hanging from the ceiling, Scott's grin displayed more enthusiasm than she'd seen all day. "You like it?"

"Yes, it's amazing. And I might even be able to find some Stickley-style seating for Lester's den, rather than ordering it. I should've come in here long ago." Shelby paused, looking up as she recalled the discussion at hand. "But why would Caitlyn ask you about removing a wall between the shop next door and this one?"

"There you are!" A voice called from behind a display of vintage window frames redesigned as wall art. A tall woman in a woven tunic of fall colors floated toward them, hands extended—Linda Culpepper. Shelby blinked, wondering how her arrival had been anticipated. But Linda approached Scott, and to

Shelby's increasing astonishment, placed a kiss on his cheek. "I see you survived the antique store, son."

"Son?" Shelby echoed.

Scott turned to her. "Shelby, if you haven't yet put two and two together, this is my mother, and my parents own Culpepper's."

Linda turned to her with a smile that melded patience and pride. "And Scott made that beautiful table I heard you admiring, as well as every other piece of furniture in the store."

Chapter Seventeen

"But—but what … why …" Shelby took a deep breath, composed her thoughts, and stared at the man whose layers just kept peeling back like an onion. Right now, a stinky onion. "When Ruby mentioned Culpepper's, why didn't you tell me that your parents own the shop?"

Scott shrugged, looking sheepish. "Sorry. I guess I'm telling you now."

Only Linda's presence caused Shelby to bite back a sarcastic response.

Linda scolded. "Scott, you should have told her." Then she turned to Shelby. "It's no excuse, but Scott's always been rather private about our family business. Only a handful of repeat clients know he's the one who crafts this furniture."

Shelby pressed her lips together so she wouldn't argue with Scott's lovely mother the first time she'd seen her in forever, but she didn't buy that explanation. Perhaps insecurity explained the reserve of the past, but this was different. They were working together, and it would have been helpful for her to know about the extent of his skills. No, this went beyond mere modesty to something she couldn't explain but didn't like. For now, she merely said to Scott, "I thought your dad owned a warehouse with old wood."

"He does." Scott's eyes pleaded for her to acknowledge that he hadn't been untruthful. "You're standing in it. The shop—the storefront—is an offshoot of the warehouse. We store all the bulk materials he reclaims in the back. Only smaller decorative pieces and furniture I craft from the salvage make their way up here."

Linda tilted her perfectly coiffed, sandy bob. "Come, I'll show you." As Shelby allowed the older woman to lead her to a barn door slider behind the register, Linda added with genuine warmth, "As I think I told you at a chamber event, I was a big fan of your show. I was beside myself when Scott came home and told us he'd be working with you."

Shelby smiled, but Scott responded before she could. "Speaking of which, this is kind of what I'm thinking of doing for the master closet door, Shelby." He reached up to indicate the roller hardware attaching the slider to the wall.

"That's fine." Shelby kept her eyes on Linda.

He didn't take the hint that she didn't want to talk design with him right now. "I've got a pallet of gray wood back here I want to show you. See what you think about the color."

"Okay. Wow, this is impressive." Shelby beheld a long showroom completely open to the brick walls except for support timbers, filled with sorted and tagged groupings of doors, mantels, spindles, columns, cornices, barn siding, baseboards, molding, and various types of wood flooring. The aisles remained wide enough for a forklift to pass through, while rolling metal doors opened onto a rear loading dock.

"This part of the business is known as Aiken-Augusta Old Woods," Linda said. "We have another warehouse in the rear where we unload new shipments for sorting, cleaning, tagging, and overflow. That's where my husband Mike and my stepson Austin spend most of their time when they're not overseeing a deconstruction crew."

Shelby finally looked at Scott. "But not you?"

He slipped his hands into his pockets. "Thankfully, Dad recognized early I preferred to build rather than take apart, and he never gave me grief over becoming a contractor. I just make the furniture. They do the hard part. That's why I don't take any credit for it."

"Yeah, but sharing about what your family does isn't taking credit."

Scott stared at the floor as he shuffled an almost invisible bit of sawdust from the walkway with the toe of his boot. "You're right."

"Scott's workshop is at our place." Linda consulted her dainty gold wristwatch. "In fact, we're closing in half an hour, and I have a pork roast in the oven. If you don't mind simple food, why don't you join us for dinner, Shelby? I know Mike would love to tell you more about the business."

Scott tensed, but Shelby accepted Linda's invitation before he could protest. She'd had enough of his silent secretiveness. She offered him a bright smile. "So if we have half an hour, I'm going to shop."

Linda clasped her hands together. "Ooh, let me help you. Scott's told me about Ruby's style, so I have a few ideas."

As Linda showed Shelby multi-purpose crates and trenchers, slat-backed chairs and benches, and the gray-flecked muntins of an old window now hung with wire-mounted glass cups that could be used for candles or herbs, her enthusiasm proved infectious. Scott disappeared into the back room until they called him to secure the smaller items in his truck. He told Shelby he'd have to get the furniture another time.

"That's fine. I don't want to dismantle your mom's beautiful dining display, anyway. As long as she promises not to sell the table out from under us." Shelby sent Linda a teasing smirk. She already liked the woman's straightforward but gracious manner.

"Of course not." Linda looked up from ringing up the sale at the register. "I'm tickled pink it will find a home with the Wentworths. I've just got to find a way to bribe you so that you let me walk through before the big reveal."

"No bribery needed. I'd welcome your help as I'm setting up."

"You would?" Scott and Linda asked at the same time.

Shelby laughed at their astonished faces. "Am I really that known for being set in my decorating ways?"

"You always shooed everyone out on the show," Linda said.

"That's because the workmen got underfoot, and Chet distracted me. No one got what I was doing." Embarrassed by the generous compliment she'd unwittingly paid the two people before her, Shelby pretended to examine a wooden bowl as she attempted to explain.

"Besides, as Scott has pointed out, this is a different style I'm undertaking. You're already familiar with it, and I do want the Wentworths to be pleased. Not pleased. Delighted. I don't count it a successful reveal unless there are tears, or at least hysterical laughter."

"Of course." The timbre in Linda's voice came across amused ... and touched. "Well, thank you, Shelby. I'll be there for consultation—and an extra pair of hands. I'll do my best not to get underfoot."

Shelby gave an incredulous glance around the store. "Oh, something tells me you won't be underfoot."

Scott asked his mom, "Should we go to Shelby's storage building to give you time to get dinner set out?"

"No, take her on home. Give her a tour. We'll be right behind you." The nod Linda gave her son seemed to hold some sort of reassurance.

Scott held the shop door for Shelby and even placed a brief hand on her back, causing her to glance at him in surprise. With a smile through the glass, Linda turned the lock and flipped the "open" sign behind them. As they stepped out to a reddening horizon and a chill hovering close to the cement, Scott commented. "Days are getting shorter. Soon we'll turn the clock back."

After that, on the brief ride down Walton Way, he remained silent. Shelby didn't speak either. As she pondered which questions to ask first, a new and uncomfortable awareness strained between them.

Scott turned onto Milledge Road and passed two Greek Revival mansions and a huge, stucco Spanish Colonial before turning into the evergreen-lined driveway of an antebellum brick Italianate with bracketed eaves, arching iron verandah, and square, two-story bays on both sides.

"No way." Shelby craned her neck to take in every detail as Scott eased the truck past the house and into a courtyard between it and a three-bay garage attached by breezeway. Another story of matching brick added living space above the addition, which somehow looked as old as the mansion.

A lean, glossy German shepherd—Luther, Shelby remembered—darted out to greet them. But after putting the truck in park, Scott made no attempt to open the door. "I have another confession to make."

"Let me guess, you actually own this place, and your parents live above the garage."

He bared his teeth in an embarrassed grimace. "Actually, it's the opposite. My parents do own the house, and I live above the garage. My workshop is below."

"Oh. You didn't want to tell me you still lived at home ... kind of."

Scott let out a breath. "Right."

"But you don't exactly live *with* them."

"No, my place is fully furnished, totally private." He spoke fast, waved his hand. "And I not only pay rent, I help with the upkeep of the property. It's not like I'm a deadbeat moocher."

Shelby met Scott's eyes. "I would never think you're a deadbeat moocher. And I can see why under certain circumstances, like having a family business, staying close to your parents makes sense. Maybe if I had been in less of a hurry to leave home ..." She let her voice trail off. Her dad wouldn't have left? She wouldn't have fallen for Chet so hard and fast?

"Thanks. Not everybody understands that."

"Well, I've seen for myself how independent and hard-working you are." As the reason behind Scott's reluctance to talk about his private life came clear, relief released some of the tension in Shelby's shoulders. But another question remained. "Why didn't you tell me your parents owned Culpepper's?"

"I started to that day your friend showed up revving the engine of her shiny sports car."

Shelby rolled her eyes. "Oh, that's no excuse. You had an opening as big as a barn door when Ruby brought up shopping there. In fact, I probably still wouldn't know if she hadn't set you up. So spill. And don't give me a sad story about how you used to be embarrassed—because obviously your dad's no longer 'the junk man.'"

Scott caught his lower lip between his teeth, then said, "I don't want to hurt your feelings in any way."

"You kind of already have, so please explain." As Shelby folded her hands in what appeared to be a composed gesture, they shook a little. Why did the prospect of hearing something negative from Scott make her nervous?

A whimper ascended from beyond Scott's side of the truck, but Scott ignored the dog. He pulled his hat off and ruffled his hair, then rubbed his eyes as if to clear his head. "You started talking about doing a TV show flipping historical houses. I was afraid my situation presented a too-neat package to fill that order. I could already envision the TV crews intruding into all aspects of my life. I know you liked the notoriety, but I'm not like that. I just wanted to do this flip with you, and …"

"Be done?" Shelby snapped, feeling defensive despite her resolve to remain impervious.

"No. I like working with you. I didn't want you to judge me because of my past or my family, or whether I was poor or wealthy. I want you to want to work with me because you like it too—because you like *me*. Not because I might represent your next career opportunity."

The vulnerability of Scott's statement pinged Shelby's heart. "I do like you. I mean, I like working with you." When he kept staring at her, she repeated herself as she reached over to give his hand a brief pat. "I like you."

The admission came out way too honest and raw in the silent cab of the truck, not at all in the cute way she intended. And when her hand touched his, Scott flipped his over and threaded his fingers through hers. The intimate touch sent fire racing all the way up Shelby's arm, but instead of withdrawing, her brain raced to picture kissing him. The force seemed so right she didn't question it, just leaned forward. His gaze dropped to her lips, but as Scott shifted, a howl of gut-wrenching abandonment launched from Luther to the sky, making both of them jump.

Scott released her hand. "Luther!" As he opened the door and leaned down to tousle the head of his pet, Shelby sat back and pressed her eyes closed. She took a moment to compose herself as Scott stepped out of the truck.

What had she been thinking? Tomorrow would be the anniversary of her husband's death, and she'd almost ushered it in by lip-locking the next guy to enter her life—a co-worker at that. But her reaction wasn't totally reprehensible, was it? Probably, it had more to do with her own loneliness and many years of conditioned response than her feelings for Scott Matthews. Yep, that was it. Too many nights of Hallmark movies and hormones.

But when Scott tilted his head up from his wagging dog and grinned at her, her resolve almost melted. He looked like a twelve-year-old boy, eager to introduce his pet.

"He's really friendly. Come out and meet him."

Shelby released her breath with the seatbelt. As she came around the truck, a rumble of disapproval broke from the throat of the German shepherd.

"Uh …" Shelby took a step back.

"Don't be scared. Come 'ere." Scott wrapped his arm around Shelby's waist, making her eyes round in surprise. He patted her shoulder with exaggerated enthusiasm, then spoke to the canine in a high-pitched voice that made her want to laugh. "See, this is Shelby. She's nice. She's my friend."

Luther ducked his head and approached to sniff in the scent of Maltie on Shelby's jeans.

She muttered through clenched teeth, "Still not sure it's safe to pet him."

Scott laced his fingers through Shelby's and lowered their joined hands to the vicinity of the dog's muzzle, a casual touch that completely disregarded Shelby's private resolution. "Scratch his ear." He glanced up at her, and she wasn't sure which jarred her most—the raspy tone of his whisper, or his shining green eyes. She could see the golden flecks in them.

Shelby slipped her hand away to comply. A second later, Luther licked her wrist and huffed up at her in approval. She released the breath she'd been holding and straightened. "Okay. Now that I'm permitted on the property …"

"Let me show you my place first."

Luther trotted behind them as Scott strode over to raise the garage door. Next to the empty bay, a table saw and circular saw occupied the center of the workshop. A workbench extended the length of the room with drawers below. Plexiglas cabinets above opened to wall-mounted clamps, sanders, nail guns, screwdrivers, hammers, and tools she had no idea how to identify. A drill press and a miter saw were secured into openings in the countertop. As Luther trotted inside with nails clicking, pencil drawings of measurement-marked furniture tacked to a corkboard fluttered in the breeze from the open garage door.

Scott hefted a long cabinet front with raised panels onto the table. "Know what this is?"

Inhaling the fresh, heady scent of sawdust, Shelby ran a hand along the curves of the raw wood. "Is it … part of the island?"

"Yep, the front piece where the chairs will slide in. You like it?"

"I do! It must be amazing to picture something and just make it. When I picture something, I have to go shopping for it."

"Or, if it involves wood, you could ask me."

"Yes." Shelby smiled. "Now I know all about Culpepper's and Aiken-Augusta Old Woods and the genius behind both."

Shelby was afraid to say more. Scott's determination to avoid publicity did barricade a future avenue she'd allowed herself to consider, one she'd thought could prove both relevant and lucrative. With the loss came a sense of disappointment ... and confusion. He said he liked working with her, but did he mean for only the Wentworth project? What if she suggested more, only to get hurt?

Renovations and woodworking already filled Scott's life. Without a TV show, he probably found her design services unnecessary. Most people wanted to decorate their homes with their own furnishings and accessories. Maybe it was unreasonable, disloyal even, believing she could replace Chet and his crew so easily. Maybe God was trying to tell her to focus on independence. Stand on her own two feet for a while rather than relying on a man.

Shelby wrapped her arms around herself as she allowed Scott to lead her upstairs. His two-bedroom apartment displayed a bachelor simplicity that made heavy use of reclaimed wood, but the occasional green plant and framed photo collage told Shelby Linda had helped personalize the space. Less really was more with the rustic style. As in a Craftsman home, the quality of each piece, including the doors, trim, and cabinetry, spoke for itself. Kind of like the man.

When they completed the brief tour, Scott led her through the breezeway and into the main residence. Expecting to glean further ideas inside the 1850s house, Shelby discovered period antiques coupled with classic oak and mahogany pieces that created a traditional *Southern Living* look.

Scott's parents added to that impression. Linda dished up generous servings of pork roast, green beans, and fresh rolls in the kitchen, while Mike Culpepper read a newspaper in the den. He must have changed from work clothes into the button-down and khakis he now wore. He stood up to shake Shelby's hand when Scott introduced her.

Shelby offered to help carry plates into the elegant dining room with its crystal chandelier, wainscoting, and massive china cabinet. As they took their places around the table—Scott and his dark-haired father on the ends and she and Linda on the sides—Shelby complimented the beautiful home.

"Why, thank you, Shelby," Linda said. "Mike wanted the house furnished authentically, but I wanted it to be livable, not like a museum."

They paused to say grace, then Mike selected a roll and passed Shelby the basket. "The house didn't look this way when we bought it."

"Oh?"

"You might be aware I worked for a historical preservation firm when I first moved to Augusta. Despite this house's prime location, an older couple lived here and didn't have the finances to keep it up. We got it for a steal considering the land value, but it required a complete overhaul."

"Which you did yourself?"

Mike nodded. "Yes, and added the garage apartment. Let's see, you were a junior when we bought this place, weren't you, Scott?"

"Sure was."

"Austin had already gone off to play football in college, so Scott helped me after school."

"This place was basically my resume for the historical contract work I did later," Scott said.

"What a resume. And what value that adds to your home on a personal level." Shelby aimed a polite smile at Scott's parents, who nodded and smiled back at her. Linda may have once struggled to survive as a single mom, and Mike may have gotten ribbed for starting a business few understood, but they now represented success in all areas of life. Impressive. No wonder Scott valued hard work so much. And no wonder he worried about freeloaders with selfish motives. She watched him cut his pork roast. "You went to college, too, right?"

"Yes. I got an accounting degree. Helps me crunch the numbers."

"Not just for his contracting work, but also for our family business," Linda said.

Shelby narrowed her eyes. "You're more involved than you let on." Shame filled her when she recalled her condescension when she'd first run into Scott on the job site. She'd behaved as though he should be honored to work with her when she should have been honored to work with *him*.

Linda winked at her son, whose face flushed. "Oh, he's very involved. Just behind the scenes, the way he likes it."

Indispensable. Far too involved to expand his business to include her. Shelby poked at her roast, separating out a small bite. As much as she might learn from Scott Matthews and admire his family, their future acquaintance would be surface. An occasional furniture order. Or crossing paths downtown if she ever got her own business going. The best thing to come out of this connection might be experience with rustic design. An expansion to her repertoire. And maybe that would eventually be enough to reclaim some business from Julian Etier.

She'd call that friend at the local magazine. A write-up with a photo spread would not only endear the Wentworths to their new neighbors, it would advertise Shelby Dodson's come-back.

On the way home, Shelby fought a strange and nauseating sense of guilt. Why did she feel guilty? She'd done nothing wrong. Fleeting moments of attraction to unlikely people did sometimes arise out of loneliness. But … She drew in her breath when she identified the source of her guilt.

"What's wrong?" As always, Scott was quick to note any change in her demeanor.

Shelby smiled and shook her head. "Nothing." She turned her face away to hide the truth.

Problem was, this attraction wasn't fleeting, and Scott wasn't unlikely. Despite all her noble self-talk about keeping things professional and impersonal, the more time Shelby spent around Scott, especially seeing him interact with his family, the more she liked him. And the more she liked him, the more she realized all the ways he complemented her. Ways Chet never had. And that was why she felt guilty.

After they unloaded their finds at her storage building, she buckled her seatbelt as he started the truck. "I have a question."

"What's that?" The street light highlighted the plane of Scott's cheekbone as he turned his face toward her.

"You've never been married?"

"Nope."

"Engaged?"

"No."

Shelby saw his jaw tighten as he steered the vehicle back onto the street. "Close?"

"Yes. Close."

"Can I ask what happened?"

"I found a girl in college I hit it off with, the first one I thought got who I was. We dated over a year. I wanted to wait to ask her to marry me until closer to graduation, so whenever she brought up the future, I avoided talking about it. I guess she took that as a lack of commitment. So … when she met somebody else …"

"No!" Shelby gasped. "You let her get away."

Scott nodded.

"Well, did you try to explain to her?"

"I tried, but her new boyfriend had this charismatic personality."

"Did she marry him?"

"She did, but it didn't last."

"Well, I guess she learned her lesson. Charismatic can turn cantankerous in a heartbeat." Shelby didn't even realize how much her statement gave away until she felt Scott staring at her.

"Thanks." His tone suggested surprise. "But it was really me who learned mine."

Shelby adopted a light tone. "You still wish it had worked out?"

"No, I got over it eventually. But I promised myself I wouldn't make the same mistake again. Even though it doesn't come naturally to me, next time I'm going to speak up before it's too late."

Why did heat rush from somewhere in her chest up to her forehead? Shelby swallowed and looked away. As they bumped over the curb into her driveway, she leaned forward, frowning. "Why is there a Cadillac in my driveway? And a man on my porch?"

Chapter Eighteen

Shelby's obvious alarm over the fact that a balding man faced Angelina at the front door made Scott hasten to park, slam his truck door, and hurry up the sidewalk. "Hey!" He barked out the greeting. "Can we help you?"

The middle-aged man turned, and a grimace twisted his mouth as his eyes locked on Shelby. "You sure can. Perfect timing, in fact." With fists balled at his sides, the visitor stepped off the porch, leaving a wide-eyed Angelina peeking from behind the front door.

"What's the problem?" Responding to the perceived threat, Scott stepped in front of Shelby. She side-stepped so she could see past him but offered no greeting.

In the faint glow of the porch light, the man stabbed the air with his finger. "Why don't you ask her?"

Scott chanced a quick glance behind him to find not fear but guilt written on his co-worker's delicate features. "What does he mean?"

Her throat worked. "Scott, this is David Barnes."

Blinking as realization hit, Scott took a moment to digest this pertinent information. David wouldn't be here for no reason. He angled toward Shelby, hunching his shoulders as he spoke in a low voice. "What did you do?"

David didn't wait for Shelby to answer. "She went to see my father, that's what! Her and that bitty sister of hers pretended to visit an old neighbor. Used the poor woman to get into the nursing home to my father and show him an old picture she found at the house, of my mother with another man."

"What?" Scott looked between them, unable to believe Shelby had found some kind of evidence she hadn't shared with him.

"I didn't think you needed to know—either of you." Shelby's statement squeaked out. "Charles was the one to decide what to do."

"He's over ninety years old!" David's face turned ruddy, and his neck seemed to bulge. "Not sound of mind or body! Why do you think he's in that nursing home? Did I not tell you when we met I wanted him left alone?"

Shelby sighed and fumbled inside her purse. "Yes, you did. But this photo could be key evidence in your mother's disappearance. I couldn't sit on it."

"So instead you made an old man wonder if his wife cheated on him forty years ago. Yeah, that's just what he needs to be worrying about."

"I'm sorry if he thought that, David, but your reaction is the very reason I went to him instead of you. Your father said you lost it any time the subject of your mother came up."

David's gaze fell on a Polaroid Shelby pulled out into the light. "I'll show you losing it if you don't give me that right this minute."

As the livid man lunged forward, Scott couldn't determine his intentions fast enough, so he put himself between David and Shelby again. Afraid David planned to hit Shelby, he grabbed the older man's arm as it arched through the air. David shoved him back and snatched the photo, then held it up in both hands.

For just a second, David glared at the likenesses in the porch light, his face twisting with pain. "This is what I think of your snooping, my mother, and the past." He ripped the picture in half and tossed both sides onto the grass, permanently dividing the man from the woman.

Shelby started to protest. "David, you don't know—"

He wagged his finger at her, starting to move toward his car. At last. "I don't care. I don't want to know. You bought the house; do what you want with it. But stop looking into my mother's disappearance, and never speak to me or my father again, or I'll hire a lawyer." David suddenly reversed course and edged up on Shelby until he stood almost toe-to-toe with her. "Do I make myself clear?"

"Yes." To her credit, Shelby didn't move or even tremble.

Scott snatched the man's elbow, jerking him away from her. "Back off, dude, or I'll be the one calling the police."

David's eyes raked fire over him. "I want to make sure you understand me this time."

"We understand you. Mrs. Dodson will be good for her word. Now leave."

"I'm holding you to it," David said on a growl. He wheeled and stalked to his Cadillac. A moment later, the engine revved, and tires squealed as he backed onto the street, then sped away.

Once the car disappeared from sight, Shelby let out a soft moan and sagged so suddenly Scott slid an arm around her. But with the threat gone, his protective instincts gave way to rising frustration. As Angelina rushed out, he settled Shelby on the front step and demanded an explanation. "So what he said was true? You two did go visit Charles Barnes?"

With a steadying hand on her sister's arm, Angelina faced him. "We visited our old neighbor, and yes, we saw Charles Barnes. We had a peaceful conversation. We didn't threaten him in any way."

"But you did threaten him." Scott went to pick up the two halves of the photo. He shook them at the girls cowering on the porch. "*This* threatened him."

Shelby protested with a soft wail. "What was I supposed to do? I couldn't ignore it. What if an innocent man's life has been ruined by suspicion all these years, and that photo provides a clue to what happened? Shouldn't Charles decide whether he wanted to investigate more himself, or take it to the police?"

"Of course it goes to the police. It always goes through the legal channel."

"Charles doesn't trust the police." Shelby wouldn't look at him. "I did what I thought was right."

"Is that really why you went? Out of concern for Charles?"

"Well, you have the photo now." Turning her face away, Angelina extended a palm in his direction. "You decide what to do. Burn it if you want."

"Did Ruby know about this?" Scott asked Shelby. He waited until her head wobbled, then nodded. "What did she say?"

With Angelina's arm around her shoulders, Shelby sank lower onto the step. "When I showed her the photo, she said she wanted to pray about it."

A piercing sense of disappointment filled Scott. Earlier, he'd almost let his attraction to Shelby get the better of him. Hadn't she told him the day he brought the soup that she wouldn't consider more than friendship? Thank the Lord, Luther's baying interruption had saved him from his own folly.

He'd almost forgotten a key fact. Yes, Shelby could be the woman of his dreams, but she was too proud. And he hated pride. Hated self-satisfied, cliquish people.

Something told him to keep his mouth shut, but a bigger part of him wanted to beat Shelby over the head with the same weakness that caused her to exclude him a decade ago. For once, he wanted to say what he really thought. "But you didn't give that a chance, did you? As usual, you were too worried about keeping up appearances. Heaven forbid somebody think bad of you."

Shelby's blonde head came up, and tears glistened in her eyes.

"Oh, stop." Angelina frowned as she snapped at him. "You have no idea how trying to determine the right thing has torn Shelby up. Or how much this job could harm her. *She's* the public face on this, not you. Not even the Wentworths. After this project, you get to keep renovating houses with your crew. But if this flip gives her a bad name and sends all her business to her competitors, Shelby won't have any clients left. Then what will she do?"

The full extent of uncertainty Shelby must be experiencing about her future hit him then. Scott fell silent. He could almost smell the smoke of the bridge he'd just burned.

On the off-chance of running into Scott, Shelby couldn't bring herself to attend Cornerstone this morning with the Wentworths. Neither could she talk herself into going back to her old church.

Yesterday had been hard, full of painful memories of shock and loss from Chet's death a year ago. Doubly hard because—before Scott had showed what he really thought of her Friday night—she'd fancied during their topsy-turvy day together that she might be falling for him.

This morning had called for a time of quiet reflection. She'd had her best personal devotion time in months, using the index in her Bible to look up those verses that talked about God being a husband to the widow.

Scott again. Why did he constantly intrude into her thoughts? Frowning, Shelby scratched Maltie's ears, gazing over the backyard. She winced when a car door slammed. From the blanket on Shelby's lap, Maltie lifted her head.

"Angelina's home." She made the announcement with cheer, although she wished her little sister would be thankful enough when Shelby let her borrow her CRV that she would treat it with greater consideration. One more pay check, and their mom would have enough for a down payment for a used car for Angelina.

Sure enough, doors closed, and steps approached through the house. A popular praise chorus sounded sweet on her younger sister's tongue. The deck door opened, and a red head poked out.

"There you are! Wow, it's beautiful out here." Responding to Maltie's frantic wagging, Angelina petted her head as she dragged a wrought iron chair across the deck.

"How was campus church?"

"It was great. I hope I'm not disappointing you, but I'd rather keep going there than Cornerstone. I mean, I understand the value of fellowshipping inter-generationally, but I feel like since it's geared toward college people, campus church will help me connect and grow."

"You're not disappointing me." Shelby smiled. "I'm glad you found a good place to worship." Although she meant it, her voice lacked its normal enthusiasm.

About to kick her feet up on the opposite chair, Angelina leaned forward and peered at her. "Wait, you've been crying?"

"I'm okay now."

"You're not okay. You're hiding at home weeping on your back deck. Did you hear from Scott or something?"

"No, nor do I expect to. That's not the way men are. Tomorrow he'll act like nothing happened, except he'll be all short and reserved. But that's all right." Lifting her chin, Shelby tapped her open Bible. "I've been reading verses I never noticed before about how God is like a husband to the widow and fatherless, and they reminded me to stop trying to take everything into my own hands. God will take care of us. Both of us."

"Shelby, don't worry about me. I love staying here, but if I need to, I can move back to the dorms—"

"No. I'm quite sure God approves of us staying together. Although … I do wish you'd keep up with your dirty clothes. And your dishes from last night are still in the sink."

Angelina cringed. "Okay, okay. I'll get on that. If finances are a problem, I could hold off on getting a car—"

"I'm not worried about finances." Well, not enough to boot her sister out.

"Or look for a job, though I'm not sure how I'd get my art done … and I just had a great meeting with Caitlyn."

"Oh really?" Shelby tried to hide her dislike for the beautiful young artist, although Angelina probably picked up on it. Today, knowing her sister planned to stop at Caitlyn's shop after church, she'd sent the old photos and menus for Lester's study along with Angelina for Caitlyn to frame, sparing herself a trip.

"Yes, I got your stuff dropped off. And Caitlyn said she wanted to feature several of my best pieces during the downtown holiday open house."

"Why, that's great!"

"She talked a lot about the store next to Scott's as a future location where she plans a proper art gallery."

"I bet she did." This time Shelby couldn't bar the sarcasm from her statement. Stroking Maltie's silky fur, she stared at the golden leaves of the poplar in her back yard. "But as long as you and she get along well, that's what's important. I won't be seeing her—or Scott, either—after next month."

"Just because you and Scott had an argument doesn't mean you end your relationship. People disagree all the time. We did what we thought was best. He would've done something different, but that doesn't mean either of us did anything wrong."

"I know that, Angelina. But we don't have a relationship, except a working one. And that's about to end."

Angelina hefted a sigh and sat up. "Wow, it's all or nothing for you, isn't it? You should try giving people a little grace."

Shelby pressed her lips together. "I'll forgive him for hurting my feelings, but I can't let my neediness and uncertainty about the future create unrealistic expectations of people. I have to turn to God."

"That's true, but—"

Having finally reached a modicum of peace after a night spent tossing and turning, Shelby had no desire to hear Angelina's analysis. "As I've been praying, I've been thinking maybe God let all this happen as a reminder to keep things in check."

"Really, Shelby? Because that's not what I see at all." Angelina looked irritated when a knock on the front door interrupted her. Sighing, she got up. "I'll go see who it is."

"Whoever it is, send them away."

Angelina's brow furrowed as she paused at the kitchen door. "I was kind of hoping to have a few friends over this evening to study. They love to get off campus, and they keep complaining we never invite them."

Shelby threw her hands up. "Seriously? Did you not just see me sitting here crying? I need quiet and recovery time, not a passel of college girls eating up everything in my kitchen. And what about all the laundry and dishes we just discussed?"

"Right. Of course." Angelina's hopeful expression fell. "I'll just … send everyone away. Everyone."

As her sister disappeared into the house, remorse stabbed Shelby. Angelina's statement, "you should try giving people a little grace," hung in the air, convicting her. But what about her? How much grace had Scott given *her* last night? And what about all those fake "friends" who deserted her as soon as she fell from local stardom? And Angelina … she should grow up and take more responsibility. If Shelby didn't enforce that, who would?

A moment later, Angelina returned, her brow raised. "Well, look who's here."

Aghast that her sister had disregarded her instructions, Shelby whirled around.

Chapter Nineteen

He held his gift on a plate, one slice of decadent, moist, triple-layer chocolate cake. One slice to make it clear it was just for her, and on Ruby's wedding china at that. But Scott's stomach dropped as he watched Shelby's surprise turn not to welcome, but to suspicion.

"What are you doing here?"

He swallowed. "Uh … bringing a peace offering for acting like a jerk Friday?"

The goofy smile that lit Angelina's face made Scott wish his contrite gesture lacked an audience.

"Thank you for your apology, but no peace offering is necessary." Sitting up straight, Shelby restrained Maltie with her hand. The dog wiggled and whined in protest.

Scott slid the plastic-wrap-covered dessert onto Shelby's table. "Maybe not, but Lester's mother's recipe was, of course, passed down through the annals of time. I can promise you've never tasted cake like this before. The Boll Weevil Cafe would love to get their hands on the recipe."

"No apology is necessary either." Shelby slid the cake back. "Like Angelina said, we saw things differently. No crimes were committed, at least not by any of us."

Scott stood there shifting his weight, praying for a crack in her armor. Since he didn't see one, he'd have to make one. "But I think I hurt you, and that's a crime in my book."

Angelina hitched a thumb toward the house. "And on that note, I'm going in to make a sandwich … since no one is offering *me* cake." With a lame grin, she popped back inside, closing the French door.

Scott seized that moment to slide into the chair next to Shelby. The sense that he'd spoken the truth without love Friday night had left him sleepless, and he didn't figure on getting any peace until he'd fixed things.

Shelby rolled her eyes. "Why do men always bring gifts after a fight?"

"I don't know, is that what they do?"

"Always, although I admit, you were quick on the draw. I expected we'd spend most of this next week not talking to each other."

Scott drew back with a grimace. "Why? Is that how I come across to you? Mean and petty?"

The surprised glance Shelby flashed him checked his words. As Scott recalled what Shelby had said about his ex-girlfriend's husband, understanding from the Holy Spirit illuminated the problem. Shelby expected what she was used to. He tried a relaxed response, leaning back and folding his hands. "Not me, no, I can't stand to keep a fight going."

To his relief, she gave a faltering but genuine smile. "Fine, but you still don't have to keep bringing me food."

Scott lifted an index finger. "But remember, Lester's courting Ruby too."

"Too?" Shelby's brows shot up.

Panic made him fumble. "Not 'too' like this is a courtship ritual. 'Too' as in, in addition. You know. I'm helping him *too*."

"Admirable, as long as you know that gifts don't take the place of an apology."

"I do know that." Scott shifted. When Maltie hopped up in response, he patted his lap. Shelby scowled as her pet leapt over to him. As much as he wanted to agree and move on to easier topics as quickly as Maltie changed laps, he'd have to push past his normal reserves if he wanted Shelby to trust him again.

Before he could continue, Shelby spoke. "I don't like feeling manipulated, like if I don't respond to the gift with all smiles then I'm in the wrong." Faint bitterness rang in her words.

"Look, I don't know what you witnessed growing up or with Chet, but that's not the way Mike and Mom did things. I don't go for the stony silences or bribery either. I didn't intend the cake to do *all* my talking for me." He shot her a hopeful grin which she met with an unfazed, horizontal pull of her lips.

It had been a long time since Scott discussed emotions with a girl. *God, help me here.* "This project's been challenging for a number of reasons. It's hard enough when people are new working together, but add to that our different renovation ideas and the fact that you're grieving your husband, not to mention this Barnes mystery, and it's been pretty obvious to the Wentworths we needed some help."

Shelby blew out a breath. "I'll own that most of that has been my fault, but I don't like being unprofessional. The client should never know if we disagree."

"They realize this is a unique circumstance."

"I do get the sense that they're more interested in us personally than professionally."

Scott nodded, hopeful at her observation. "Definitely. And honestly? I've been thankful for their advice and patience. Lester's cake gave me the courage to show up here today. It's not easy for me to say what I think."

"You didn't seem to have any trouble the other night."

Ouch. Scott grimaced again. "I know, I'm sorry." *Say the rest,* the gentle whisper in his spirit urged. He sighed. And talked, even though he'd surpassed his daily word limit a few minutes ago. "I have this problem of believing I have to fix something if I think I'm right. Or saying what I think when I'm angry. I'm sorry for that. I hadn't thought through what a threat to your career means right now."

Lips parted, Shelby stared at him. Finally, she said, "Okay, and I'm sorry if I disappointed you … or the Wentworths. I did what I thought was right, but I do intend to leave things alone now." She smiled. "Obviously, I don't want a lawyer breathing down my neck."

Scott grinned back, feeling the weight lift off his chest. "Obviously." Then, like a splinter in a wound, something else forced its way out. "I think … I wanted your approval too much."

"*My* approval?"

"Yeah. I guess … I never got over that from high school."

Shelby let her breath out in a soft laugh. "But that's the thing, it's your approval *I* wanted."

"You did?"

"Yes. I felt awful for disappointing you. I may not agree with you all the time, but I totally respect what you think."

Scott gaped in astonishment that God gave him the very thing he longed for after he quit demanding it. Whatever happened with Shelby after this project, he never had to wonder again if she looked down on him. The freedom of that released something from his past.

Shelby took a breath and pulled Ruby's china plate closer. For the first time, her eyes lit with the interest he'd expected a girl to show chocolate. "Can I still accept your peace offering?"

"For sure." No way was he going to reveal that this time, *he'd* called Lester.

The morning of the excursion to North Augusta Living History Park dawned crisp and clear. After a week of hard work, Shelby looked forward to going out for fun in stylish, short boots, colored jeans, and a long cardigan over her fitted blouse. But she couldn't quell some anxiety as she parked her CRV in the lot off Lake Avenue. What if Ruby planned a scolding over Shelby's visit to Charles after she'd promised she'd wait and pray? Best address the problem right out of the gate.

Scott leaned against his truck, chatting with the Wentworths as they waited for her. Shelby was annoyed to find him looking like his Sunday self, clean-shaven, wearing a casual jacket over a dressy navy sweater and jeans with loafers.

"Hey," he said with a grin after Shelby greeted everyone. "I was just giving Lester and Ruby an update, telling them about the paint crews coming in."

"What did you guys do, take a beach vacation?" Lester joked.

Shelby grinned. "Not hardly. He still found ways to keep me busy, putting down plastic, taping the windows and hinges, cleaning and sanding walls, touching up." She couldn't resist poking Scott in the side with her elbow.

Ruby's gaze followed her gesture, and a smile played around her lips. "I'm glad things are progressing despite a rough start to the week."

"About that, I want to apologize, Miss Ruby. I know Scott told you what happened. I thought I did the right thing to visit Charles Barnes, but after what Scott said over the weekend, I spent some time thinking and praying."

Ruby gave her an encouraging nod, but Shelby forced herself to address Scott before turning back to the Wentworths. "Your honesty about what made you so angry with me made me look a little deeper. The truth is, someone told me that my old clients were going to my competitor now, and I let that goad me into action. Even if taking the photo to Charles needed to happen, I shouldn't have done it out of fear. If I had waited on God's timing, it would have all gone smoother. I do hope you're not mad at me."

"Of course not, dear." Ruby reached over to pat Shelby's hand. "It sounds like you've learned what you needed to. Now we just trust that God works all things for good, like He promises."

Here was the second time this week that forgiveness issued so freely amazed and convicted Shelby. Her father and stepmother flashed to mind—and David Barnes. Shelby grimaced. "I think I need to apologize to the Barnes too. It might help calm the waters. What do you think?" She grinned. "I promise, I'll really listen this time."

As Lester and Ruby smiled, Shelby almost jumped when Scott rubbed a hand up and down her arm. She glanced at him to see approval written on his handsome features. Approval, not flirtation, she told herself, although somehow that tunneled deeper into her psyche. And handsome? When did he go from normal to handsome?

Temporary. Professional, she told herself. Surprises always lurked beneath the surface. There was no way Scott was all he appeared to be.

"Maybe you could call David." Lester turned to his wife with a speculative glance. "Let him know Shelby wants to apologize and we have no intention of stirring up any more trouble for them. After all, you're the least threatening person possible."

"Oh, I am, am I?" Fixing a fist on her hip, Ruby mock-glowered.

"Well, when you're not mad at *me.*"

"He does have a point." Scott laughed.

"Let me think on that," Ruby said. "For now, let's enjoy our day. Are you ready for all this history, Shelby?"

She gave a wry grin. "I'm sure it will be very … educational, Miss Ruby."

As they entered the seven-and-a-half-acre park past a guard house where a Colonial sentry stood at attention, Ruby told them that the young family that had viewed their current home seemed likely to put in a bid.

"That's wonderful." Shelby paused under a shingle that read "Print & Post" on the side of an adorable yellow building with light-green and black trim. Letting Scott lead the way, she followed. The cool air scented with the delectable aroma of meat cooking—and a lighter conscience—put a spring in her step.

Scott set out for a dormered, blue building. On the porch of the two-and-a-half story New Windsor Cabinet Shop sat buckets, chairs, churns, and smaller items, apparently for sale, while a rhythmic thumping sound issued from the open workshop.

As she trailed Scott inside, Shelby inhaled the clean scent of fresh wood.

"This is what my shop would've looked like two hundred years ago," Scott said.

The source of the thumping became apparent, although the man pumping the foot-powered treadle lathe stopped the minute he noticed Scott.

"Keagan." Scott went over to clasp forearms with the living historian clad in tan knee breeches and full-sleeved muslin shirt. "How're you doing, man?"

"Good morn to you, Scott Matthews. It looks like the good Lord sent me a helper on this busy day!"

"Afraid not, although I'd love to. I'm with some clients today." Scott introduced the Wentworths as the clients and Shelby as his co-worker on their renovation project.

As thirty-something Keagan, with his sandy, shoulder-length hair tied back with rawhide, bent over her hand, Shelby fluttered her lashes in surprise. Westley from *The Princess Bride* sprang to mind.

Keagan seared her with his charming, dimpled smile before turning back to Scott. "If you refuse to work, and you can evade being drafted into the militia, you must take the fair maid a'dancin'."

"Oh … no. No dancing." Shelby took a step back.

A little boy sucking on a striped candy stick sidled up, nodding toward the lathe. "Whatcha makin'?"

"A spindle for a Continental officer's chair, my lad. See how it works? I have secured the wood on the screw, held up by this adjustable tool rest. I pump this pedal with my foot and apply this tool as 'tis turning."

"Cool, can I pump it?"

Noticing a good moment to escape, Shelby waved and headed onto the porch, where Ruby admired the merchandise. After calling out a goodbye to Keagan, Scott followed her.

"I saw a basket demonstrator over there under those trees," Ruby said. "You can use baskets in the decorating, can't you, Shelby?"

"Of course. I'll help you pick them out."

"Oh no." Ruby waved her hand. "I can't mess up basket selection, and besides, I've got to stop by the restroom."

"Already?" Lester groaned.

"Well, I did drink two cups of coffee. I hear music coming from the event barn. Scott, why don't you take Shelby over, and we'll catch up with you in a minute."

Shelby's mouth dropped open at Ruby's desire to part ways so soon after arriving. "But—" To her amazement, Scott agreed with Ruby, took Shelby's arm, and steered her across a meadow. "Doesn't it seem to you like they're setting us up?"

Scott winked. "Let's just let them have their way. Keep the clients happy, remember?"

"Fine, but the clients are getting rather pushy."

Scott chuckled.

As they approached the huge, sliding door at the barn front, the wistful sound of a string ensemble stirred Shelby's emotions. She stood next to Scott to admire several men in waistcoats and breeches and ladies in gowns with paniers. They glided through the steps of an elegant reel under a huge, black iron candelabra. Scattered on benches around the horizontal, light-wood walls, spectators of all ages smiled their approval. When the dance concluded, they applauded.

The most elegantly clad, middle-aged female dancer addressed the crowd. "That was the Hole in the Wall, which you might recall from the romantic ballroom scene in *Becoming Jane*."

Allowing for gasps of recognition, she folded her hands in front of her laced brocade bodice. "And now, as promised, I invite you to join us for instruction in Christ Church Bells. 'Tis easy to learn, so come out and form sets of three couples."

Scott turned to Shelby with a gleam in his hazel eyes. "You want to go?"

She took a quick step back. "No! Didn't you hear me in the cabinet shop?"

"Yes, but I think you might like this almost as much as laying tile."

He held out his hand, but Shelby tucked hers behind her back. "I'm totally uncoordinated. My mother had to pull me out of ballet classes when I fell on another little girl's head." No way could Scott understand the social disaster her withdrawal from that class had become. She'd lost all her friends, who continued dancing gracefully—and many, competitively.

Scott glanced at the people filling the dance floor, then gave her a quick once-over. "I'd say you've outgrown any childhood awkwardness. Weren't you a cheerleader?"

"That wasn't the same. Those were routines." Routines she'd painstakingly rehearsed to get back into those same social circles years later. It had always stuck in her craw that some people said her appearance and not her talent had earned her spot on the squad.

"Well, these are routines also." He held out his hand again. "Come on. Please?"

"What happened to you being shy and quiet?"

"If you haven't noticed, I'm not as shy as I used to be, and I love this stuff." Scott's face glowed with hopeful enthusiasm.

She shook her head. "Sorry. You're welcome to go ask someone else."

Scott's expression fell as he stepped to her side to observe the dance mistress organizing the volunteers. He so resembled his awkward high school self that her heart squeezed with conviction. She'd done that—squashed his confidence and joy as fast as she had years ago, and for a silly, selfish reason. But why should she always be the one shoved outside her comfort zone? Irritation and guilt warred within her. Finally, guilt won out.

She tugged him forward by his arm. "Forget what I said. Let's go."

"Really?" Scott looked amazed and delighted as he lined up opposite her, but the best she could offer in return was a tight smile.

The dance mistress gave instructions for the formation. "I have placed one experienced couple per set who will guide you through the steps. Now, we shall begin by bowing in line, acknowledging the band. Then, a bow to one's partner."

Scott bent at the waist, while Shelby curtsied as she saw the other ladies do. She might as well make the most of this. Deciding to swirl through the dance with exaggerated elegance, Shelby paid close attention to the instructions to promenade and star, first with Scott, then with the next man in line. Problem was, both moves required holding hands with her partner. And problem was, every time their hands touched, warmth flushed from her chest up to her face. And every time she saw Scott approaching, her heart performed a little dance of its own.

They skipped in a circle with the couple next to them, back to place, and then slapped right hands and left. By the second time they did this, Shelby's mounting irritation at her body's subversive reaction made her slap Scott's palm a little hard.

"Ow." He shook his hand in the air as they cast off.

"Excellent. Now, back to places, and we shall have music." The dance mistress held her clasped fingers out to each side like a conductor about to initiate a symphony.

As they executed the first bow of Christ Church Bells, Shelby noticed Ruby and Lester grinning and tapping their toes on the sidelines, but after that she could only see Scott's hazel eyes. They didn't leave her face, even when she tried to look away. Shelby wasn't sure which was worse, looking or not looking. Why had he put her in this position? And why did she feel like an eighth grader at her first dance? Like she'd felt when she realized Chet stared across the room at her that day they met?

Finally, it ended, applause and laughter erupting. The dance instructor passed by them, exclaiming, "Lovely! Lovely!" She slipped Shelby a business card and murmured *sotto voice*. "You two make a perfect pair. We could use another couple in our performing repertoire."

Laughing, Scott stepped closer as the lady glided away. "Shall I escort you to the sutler to purchase a period gown, m'lady?"

Shelby blew out a scornful breath. "No."

As she shoved the card into her pocket, Scott reached for her hand and bowed over it like Keagan had. Only he let his lips brush her knuckles. He was playing a part, she told herself. But the guilt and irritation bubbling up inside caused her to blurt out, "I'd appreciate it if you wouldn't flirt with me. As I said before, it's best we keep to business. Now, I've seen your rustic simplicity, I've done your dance, and I'd like to go home."

She walked away before she could feel guilty for the wounded look she'd put in Scott's eyes.

Chapter Twenty

Ruby's phone call late the next week took Shelby by surprise. To make sure she heard her client's request correctly, she closed the bungalow's living room window. The workers created a teeth-jarring racket, jackhammering the front driveway, then hauling off the concrete chunks in the shovel of a bobcat. Behind the house, Scott added to the din by revving up an old auger to dig the pergola post holes.

Shelby put the paint scraper down and brushed off her jeans. A miasma of dread at the thought of talking to Scott engulfed her as she stood. She'd finally elicited the stiff reserve she'd expected from him, but by rebuffing his attentions rather than disobeying his wishes. While they'd concluded their visit to the living history park with a polite lunch, the shutters had come down over Scott's hazel eyes. The subtleness of the loss ached more deeply than any vindictiveness. But she could hardly complain. She wanted a co-worker, she got a co-worker.

This week, Scott always seemed busy when she arrived, while Todd met her with suggestions of what she might do and fetched her supplies. But she chose to work rather than stay home, telling herself the more hands on the job, the faster it would be completed. Tomorrow Shelby had an appointment to look at several office spaces, none near Culpepper's.

Exiting through the master bedroom, she admired the barn wood closet door slider Scott had just installed. She'd feared it might detract from the light, airy color scheme, but instead, the touch of color and texture brought warmth to the room. When she found the master carpenter himself jerking the pull cord of the detached post hole digger engine, she waved and yelled to attract his attention.

Scott peered up past the brim of his ball cap.

"I got a phone call from Ruby, and she wants us to meet them right away."

"Could you just go? As you can see, I'm busy here." He indicated two other two-foot-deep holes, along with markings for more. Pergola poles and beams waited beside the house, which was now painted a rich medium-gray.

"Ruby says we should both clean up quick and meet her and Lester at this address." She held up her phone to double check the details their client had texted. "Twenty-four North Broughton Street. I think that's near the West End car dealership."

"Whose address is it?"

"David and Leah Barnes'."

"What?" Scott dropped the pull cord.

Shelby shrugged. "Ruby said she decided to call David to tender our apologies, and as luck would have it, or God would have it, his wife answered. It seems Leah is a Christian. She believes all this was meant to happen because she's seen how tormented her husband has been over the years, even though he tries to hide it. She has something important to tell us."

The stunned expression of hope on Scott's face made Shelby's heart beat faster. Maybe something so good would happen, happiness might override his hurt.

"How long do we have?"

"Less than an hour. Would you want to stop by my house to freshen up? It's closer—on the way." She stepped back as Scott moved the heavy auger motor inside the French doors, then tamped the dirt off the separate, red spiral blade.

He answered without looking up. "I don't want to inconvenience you."

"Scott, it's not an inconvenience. It's silly for both of us to drive when we're coming back—"

A voice, no thinner for its owner's effort to broadcast it, came from the corner of the house. "Excuse me?"

Scott and Shelby glanced up to behold Betsy Lou Clark approaching in a flowered house dress, cardigan, and white walking shoes.

"Why, Betsy Lou!" Scott actually sounded pleased to see the elderly neighbor. "What can we do for you?"

"You can cease all this awful noise, for one, then you can tell me when you're going to get this mess cleaned up."

Shelby stuck her head out the door. "Remember what we talked about, Miss Betsy Lou? Unfortunately, we have to make a mess and a lot of noise before we can clean everything up."

"How much longer? The Summerville Tour of Homes is this weekend, and my house is going to be featured. I guess they decided enough time has passed that it's historic. But how will folks even get in if y'all have all that equipment and trash in the way?"

"That's great news." Scott offered a diplomatic smile. "We'll have a new driveway poured by the end of the day tomorrow. Your place will be looking even better with fresh cement next door."

Betsy Lou pursed her lips and harrumphed. "But not fresh grass. All that dirt's an eyesore."

Shelby bit her lip to keep from instructing the combative old sourpuss to get back home and mind her own business, but to her astonishment, Scott rocked back on his heels and rolled his eyes up as he appeared to give consideration to her words. "Well, I had scheduled to have sod laid Monday, but I tell you what. I'll put in a call and see if they have time to come Friday."

The pursed lips twitched. "What about bushes? Flowers?"

"Now, being as I'm not a miracle worker, I can't promise that yet, but you're welcome to come over and transplant some of yours, Miss Betsy Lou. We could use the help, and it looks like you've got plants enough to share."

The teasing words, accompanied by the glint in Scott's eye, made Betsy Lou crack a smile. "Not only are you stealing my nap, now you're trying to put me to work. Have you noticed how old I am, young man?"

"No, ma'am, and I wouldn't venture to guess. We're fixing to leave for a while, so I'll see if they're almost done with the driveway. And I'll wait to complete the pergola tonight. That gives you a nice nap time. Do we have a deal, Miss Betsy Lou?"

The woman struggled to maintain her disgruntled demeanor. "I'd better take what peace I can get because I know you'll be at it again soon."

As she turned to walk away, Scott called after her, "I promise it's almost done."

Betsy Lou waved behind her and kept walking.

"Forty-five minutes." Shelby looked at her watch. "Now we might not have time to stop by anyone's house. Why'd you placate her? She'll just be back complaining about something else."

As Scott stepped into the house and closed the French door, he fixed her with a steady look. "Because sometimes, the person is more important than the job, even when we think that person is below our notice. *Especially* when we do."

As a sickly cocktail of dismay and conviction swirled in Shelby's stomach, she swallowed, but as always, her first response was to defend herself against Scott's poor opinion. "I don't think that. I stay focused on what's most important, which right now is meeting Ruby and Lester. Do you want to stop by my house or not?"

He removed his work gloves and tossed them on the floor next to the machinery. "I want to change. I'll meet you there, and don't worry, I won't be late."

Great, thought Scott, heavy on the sarcasm, as he pulled up at the Barnes' black-shuttered, red-brick Colonial the same time Shelby did. In his rearview mirror, he saw her get out of her CRV and stand on the sidewalk wearing a cute little denim dress and short boots. Looking at the house, she nibbled her lower lip … and waited for him.

He didn't want to talk to her. He didn't want to walk in with her. He'd been stupid to hope that observing him with his family and hobbies, and the fact that they'd started agreeing on the job, meant Shelby considered him an equal. He'd been stupid to imagine her face flushed with pleasure rather than embarrassment when they danced together. He'd been stupid to feel something for her. Her reaction to his theatrical kiss on her hand showed she'd only danced with him out of pity. And now he just wanted to get this job over as soon as possible.

Sighing, Scott opened his truck door and walked around to the yard.

Shelby greeted him with a fleeting smile. "So you see what I see?"

"What's that?"

She framed the white-columned Colonial with both hands. "The perfect flip. Imagine how light-gray paint and a new roof would update this house."

Why was she trying to connect now? And always put a pretty veneer on things? Or maybe it just annoyed him that he agreed with her. "Nothing wrong with plain brick. Wentworths are already inside. Let's go."

Hands clasped beneath her chin, Shelby hung back. "I'm nervous. What if despite what his wife thinks, David doesn't accept my apology?"

Just like a woman to expect emotional support after shutting a guy down. "Ruby will keep things moving in the right direction." As he walked ahead of Shelby, Scott's work boots crunched across red dogwood leaves.

She scrambled after him. "Well, nothing like you acting mad at me too!"

Scott turned around so fast Shelby almost bumped into him. "What do you want from me, Shelby? Maybe you can clarify. Because I can't seem to get it right."

Astonishment and hurt clouded her blue eyes. "To be friendly and professional. Is that so much to ask?"

A muscle worked in Scott's jaw. "I don't want you to mistake friendliness for flirting again, so maybe we should stick to simply professional." Shutting someone else out behind a wall provided a grim sense of satisfaction. He ignored the guilt that partnered the sensation.

Shelby's lips parted, and her eyes sparked with the potential for a fight. "Fine, but you need to add one more thing. Respect."

His mouth fell open. "Respect? When have I failed to respect you?"

"How about all the times you pushed me into doing things I didn't want to?" Cocking her head to one side, Shelby planted her fist on her hip.

"I told you why I wanted you to participate in the house reno." Scott held one of his hands to one side, palm up. "And not only did you end up learning new skills, you liked them."

"Even so, you could have asked. Explained straight-out."

Scott thought they'd cleared the air of all this stuff already. He ran a hand over his hair in frustration. "Well, again, I'm sorry."

Shelby's other fist contacted her other hip. "Then there was the way you made me feel today."

His eyebrows flew up. He briefly considered walking back down the sidewalk to his truck. If they were in this bad a shape, how could they face the Barnes? Might as well hang it up. But that would be childish and wouldn't solve anything.

"What you said about Betsy Lou—I know I need to work on my patience with people who interrupt me, but I don't think she's less than me in any way. You assumed the worst about me. Even if it had been true, you certainly weren't 'speaking the truth in love.'"

Scott's jaw dropped again, but this time, not from righteous indignation. Because she was right. Dead right. He'd fallen back into judging her the minute she rejected him. It might make him feel better, but it certainly wasn't Christlike. It made him what he accused her of being—prideful.

Before he could reply, the front door of the two-story house opened, and a middle-aged woman with short, brown hair looked out.

"You must be Scott and Shelby." Adjusting a burgundy cardigan over her slightly rounded middle, she stepped onto the rocking chair porch framed by the dark-red leaves of Virginia sweetspire shrubs. "I'm Leah Barnes. Thank you for coming! Please, come in."

Shelby smiled and stepped forward quickly, while Scott took deep breaths in an attempt to cool the heat he felt coloring his face. After shaking Leah's hand, they entered a traditional foyer with a parquet floor, crystal chandelier, and stairs with a Persian carpet runner, elegant if a bit dated.

Leah smiled, noticing him inhaling the tantalizing aroma from the back of the house. "That's my pumpkin bread. Would you like a slice and perhaps a cup of coffee?"

"I won't turn you down on that, Mrs. Barnes." Scott grinned. Pleasantries felt like a relief after the encounter with Shelby—and his own inadequacies.

"I'm glad to hear it. I made it especially for my guests today." She gestured to a parlor through a wide, cased opening on their left, where a baby grand piano added an extra touch of class to long drapes and plush, light-blue carpet. Scott immediately pictured the room with hardwoods. Shelby's speculative assessment told him she did the same. He ventured a tentative, knowing smile at her, which she returned. "Please, have a seat, and I'll bring you the coffee. Sugar and cream?"

"Yes, thanks."

"Shelby, would you like some too?" Leah leaned close to Shelby to get her attention.

"Oh. No, thank you." Shelby clutched her purse close to her side as she entered the parlor, casting a quick glance to David Barnes before smiling at Ruby and Lester, seated on a button-tucked sofa.

Their last encounter with the man all too fresh in mind, Scott resisted an irritating instinct to keep Shelby behind him—though she'd probably rebuff his protection today—but thankfully, David stood from a wing chair with a conciliatory expression and held out his hand.

"Welcome." He shook hands with Scott, then Shelby. When she stood as far back from him as possible, David ducked his head. "I promise this isn't an ambush. I'll be on my best behavior today. I'm rather ashamed of how I acted when we last met."

Shelby accepted a spot on the cushion Ruby patted next to her, leaving another wing chair for Scott. As she took her place, crossing her legs, she said, "I'm sorry, too, and that's why I asked Ruby to contact you. I regret upsetting you and your father. I just … didn't know what else to do with the photo I found. But I shouldn't have seen him without your permission."

David nodded. "I understand, and I'm sorry you got dragged into my family's sorry mess. We hoped the sale of the house would go off in a quiet manner. Wishful thinking, right?"

"But according to what Leah told us earlier, God has been at work, so some good's coming out of all this," Ruby said.

"Needless to say, I'd buried the anger toward my mother I thought I'd dealt with." David glanced at his wife as she entered with Scott's coffee and a slice of pumpkin bread on a small stoneware plate. "Leah knew it all along. She suspected my health problems over the years stemmed from those unresolved issues. But I refused to discuss it with her. Until now."

"David came home very upset that night." Leah handed the refreshments to Scott before lifting a laptop from a white-padded chair near the window. "When he told me how he'd threatened you, I felt so bad. Of course, we'd never bring legal action. Please know he spoke from a sense of self-preservation. But what he shared about the photo made me start searching online."

"Did you find anything?" Propping his hands on his knees, Lester sat forward.

Leah nodded, opening her laptop. "I did. The next day, I traced Jeff Wilson's accounting firm to Philadelphia, where his family came from. Jeff's son, Matt, was pictured with him on the website. And look at this."

Leah tapped on the keyboard then came to kneel between Scott and the group on the sofa. Scott took a bite of the still-warm pumpkin bread as he leaned over to see. Under a banner headline that read "Wilson Accounting," the screen displayed an older but still handsome, salt-and-pepper-haired man in a suit, standing beside a younger, shorter accountant. "This is Jeff's son, Matt." Beside the computer screen, she held up a photograph of her husband, twenty pounds lighter and with a full head of hair. "And this is David, ten years ago."

"Different hair color and face shape, but look at those eyes!" Shelby pointed to the computer screen. "Practically identical."

"Exactly." Leah glanced around at them, waiting for the realization of what she was saying to sink in. "I stared at the two of them for an hour before I worked up the nerve to show David. Then, with his permission, I searched for Matt on social media. And we found this."

Settling on the floor, Leah opened another web browser, and they all strained to see as an enlarged, close-up photo of Matt Wilson appeared. His head tilted in a familiar pose against that of a woman Scott immediately recognized, despite the ravages of age and probable hard living.

David muttered from his wing chair. "As you can see, my mother is alive."

Chapter Twenty-One

With a glow of satisfaction, Shelby finished wiping down the new, stainless steel oven in the Wentworths' kitchen and turned the dial to four hundred. Sensing someone behind her, she whipped around to glare at the trail of sawdust Scott's bag-covered shoes made across the floor.

"I just finished cleaning everything in here, and I do mean everything." Shelby made a gesture that encompassed the refinished and repainted off-white cabinets, as well as the floor itself. Just the small movement made her wince. The day before, she'd helped the crew not only roll out plastic and drive in uneven nails for the floor sanding, but also tape shut vents, lights, and fireplaces.

Scott froze. "Sorry." He watched her retrieve a pizza from the freezer. "That looks good."

Shelby smiled as she opened the cardboard box. Knowing Halloween promised to be another long day, she'd brought several pizzas and garden salads to feed everyone. She'd made sure the men sanded the hardwood floors in here first—early in the morning when they threw open the doors and windows—so she could access the kitchen in time to make dinner.

Now, the men worked upstairs, but the pervasive dust made her grateful she'd spent most of the day outside. Even though she had to put plants in the ground where she sometimes encountered earthworms. She hadn't screamed. Not once. But a couple of breaks had been required to provide time for the disgusting creatures to burrow deeper.

She wanted to know if Scott approved her efforts but didn't dare ask. They were back on friendly terms, but not of the joking variety. Just business. After leaving the Barnes residence, he'd pulled her aside to apologize for his condescending attitude. When he'd actually thanked her for reminding him to speak the truth in love, she'd stumbled into an explanation of how dancing brought back bad ballet memories and how she hadn't meant to hurt his feelings.

A shutter had come down over his eyes, and he'd waved a hand to stop her. "Regardless of why you didn't want to dance with me, I shouldn't have acted like I did."

Now, taking extra-large steps to limit the tracks he left, Scott laid a spackle, a tube of wood filler, and a huge bowl filled with bags of candy on the counter.

"What's that for?"

He looked askance at her. "Trick-or-treaters." Ripping open the first bag, he started pouring in the mini chocolate bars.

She wanted to protest the dust on his clothes and hands but decided it wasn't worth it since the candies were individually wrapped. "Who's going to answer the door? I'm preparing dinner."

"I will. I'm ready to clean up and wipe down the floors with mineral spirits. We're on schedule for three coats of polyurethane tomorrow."

"Yea, more stink." Shelby pulled the pizza pan she'd brought from home out of a lower cabinet.

Adding the contents of the final bag of candy, Scott mixed with his fingers. "You don't have to help."

She bristled. "I can wipe floors too." Then she softened. "Actually, I can't believe all I missed during every renovation. Now, it feels like if I miss a day, I miss something important."

Hoping Scott might affirm her commitment, Shelby ducked her head and jerked apart the pizza wrapper. But when his phone dinged, he pulled it from his pocket and held it up. Shelby darted a glance from the corner of her eye, but she couldn't make out who sent the text. Not like the day at the Barnes' when, after tendering his apology, he took a call from Caitlyn Curtis. Talking with his phone to his ear, he'd gotten into his truck with just a wave goodbye. But both times, the same slightly frazzled smile had flitted across his face.

Shelby's confession didn't seem to register. He texted as he walked away, mumbling, "Okay, I'm going into the bathroom for a minute."

A minute later, Shelby heard the water turn on at the newly installed dresser vanity. Sighing, she slid the pizza into the oven, then unwrapped the other paper goods.

He wasn't cruel, she told herself. Just disconnected. Which was good considering they'd soon part ways. It wouldn't be fair to keep him dangling. But it didn't feel good.

And it gnawed at her that he didn't understand the reason behind her rejection. He thought he had to protect his heart from a cold woman. Problem was, she wasn't cold. But she couldn't tell him any of that without revealing some very warm feelings she was not ready to examine. Still, the steady ache in her chest felt like she'd lost a close friend, and she couldn't seem to stop herself from attempting to build a bridge.

Scott emerged, stripped free of plastic booties, outer shirt, and the fine layer of dust that had covered his skin. He'd slicked his hair back with water. Shelby frowned at this rare attention to his appearance while still on the job.

"Is there a reason we're concerned about trick-or-treaters today?" She glanced over her shoulder as she tossed the salad.

"Besides joining in on the holiday fun? Caitlyn said she might come by and bring the framed prints your sister made for the house, as well as the restaurant memorabilia."

Shelby's tongs stilled. "Oh. And she needs candy?"

A wrapper crinkled as Scott opened a chocolate bar. "Her three-year-old daughter might."

"What?" Shelby whirled around to stare at him.

He met her eyes matter-of-factly. "Yeah, Caitlyn's a single mom."

"I … I didn't know that." The memory of Scott holding his toddler niece pierced Shelby's consciousness, filling her with unease. Caitlyn possessed more motivation for romantic connection than Shelby had even imagined. No doubt the woman had already pegged steady, loyal Scott as a frontrunner for stepdad.

Popping the candy into his mouth, Scott turned to walk into the dining room. "Yeah, well, there's a lot you don't know."

A male voice boomed from the foyer. "Hello, the house!"

"David!" Scott strode into the living room to shake the man's hand.

Shelby leaned against the counter, closing her eyes a brief moment in an attempt to calm her thoughts and emotions. Despite the unfamiliar sensation churning in her middle right now—though it reminded her vaguely of the beginning stages of the flu—she needed to show David Barnes nothing but kindness and absolute focus. Last she'd seen him, he'd been wiping tears from his eyes after Ruby prayed over his indecision about what to do about his mother.

"Man, it looks good in here." The older man looked around with appreciation as he strolled through the dining room with its freshly repainted trim and window seat. "And the kitchen … wow. This sure doesn't look like the house I grew up in."

Shelby turned from pulling the first fragrant pepperoni pizza out of the oven to offer David a half hug. "We're not nearly done yet."

Why did David look so different? Ah, the smile he now wore. And he held his shoulders back and chin up. "Scott's new gray island with marble countertop will go right here." Shelby indicated the area separating the kitchen from the dining room. She tried smiling at Scott. "I can't wait to see it."

Focused on David, he didn't respond to her comment. "I'm happy to show you around, but did you really come by just to see the house?"

"No." David ran a hand over the slight growth of tawny stubble on his chin. "To be honest, I was out driving, just thinking, and I ended up here. I feel like you guys need to know what happened with my mom, and I wanted to tell you in person."

Shelby asked, "Will you join us for pizza? We can sit at the built-in table and benches in the eating nook."

"I guess I could eat a slice."

A minute later, after delivering the second pizza for the crew to the oven, Shelby slid in by David, lacking the courage to join Scott. Scott said a brief blessing, then Scott and Shelby both looked at David while his slice of pizza lay untouched on his paper plate.

"So … I decided to contact Matt Wilson."

"You did?" Shelby blinked, trying to separate a string of cheese between her plate and her lips before Scott happened to glance over at her. She quickly set the slice back on her plate, her cheeks heating.

"Yeah." David took a swig of soda, and his eyes briefly squeezed shut in that tic he had. "I sent him a message on social media. I just laid it out there, told him who I was, and how I thought we were connected. I mean, I didn't go into the lifetime of hell our mother put me through, but apart from that …"

"Do you share the same mother?" Scott asked.

"Turns out, we do. Jeff helped my mother disappear back in 1976. Back then, she thought she was in love with him, and she was miserable with my dad. She also knew he'd never grant her a divorce. Jeff came up with the idea to move her to Philadelphia near his family, get her settled there under a new name, and follow her when enough time had passed to allay any suspicion."

Scott polished off his first slice of pizza and wiped his mouth. "But wouldn't the police have traced the name change?"

Reminded of his cooling dinner, David reached down for his own slice and took a quick bite. "The Wilsons are very connected in Pennsylvania. Typically, a name change is announced in the newspaper, but under the right circumstances, that can be … overlooked. The next step is to apply for a fresh social."

"And she married Jeff Wilson?" Afraid to take another bite of pizza, Shelby removed a pepperoni and laid it to one side.

David nodded. "They stayed together for ten years. Divorced when Jeff had an affair. Big surprise, right? But my mother got custody of Matt, and they remained close after he grew up. Thus, the picture we found online."

Shelby marveled at David's calm delivery. She had to believe the abandonment and betrayal he must have felt—that she herself felt for so much less—swirled just beneath the surface. She leaned forward. "But how did Matt respond? Did he even know you existed? And how did you feel to learn all this?"

The soda can shook in David's hand, and he placed it on the table. "He did know about me, but he hadn't contacted me because Mom asked him not to. At least, she asked him to wait until she was ready. He was thrilled by my message because he said Mom's been trying to work up the courage for some time to reach out to me. You see … Mom has cancer. She's terminal."

"Man," Scott whispered before silence descended in the kitchen.

Watching a muscle in David's throat work, Shelby pictured the abandoned little boy—about to be abandoned again—and checked a misting of tears in her eyes. "I'm so sorry, David."

"Yeah." He blinked, cleared his throat. "Matt said Mom has always expressed remorse and guilt over leaving me. So much so that she was afraid to contact me. Afraid I'd hate her. This afternoon, I got to talk to her myself. She explained a few things about the past and asked my forgiveness."

"That's wonderful, David. Were you able to?"

David nodded again, wordless for a moment. "She apologized for her selfishness, said it was almost like she lost her mind over Jeff. He was everything she thought Dad was not, charming, successful, handsome, and willing to empower her freedom. He fed her disgust with Dad by agreeing how controlling he was. But she didn't see the bondage forming with Jeff. Their relationship was … obsessive. Nothing else seemed important but him.

"By the time she realized she'd bought a lie, she already had another child, one she didn't want to abandon like she'd abandoned the first one. She decided to stay in the area and start making her own way. She said my contacting Matt was an answer to prayer. When she got sick, she found a church, a good pastor, and a support group. Most important, she found God, and took the first steps toward forgiving herself for her past. She said … knowing I could forgive her lifted a crushing weight off her that she'd carried for years."

Scott folded his hands on the table and bowed his head. When he said, "praise God," moisture glistened in his eyes too.

"We're flying up to see her at Thanksgiving."

Unashamed, Shelby wiped a tear off her cheek. "That's wonderful." When her voice caught, she covered her nose with her napkin. Amazement at God's handiwork and joy for David pried the lid off her emotions about her own father and stepmother, birthing a sense of bittersweet longing she didn't want to feel.

She sensed Scott studying her with an expression of concern. But David laughed and reached out to clap her on the shoulder. "Don't cry. You see, your meddling brought about a good result after all."

"No, *God* brought about a good result." Shelby smiled at David, while Scott nodded his approval.

"That's true enough." David grinned back. "Well, guys, I've got to get going. The kids are having some friends over for a party tonight, and if I'm not there to keep all the teenagers in check, Leah will kill me." He stuffed the last couple bites of pizza in his mouth and shifted in a way that let Shelby know she needed to let him out of the booth.

"We're so glad you came by. Best Halloween ever—"

"Knock, knock." A feminine voice sang from the foyer. "We saw the front light on."

—Or not. Caitlyn Curtis approached with a coy smile, holding a plastic, hot-pink jack-o-lantern bucket in one hand and the hand of a tiny girl in the other. Both females sported pink-and-white bunny costumes with stand-up ears and tiny skirts that had the effect of being adorable on the toddler but eye-popping on the mother. In fact, Shelby saw the gaze of the man who must have turned on that front porch light slide to that curvy expanse of black tights-clad legs. He quickly redirected his eyes, but Shelby still felt indignant heat build in her chest.

"Uh, hi, and I better get home to my wife." Like Scott's, David's exaggerated efforts to focus far above the slinky hose and cotton-tailed bunny bottom were almost comical.

Before he could run out the door, Shelby snagged him for a real hug. David patted her back with genuine affection. She forced her attention away from Scott bending down to Caitlyn's brunette little girl with the bowl of candy. "Tell her hello for us. And please, feel free to bring her by after the reveal."

After the child made her selection, Scott stood up and shook David's hand. "I'm so happy for you, man. God bless."

After David left, Shelby had no choice but to greet Caitlyn. Bunny mom approached with the barest hint of a smile, her eyes sweeping Shelby from top to toe. Imagining dirt left over from planting oak leaf hydrangea, Shelby brushed a hand over her cheek.

"Hello again, Shelby."

"Hello, Caitlyn."

"Meet my sweet little Ashlyn."

Caitlyn and Ashlyn, how clever. Shelby smiled at the smaller bunny. "Hi there. You getting a lot of candy tonight?"

Poking out a lower lip, Ashlyn tilted her almost-empty bucket for Shelby to see. As Shelby broke into laughter, Scott dropped in a Jolly Rancher.

"We're just starting." Caitlyn grinned. "I have the prints in the car, but first, I'd love to look around." She turned an expectant expression on Scott.

"Oh, sure!" He jumped up, shoving the candy bowl into Shelby's arms. Frowning, Shelby took a step back.

"I'd be happy to give you a tour, although we need to stay down here for now since the guys are refinishing the floors upstairs. They'll come down for pizza when Shelby gets it ready, but it will still be a mess." He glanced pointedly at the laced, high-heeled black boots on Caitlyn's tiny feet.

Caitlyn nodded. "Of course. We're standing in the dining room?"

Shelby moved in front of Scott. "Yes. I selected one of Scott's beautiful tables from Culpepper's the day you saw us in town—to go right here. The island he's making will separate this room from the kitchen, and we found the best chairs that day, too, didn't we, Scott?"

"Um, yes."

Shelby swept an arm to indicate the ceiling. "Above the plate rail, we'll do a stencil. I'll start that next week."

"Oh? What kind of stencil?"

"The Craftsman aesthetic calls for something either geometric or natural." Shelby added a polite smile to the professional vibe she tried to emit. "I was planning on a print that will tie in that beautiful view of the trees from the window seat."

Caitlyn squinted her eyes and twisted her lips to one side in thought. "I have a great pinecone template at the store I could bring by."

"Well … I'm not sure if pinecones would be elegant enough."

"Free form is no problem. I can do whatever you want."

"I think pine cones would go great with my table." Scott glanced up from unwrapping a wad of bubble gum for Ashlyn, who stuffed it in her mouth and handed him back the paper. Caitlyn looked on with an approving smirk.

Shelby said, "I've got it covered, and besides, I prefer to avoid last minute budget adjustments."

Caitlyn's long, mascara-encrusted lashes gave a slow blink. "Oh, no charge. I love to give back to the community. Consider it my mark on the Wentworth project." Sidling over to Scott, she snaked a bare arm through his and gave a squeeze.

At least he had the grace to look a little embarrassed. "That would be super generous, Caitlyn, but we can decide for sure later. Uh, Shelby, do I smell a pizza burning?"

Shelby raced into the kitchen to rescue the crew's supper. As she picked off seared sections, Scott and Caitlyn trailed her. Caitlyn admired the cabinet fronts and ran her hand over the beadboard, then they wandered into the master bedroom. While Shelby cut the pizza and got drinks out of the fridge, she noticed them out the window, inspecting the pergola in the fading orange evening light. Caitlyn's silky laughter drifted to Shelby's ears. When they returned, Scott carried Ashlyn.

"Scott, can you please go upstairs and tell the guys to come down?" Shelby asked.

"Yeah."

"Wait, you've got ..." Caitlyn edged close and swiped a smear of chocolate from Scott's cheek. "Ash, baby, let me see your hands." When the child extended all ten splayed fingers toward her mother, Caitlyn chuckled and licked the incriminating evidence off her daughter's thumb.

Shelby gave the salad another unnecessary toss, muttering in a flat voice. "I had a napkin right here." Didn't Scott see through such antics?

"Oh, it's okay. We moms can hardly be squeamish. I probably have the germ tolerance of a preschool teacher. But you!" Caitlyn growled at Ashlyn and pretended like she'd gobble up her hand. "Stay out of the candy."

The child tucked her head against Scott's chest the same way his niece had in church, earning his indulgent smile.

Shelby stifled a laugh a minute later when Scott exclaimed over the chocolate Ashlyn's mouth had transferred to his clean shirt. She handed him a wet dish cloth. Caitlyn plucked it from his hand and started wiping the splotch with giggles and apologies.

Finally, Scott pulled free, and Caitlyn put the cloth back on the sink. Scott shifted the mini-bunny on his hip as he faced Shelby. "We can't leave Caitlyn's prints here yet. Do you want to come out with us and put them in your CRV?"

She wanted to tell Scott to put them in his truck, but that would give him and Caitlyn more time alone. "Sure. Let me get the crew to come down for supper."

After calling up the stairs to the workers, Shelby followed the trio down the front walk. Framed against the golden leaves of the gingko Todd had just planted, the neighborhood looked enchanting in the October dusk. Candles and jack-o-lanterns lit historic homes as children in costumes scurried along the sidewalks, trailed by protective adults. At Caitlyn's red Civic, Scott buckled Ashlyn into her car seat.

"I want trick-or-treat," Ashlyn whined to her mother. "Scott come too!"

Caitlyn laughed. She pressed against her car—and Scott—as a cluster of black-caped, preteen vampires traipsed past her, dribbling fake blood and swinging bulging plastic bags and Halloween-printed pillow cases. "Do you want to? That would be fun."

Scott straightened. "I haven't gone trick-or-treating in fifteen years."

"Well, I would hope not."

"You don't have a costume," Shelby said.

"I could put on my sanding bags and mask." Covering his mouth, he waggled his eyebrows, causing Ashlyn to giggle.

"Clever." Caitlyn winked at Scott.

Shelby cleared her throat. "Could we get the prints? I need to put a third pizza in the oven."

Caitlyn twisted her wide, bow lips, painted a deep red, and clicked the remote for her trunk. "Sure."

Scott followed her to the back of her car. "I appreciate the invitation, but I shouldn't leave until the guys have all cleared out."

"Call you for a rain check? Builders' Expo next weekend and dinner?"

Scott bit his lip. "Ooh, you drive a hard bargain." He tilted his head to one side. "Okay, yeah."

Yeah? Wait, had they just set up a date right in front of her? Shelby remained rooted to the sidewalk as her co-worker and the bunny mom leaned over the trunk. Caitlyn's white bob tail wobbled as she shifted items around.

"Shelby, you've got to see these! Get over here!"

Scott's enthusiasm drew her. Shelby didn't know whether to be dismayed or overjoyed that the framing of Angelina's whimsical neighborhood prints and the photos of Lester and his restaurant employees turned out better than expected. Against a backdrop of soft red velvet, Caitlyn had even shadow-boxed an old, leather-covered menu.

"And here's the *piece de resistance.*" Caitlyn lifted a foursome of recipes mounted in a single rectangular frame. "Copied from Lester's mother's beloved cookbook. Will this not warm his heart every time he goes into the kitchen?"

Shelby swallowed a lump in her throat. "Yes, it will." More importantly, it warmed *her* heart. Because, ironic as it was, the four recipes displayed were the very four Scott had cooked for her. She couldn't stop her eyes from raising to seek his. And he was looking at her.

Caitlyn nudged Scott. "Don't you like it?"

He turned his head. "Yeah, I love it. Let's get these transferred."

"She's something else." Scott grinned and shook his head after the artist drove away, waving.

He'd given Shelby the perfect opening. "That's for sure. Not only did she practically force her services upon us, she asked you out right in front of me."

Scott looked at her. "Is there a reason she shouldn't?"

"Well, it was … awful bold, considering you've only had a business acquaintance since college."

"I never said we only had a business acquaintance."

A pit formed in Shelby's stomach. "Well, how close were you in college?"

He crossed his arms. "Very close. Caitlyn's the one I told you about that got away."

Chapter Twenty-Two

The kitchen subway tile was taking longer than Scott had estimated. Trowel in one hand, he glanced at his watch. He knew Shelby would take over if he asked her to, but he didn't want to make her aware of his plans. Why it mattered, he didn't know. He had to stop needing Shelby Dodson's approval.

When he reached the final stretch below the fancy wooden oven vent hood, Shelby slid a hip off the nearby counter where she screwed new handles onto the upper cabinets and came to stand beside him. Assuming she assessed his progress, and not wanting to notice again how cute she looked in her plaid flannel shirt and jeans, he kept working. She'd finally traded dresses, or silk blouses with designer pants, for more sensible clothing while on the job. She probably had no idea the transformation made him want to sling her up in his truck and blow through the last stoplight leading out of town. But she insisted on claiming his attention by placing a decorative gray mosaic tile cluster in front of him.

"Why did you buy that? We talked about plain subway tile."

"When I went back in there, and I thought of how big this expanse of white is under the hood, I couldn't resist. Just try it. Hold it up."

Scott sighed and let his arm drop to the counter. Stared back at her pleading expression with his mouth flattened into a thin line.

"Hold it up." Hector echoed Shelby from his ladder over the island where he installed the third pendant light shaped like a downward white tulip on a rod of black metal.

Scott glowered at him. "Fine." He took the section of tile and did as Shelby asked. He didn't want to get into another disagreement with her. In fact, he wanted to talk to her as little as possible. Avoiding her made it a little more bearable that after two weeks he would never see her again.

Shelby obliged his unspoken wishes by stepping back as she assessed the effect of the tile. "Picks up the color from the island beautifully."

"I do like the color." He could agree to that much.

"But it's too fancy. Too modern." Shelby shook her head and held out her hand for the sample. "Ruby will hate it."

"Wow." Scott blinked in surprise as he handed it back and Shelby laid it on the counter. She no longer needed him to interpret the rustic charm of the bungalow.

Shelby returned to her cabinets. "It's a shame. It's not like they can hang anything there."

"I have no doubt you'll find the perfect solution, Shelby." The electrician grinned down from his perch with an obsequious amount of enthusiasm.

"Thanks for your support, Hector."

"You're welcome. I believe in you. Now, I need your help with the chandelier in the dining room."

Scott laughed. "Brownie points don't count when you want something, man. But for the record, Shelby, you made a good call. I know you'll figure out something even better." Even though he needed to stay off personal ground, professional encouragement could help them all finish this job well.

Shelby glanced over her shoulder at him. Several times during the day, he'd felt like she wanted to tell him something, but she'd reverted to talking shop. At that moment, her cell phone rang. She pulled it out of her pocket, looked at it, then headed for the back door. The tentative tone of Shelby's response caused Scott to pause. He'd never heard her that quiet, that nervous.

"You're sure?" He could hear her speaking from outside. "Okay, if you're sure and Aubrey is, too, we'll drive down the day before. Yeah, Angelina's eager for a break. We'll stay through Sunday. That would be great. Is there anything I can bring? … Thanks." In the light of the new side lantern Hector had mounted by the back door, Shelby bit her lip. "Love you too."

Shelby stood there clutching her phone. An urging in Scott's spirit told him to go to her. He didn't want to open up his emotions to this woman again, but this sounded huge. Spiritual stuff trumped his own trampled feelings.

Scott cracked open the door. "Sorry, but … was that just your dad?"

Shelby nodded, and a tear ran down her cheek. "After the courage and forgiveness David showed his mom, I couldn't let things go on. My mother's visiting her sister for Thanksgiving, so I left a message this morning asking my dad if I could come with Angelina for the holiday."

Scott felt a grin crack his face. "And he said 'yes.'"

She gave a soft laugh and covered her eyes. "Yeah, I can't believe it. God's going to have to give me grace for Aubrey, but we're going."

"He will."

Shelby laughed again and stood up straight, lifting her chin as she tucked her hair behind her ears. "Sorry, I don't know why I'm so emotional."

"Don't apologize. It's a big deal. I'm happy for you." Apparently triggered by his supportive words, another renegade drop of moisture hurtled down Shelby's face. Before he could stop himself, Scott reached out to wipe it away. To his surprise, Shelby caught hold of his hand.

"I do need to apologize."

He pulled away, refusing to allow her to arouse his hope again only to short-circuit it. "No need. I understand now where you were coming from. And for the record, that was comfort just now, not coming onto you."

"I know that. Scott ..."

He turned toward the kitchen, answering over his shoulder in what he hoped was a light manner. "Gotta get this finished. I'm running late."

She followed him inside. "For what?"

Scott closed his eyes a second before he started smearing putty again. "I'm helping Caitlyn move tables and big pictures around tonight for her holiday open house. Basically, I'm helping out for your sister's showing."

Shelby frowned. "Funny she had to wait 'til dark."

"*I'm* making her wait 'til dark."

"Ooh." From the dining room, plastic and cardboard rustled as Hector unpacked the intricate wrought-iron wheel supporting electric candles Shelby had ordered.

"Seems like she's calling on you more and more. Doesn't she have a dad or something? Or does she like to just play the 'I'm all alone in the world' card? Maybe I should've tried that. Being a widow should elicit more sympathy than being divorced."

When Scott widened his eyes and blinked at her, Shelby pinched her lips shut as though realizing she'd said too much. To this point, Shelby had attempted to veil her dislike of Caitlyn. Done with that now, apparently. The hot bunny costume must have put her over the edge.

"I'll be her dad," Hector said. "Her sugar daddy, that is."

Shelby ignored him, narrowing her gaze on Scott. "You know she likes you, right? You're not actually doing this because you feel sorry for her?"

"I'm doing this because she needs help. And so what if she likes me?"

"Um, maybe I'll just come back tomorrow." Hector eased the chain of the chandelier back onto the floor and backed away with a wave. "Night, night, y'all."

Barely noticing the employee's retreat, Scott rounded on Shelby. "What do you care, when you've made it clear you're keeping things professional? You think you can boss people around like you did in high school, just snap your fingers and they do your bidding. Just because you don't want any love in your life, you don't want anybody else to be happy either? Well, maybe this is my second chance, whether you want one or not."

As he spoke, Shelby shook her head, and her eyes filled with tears. Everything in him screamed he was settling for cheap laminate when two-hundred-year-old heart pine stood right in front of him. But what choice did Shelby leave him?

He quieted his voice. "Or maybe you just don't want one with me." Scott placed the spatula atop the putty bucket. "I'm done here too. See you tomorrow. Or if it's not too much to ask, maybe you can stay home so I can complete my work in peace."

On the way out, Scott grabbed his jacket from the stair post. He walked as fast as he could away from the second-class way Shelby Dodson still made him feel. A half-moon rose over Augusta, adding its light to the street lamp where his truck waited. But before he got there, steps pounded on the front porch, and Shelby called his name as she ran after him.

Hands in his pockets, he turned around with an expression of exaggerated patience. He prepared himself for another apology, because no matter how often "the special people" climbed over others, they never wanted to look bad doing it.

"You're wrong. I do want a second chance at love. And … I want it with you."

His mouth fell open as Shelby continued, her words running together.

"I'm scared, and I feel guilty, because, because … I feel more for you than I was ready to. Honestly, more than I felt for Chet. And what kind of wife betrays her husband that way a year after he dies? And I can't believe you're for real, because people just aren't that good. But now I see you are for real, because otherwise you'd never be interested in that prissy little—"

Shelby didn't get any further because Scott did what he'd wanted to since high school. He reached out and pulled her to him and pressed his lips to hers. They tasted just as sweet as he'd always dreamed, and they yielded to the searching pressure of his before firming in a very encouraging passionate response. With a hand at the soft curve of her waist, he held her close, savoring the way her slender form fit against his.

But the next second, Shelby sprang away, shaking her head. "Oh no. Oh no, oh no!"

Scott drew back in alarm. "What?"

She turned her head from him. "Dang it, that was really good. I was afraid it would be."

As the full meaning of her words hit him, he started laughing in relief. "You don't make any sense, woman."

"I know. I'm sorry. I've always known my own mind, but now … I'm finding I didn't know my heart."

"But I knew it. Ten years ago, I knew it. I just couldn't get your attention long enough to tell you."

"Well, you have my attention now."

And that was an invitation for another kiss if he'd ever heard one.

Above Shelby's hissing gas logs in the fireplace, the mantel clock struck nine.

Scott barely sat down before she exclaimed, "I can't believe I ran after you like that!" Wanting to disappear into the sofa cushions, Shelby covered her face with the sleeves of her sweater.

"I can't either."

"I couldn't take it, the thought of you going off to that, that …"

Scott smiled and pulled Shelby's arms down. "No name calling is necessary."

Shelby sighed and reached for the Bible she'd left on the coffee table next to a tray of hot chocolate and shortbread cookies. "You're right. I was trying to settle myself down after I got home, and I was reading in Romans 12. It really hit me. Listen to this." Shelby raised the Bible to read out loud. "'Be kindly affectionate to one another with brotherly love, in honor giving preference to one another; not lagging in diligence, fervent in spirit, serving the Lord; rejoicing in hope, patient in tribulation, continuing steadfastly in prayer; distributing to the needs of the saints, given to hospitality. Bless those who persecute you, bless and do not curse. … Do not set your mind on high things, but associate with the humble.'"

Scott nodded. "That's a great passage."

"One I've been terrible at." Shelby put the Bible back on the coffee table. "You've been right, I've been selfish most of my life. When Chet died, I felt like everything I'd worked for could be stripped away. That insecurity made me worse. You've called me on it. I don't offer Angelina and her friends hospitality. I get annoyed with people like Betsy Lou. And Caitlyn …"

"You don't exactly want to bless her, do you?" Scott tilted his head and gave her a teasing but understanding smile. When Maltie trotted into the room, he held a hand down close to the floor and snapped his fingers.

Shelby ignored her dog licking Scott. "No. I was a mess the whole time you were with her tonight." Shelby couldn't help herself. She leaned forward, and the questions popped out. "What happened? Are you still going on that date with her?"

Apparently put off by Shelby's intensity, Maltie hopped onto Scott's lap and sat looking at her with a smug expression. "No, I am not going on that date with her."

As Shelby released a breath of relief, Angelina jogged down the stairs in Augusta State sweats. "Hi, guys."

"Hi," Scott said.

Shelby frowned, then caught herself and laughed. "Hello, dear sister."

Scott offered an encouraging nod at her response, then continued his explanation as Angelina walked behind the couch. "I moved the stuff she wanted me to move, then when she asked about where we should eat after the Builders' Expo, I explained there was something between you and me, and I needed to back out of my plans with her."

"Speaking of between you …"

To Shelby's dismay, her little sister launched into speed mode, darting around the coffee table and depositing herself on a leg of both Scott and Shelby until they wiggled over to make room for her. She looked between them, then fixed on Scott. "Hi, friend."

He attempted to shift away from her. "I already said 'hi.'"

Angelina draped an arm around Shelby's neck, then Scott's. Shelby got a face full of red curls as Angelina said to him, "So. I hear you kissed my sister tonight."

"I … uh …"

"Angelina!" Shelby wrenched a hand under her sister's arm and pried with all her might. "Get! Out!"

Angelina popped up like a jack-in-the-box. "I just wanted to say … good job. High time. And high five!" She swiveled around and held out a hand to Scott. Mouth in a flat line, he gave it a smack. "Now, I'm going to get my ice cream and watch Netflix in my room. But don't forget I'm here. I could show up at any time."

Shelby swatted her sister's bottom as she passed.

Angelina almost upset the hot chocolate. "Oops." She did a little dance.

"I'm sorry." Shelby shook her head once the troublemaker disappeared into the kitchen and they heard the sound of singing accompanying the squeak of the freezer door.

"Don't apologize. I like her a lot."

"Well, that's a relief, because she could be a deal-breaker." Shelby settled back onto the sofa. "So you were saying, about Caitlyn …"

Scott gave a half laugh. "Well, I'm guessing you're back to doing the stenciling."

"Okay by me. And she won't be setting up shop next to Culpepper's?"

"I dare say not."

They both fell silent as Angelina passed by, digging a spoon into a generous serving of moose tracks. "I promise I won't leave the bowl upstairs this time."

"For tonight, you can, if it means you won't come back through here." Shelby sent her a teasing smile. "And you can ask your friends over too. Friday or Saturday. I'll be decorating for the big reveal. I'll even make lasagna and leave it in the fridge."

Angelina's eyes popped open wide. "You will? Sweet."

After her steps sounded on the floor above, Scott grinned. "Way to apply that Scripture."

"Thanks."

"I always got the feeling the real Shelby was hiding under there. I know I pushed you too hard at times. Man, I really wanted you to notice me."

"Well, I did. But when I started to …" Her voice trailed off. "You're just so different from Chet. It scared me when you brought out things about me that he never did. How I liked things about you that … he didn't have."

When Shelby's chin dropped, Scott shifted, putting Maltie on the other cushion. He slid an arm around Shelby and lowered his voice. "I'm picking up on the fact that life with Chet might not always have been as glamorous as it looked from the outside."

Shelby bit her lip. "The flip side of possessing all that charisma can be tumult. Or silence. Or both. Chet had high expectations … a lot like my dad, come to think of it. Not like you, wanting me to be my true self. Like wanting me to always be more. Perfect. It was exhausting. But don't get me wrong, there was a lot of good too. Laughter, romance, adventure. And I know he loved me very much. Life with him was always exciting."

"Of course, and those are things you can always treasure."

"I will, but it feels disloyal to speak badly of him."

"To speak badly of him, maybe, but you do know it's okay to learn from the past and choose some things differently in the future, right?"

There was that maturity and wisdom again. She could only guess it came from lots of time alone with the Lord. "The fact that I wanted different things in my future felt like a betrayal of my marriage to Chet."

"I can understand that."

Shelby offered a shy smile. "I really admire how you put people ahead of business, ahead of money, ahead of appearances."

"I try." Scott squeezed her shoulder.

"I'm sorry I gave you mixed signals."

"Having been married before, you're coming from a place I've never been. I know you need time, and I can give that to you. Maybe we can just try not to get our wires crossed again?"

Scott's hand sliding up and down her forearm fed a lonely void in Shelby's heart. She'd missed this. And now that she trusted it, she didn't want to ever let it go.

Shelby grabbed his hand and kissed the work-roughened fingers. "I won't cross my wires, because I know what I want now, and I know it's okay to want it. I think I'm falling in love with you, Scott Matthews."

"Shelby Holloway." He got her attention by using her maiden name, even before he leaned his forehead against hers. "I'm already there. I already love you."

Her heart might melt and overflow her chest. Shelby hooked her hand at the back of Scott's neck and pressed her lips against his, letting the kiss make promises she still felt too shy to speak. She ran her fingers over the sandy stubble on his jaw and pushed them into the soft hair at the back of his neck. Everything about him felt different but so right. Close to him, she fit into a place she'd been looking for her whole life.

Chapter Twenty-Three

Shelby worked into the wee hours of the morning on the scheduled reveal day. After a check of every light, she sent Hector off. After Todd helped Scott bring in the island and the dining room table—both finished more beautifully than Shelby had even hoped—she sent Todd off. After Scott brought soup and gourmet sandwiches from the Boll Weevil, she gave him a peck of a kiss and sent him off as well. But Linda Culpepper she kept. For the first time, she had someone who could actually help her decorate.

Shelby returned to her four-square in a state of exhausted excitement. She knew better than to attempt sleep. Instead, she hit the shower, blew her hair dry, and applied fresh make-up. She selected a rust-red, cable-knit sweater dress, accented by a topaz pendant necklace and brown boots. But she paused over her jewelry cabinet. In the light of early morning illuminating the scarlet-tinted oak out her bedroom window, the diamonds of her wedding set winked at her.

Time seemed to stop. Breathe in, breathe out. Choose to embrace the future.

Slinging on her watch with the click of the clasp, Shelby tiptoed to the door. A day like today called for not only a cinnamon latte but a whole grain muffin from Buona's. Drawing her coat tight around her, Shelby headed for her car. Just as she unlocked the door, Scott's black Chevy pull into her driveway.

When Scott jumped out, she stepped forward to greet him. "Is everything okay? I thought you were picking up Lester and Ruby this morning." On the chilly air, her breath formed a little white cloud.

"I am. No worries, we've got time. Man, you look gorgeous. I'm so glad I can say that out loud now." Grinning, Scott slid a hand under her coat and pulled her to him.

A second later, his warm lips covered hers. She relaxed against him and kissed him back. Dressed in slacks, a sweater and dress shirt, and an overcoat, he smelled like aftershave and looked considerably better rested than she imagined she did, despite his compliment. "Well, I'm not complaining, but why are you here?"

"Come sit in the truck a second. It's freezing."

"Okay, but I'm on my way to Buona. Did you want to go with me?"

Just smiling, Scott held open his passenger side door.

When Shelby got in, she realized why. Steam curled from the slitted lids of two coffees waiting in the cup holders, while a paper bag rested on the dash. She reached for it with a squeal. "You *are* too good to be true." She opened the bag to discover not only a muffin but a slice of quiche, still warm. "You brought me breakfast."

Scott slid in behind the steering wheel and shut the door. "I figured we should celebrate a job well done."

"Mm." Shelby agreed as she sipped the rich, foamy cinnamon latte. "Thank you so much."

As the truck heater spewed toasty air into the cab and the radio played a soothing praise song, they dug into the food. After a minute, Scott said, "Mom told me how well things went last night."

"She did? You didn't stop by and look, did you?"

"No, although I was tempted."

"Good, I want you to be surprised right along with Ruby and Lester."

Scott crumpled his bag. "I know you worked your magic."

"Your mom stays so focused. She calms my jitters and gives me new ideas." Shelby opened the lid of her coffee to better savor the flavor.

Scott smiled. "You think you might need an assistant in the future? Because I believe she's up for the job."

"Really? Oh, I'd love that. I'm just not sure how soon I could pay her."

"I don't think you have to worry about that."

Before Shelby could ask what he meant, Scott scooped up her fingers. He stared at the bare fourth digit before looking at her and asking in an amazed, almost fearful, voice, "Shelby?"

She curled her fingers in a protective fist while a fierce blush swept her cheeks. "I thought it was time." Sudden, nauseating fear swirled in dizzying waves, making her question if Scott would consider her decision premature, hasty. If he might feel pressured.

His gentle laugh alleviated her doubt. "Well, I have to admit I'm relieved. I didn't want people to think I was dating a married woman."

She reached over to swat him.

"I've got something else for you. Look in the glove compartment."

Cocking her head, Shelby released the lever on the compartment, then reached for the small, brown paper-wrapped item inside.

"I've had it since the River Market, but your distaste for gifts and bribery kept me from working up the courage to give it to you until now."

"What ..." Shelby opened the bag and pulled out the delicate leather bracelet with the hammered bronze cross she'd admired at the jewelry booth back in September. "You didn't."

"You're right, I didn't. I actually texted Caitlyn that day to pick it up for me, and I paid her later. Even though I didn't tell her, I'm pretty sure she knew it was for you."

Shelby's mouth dropped open. "Maybe that was what amped up her competitive juices."

"Maybe." Scott took the bracelet and put it around her wrist. "Looks good on you. Doesn't exactly take the place of a wedding band, but for now ..." He gave her a shy smile.

"It's a great start. I can't believe you bought it for me way back then." Twisting her arm from side to side, Shelby admired just how perfect the piece of jewelry was for her now—quality, without being pretentious. "Thank you. I love it."

"Let me take you to dinner tonight. Our first proper date."

Shelby nodded. "I'd like that. Now, you'd better get going if you're driving out to the Wentworths' old house—which, by the way, I heard they just sold."

"Perfect timing." Scott closed the distance between them for a kiss.

Shelby almost forgot about the big reveal. Almost.

When he pulled back, she touched her lips, laughing. "You'd really better go."

"Okay." He gave her a mischievous grin. "You getting out of my truck first?"

Shelby shoved him. "Text me when you get back into the city, and I'll meet you out front."

Almost an hour later, Shelby waited on the Heard Avenue sidewalk, shuffling her feet to keep them warm. She and Scott had agreed that the work crew didn't need to be present for the initial walk-through—although they'd planned a little surprise for afterwards. It dawned on her that while one couple entered their twilight years together, the other began a journey ... toward what? If she was honest with herself, she hoped it was a long future together.

When the Chevy pulled up, Lester and Ruby wore blindfolds as prearranged. Shelby hurried to Ruby's door to help her out, while Scott assisted Lester.

Ruby's hand groped for Shelby's arm. "Oh, Shelby, I'm so excited."

"Me too. Miss Ruby, this has been the best house flip I've ever done." Shelby's gaze flitted to Scott's as she realized what she admitted. His eyes lit, and he smiled. "And we want to thank you for letting us do it. You've blessed us in more ways than we could ever have blessed you."

Ruby patted her hand. "Oh, honey, if you and Scott are a couple now like he told us on the way over, it would be worth it even if we didn't get a house."

"Now, wait a minute," Lester protested. "I seem to recall writing some rather large checks."

Shelby laughed. "Well, the good news is, you get both."

"Okay, all this personal stuff is embarrassing me. Are you ready to see your new home?" Scott asked the Wentworths.

"Yes! This bandana makes me feel like I'm being kidnapped," Lester said.

"You can take them off when we count down in …" Shelby met Scott's eyes, and the connection between them pulsed with life, giving her a flash forward of a hundred other such moments. They counted together. "Three, two, one!"

Lester gasped, and Ruby squealed. As she covered her mouth, her husband put his arm around her shoulders. Shelby tried to see it with their eyes. The bungalow's white trim and rust-red muntins and front door popped against the medium-gray paint, offering the welcoming feel of a historic cottage, while the expert gray stonework lent a touch of class to the porch and chimney. A stone-lined walkway cut from the concrete drive through fresh green sod. Under the bracketed eave, silver house numbers broke the white trim above the front porch. White pumpkins and terra cotta planters spilling over with autumn flowers flanked the entrance.

Ruby threw her hands wide. "It's so beautiful! It looks like it needs a B & B sign in the front yard!"

"No!" Lester sounded genuinely alarm. "We'll have more than enough company with family members. Please don't invite anyone else."

Scott and Shelby laughed.

"Can we go in now?" Rubbing her hands together, Ruby glanced at Shelby.

"Of course." Shelby led the couple up the walkway and held open the front door. As she'd come to expect with reveals, Lester and Ruby stopped short on the threshold, frozen in another moment of disbelief. Shelby stepped through so they would follow. She could tell from Ruby's big eyes that the classy ivory-and-gray palate of the living room drew the older woman, so she guided them first toward Lester's den, lest it be forgotten. And she was maybe most proud of it, in an odd way.

"Lester, do you recognize some things in here?"

"Why, yes. This looks like my desk from the restaurant office." As he approached the piece of furniture, he brushed his fingertips across an antique fan, then a photo displayed in front of it. "And here's my old team, the year we won the championship."

"We've got your coach of the year certificate right there." Scott pointed to the wall behind the desk.

Ruby admired the "office" sign next to the certificate along with an old vertical wall filer. Then her gaze skipped over to the collection of photographs and the shadow box menu. "Lester! Look at these."

"Oh my." Lester stopped in front of the grouping. When he ran a surreptitious hand over his face, Scott exchanged a smile with Shelby.

She let the former coach and restaurateur have a moment to reminisce before pointing out that Scott had made the 1920s-style slatted chairs. "And did you realize this is the waiting bench from the restaurant foyer?"

Lester turned around. "So it is. And I like the one rustic shiplap wall. Scott, Shelby, amazing work. Y'all can finish the house tour. I'll just wait in here."

"You certainly will not." Ruby grabbed his hand.

"That's exactly how we wanted you to feel, Lester," Scott said. "Like you have your own space. A space to commemorate your years of hard work and accomplishment."

"Well, I have a feeling if Ruby has anything to say about it, my real 'accomplishment' will frequently be gathered in the living room, in the form of my family."

"Well said." Hands on his hips, Scott nodded.

"Let's go see it." Lester allowed Ruby to lead him across the foyer.

The fire Scott laid the night before and Shelby started that morning provided crackle and cheer to the main family area. Tall lanterns from the antique store topped the built-ins on either side, while the spot above the mantel showcased Angelina's watercolor of the bungalow. Ruby responded to it with a sentimental cry. Caitlyn's neighborhood print and the rustic vintage window frame from Culpepper's accented the main walls. A collection of the blue-and-cream, salt-glazed pottery, accent pillows, small green plants, and blue depression glass in the colonnade separating living from dining space provided pops of color to neutral furniture and rugs.

Shelby had carried the fabrics of the living room into the dining room window seat, which overlooked the side yard through a frame of white sheers. She'd decided to stencil ginkgo leaves above the plate rail. But the focal point of the room remained Scott's long, rustic table, set as it had been in Culpepper's by Linda and highlighted by the black, circular, wrought-iron candelabra. Ruby appeared to lose the ability to speak when she took it in.

While Ruby admired her immaculate kitchen, Lester teared up again over the framed recipes mounted above the eat-in nook. "Now I swore I wasn't going to get emotional, and you go and do stuff like this."

Ruby left off stroking the padded, gray-striped back of the slipper-style island chair to come to her husband's side. "But this is worth getting emotional over. These are the dishes you made me this fall."

Lester nodded. "And Scott made Shelby. And you see? It worked for him just like it worked for me. A woman can't resist a man who can cook."

"Lester, you're a stinker." Shelby laughed as Scott drew her to his side. "I knew you and Miss Ruby were plotting to get us together all along."

Lester didn't hesitate a beat. "Well, of course we were."

"Bless God." Ruby sank down onto the bench, wiping both cheeks. "I'm sorry. I need a minute. This is all too much."

"It's okay, take all the time you need." Shelby gave Scott a nod, prompting him to send a text as she stood over Ruby and rubbed her shoulder.

Lester handed his wife a handkerchief. Patting her face with it, Ruby looked up at Shelby. "I told you we'd redeem this house, didn't I? And look at all that has happened. God's worked restoration in the Barnes family and also brought you and Scott together. See how He brings good out of all things?"

Shelby nodded. "As usual, you're right, Miss Ruby."

"I think we should have a prayer over the house after we finish the tour." Scott slipped his phone in his pocket. "Do you feel ready to check out your master bedroom?"

Ruby agreed and rose. She adored Scott's barn door slider and the matching headboard he'd made along with Shelby's rustic accents, including a collection of old books and a nod to Augusta's past in the form of cotton boll stems gathered in a vase. The silk jacquard Lili Alessandra comforter Shelby had chosen in shades of blue, champagne, and silver retained an elevated sense of elegance in the room.

In the master bath, folded, fluffy white towels waited in an antique crate. A greenish Verdigris pedestal dish vase offered wrapped K. Hall soaps. Robes hung on the back of the door. And the gray dresser vanity and paint on the upper portion of the walls provided a satisfying contrast to white subway tile, beadboard, and Ruby's slipper tub.

Upstairs, Shelby attempted to stall the couple and talk loudly, hoping they wouldn't notice any noise from below. But she could only point out vintage wallpaper accent walls and mini-chandeliers for so long. When they made their way back downstairs, she hoped everyone had made it to their place.

"Let's make some coffee and talk about the equity in your house." Scott held an arm out toward the kitchen, urging the couple in front of him.

Lester's eyes lit up. "For sure—" he began, but he got no further, for as soon as they rounded the corner into the living room, a huge group of people overflowing the kitchen and dining room shouted, "Welcome home!"

Lester and Ruby started laughing with joy as they recognized their children, grandchildren, siblings, and cousins. They hurried forward to embrace the family members. Behind them, Shelby saw Scott's mother beaming with triumph. The spread of breakfast pastries, fruit, and quiche she'd hauled inside while they toured upstairs covered the kitchen island. A tall, muscular man and an attractive brunette stood beside her, holding three-year-old Lexie.

"Come on." Grabbing her hand, Scott pulled Shelby through the crowd. "I want you to meet my brother Austin and his wife, Kaleigh."

When Scott kissed his mother's cheek and thanked her for her efforts, Shelby followed it up with a hug. Linda patted her back. "Good job, Shelby."

"Shelby Holloway!" Austin edged his substantial form past the smaller people chatting around him. "I remember you. You haven't changed a lick since high school."

Kaleigh elbowed him. "Dodson."

"Oh right." Austin looked apologetic and stuck out his beefy hand.

Shelby slipped her palm onto his. "You haven't changed much either, Austin. Nice to meet you, Kaleigh."

"I guess we'll be seeing a lot more of each other, now that you're dating my little brother." Austin paused to elbow Scott in the ribs, causing him to double over. "Congratulations on getting the girl, Scott. Took you long enough."

Scott pushed him. "Go eat a bagel."

"Better yet, I want to see the house," Kaleigh said. When Lexie flexed her fingers toward a donut, her mother patted her hand down and edged away from the food. "Come on, Austin. We've got to get our sugar monster out of here."

As Kaleigh attempted to tug her husband out of the kitchen, Lexie made her desires known. "I wanna stay with Scotty!"

Linda intervened. "Go with your mama right now, Lexie, and let her show you the pretty things in the house. Uncle Scott has something he needs to talk to Shelby about. And I need to serve coffee." So saying, she pulled a folded paper out of her coat pocket and handed it to her younger son, then offered them a smile. "Go. Steal a quick minute alone."

As Linda nodded toward the back porch, Shelby frowned in bemusement but allowed Scott to lead her outside. When he closed the door on the gathering, Shelby could hear the musical tinkle of water from the fountain installed near the pergola. Scott sat on the bottom step and patted the spot next to him. Lowering herself onto the cold concrete, Shelby realized it was the exact spot she'd sat crying three months before, when she'd first met Scott again after a decade apart.

"What's up?"

"Okay." Scott fiddled with the corner of the paper Linda had given him. "I asked Mom to bring this because I've heard you talk about starting your own interior design company. It so happens the store next to Culpepper's remains vacant. This is a copy of the lease agreement Caitlyn, uh, decided not to sign."

Shelby started laughing, then faded into silence as she realized what Scott suggested. She snatched the paper and opened it, staring at the figures spelled out inside. "This … is a really good rate. Too good for that size space. A space that's honestly too big for an office."

"Not just an office, but a storeroom behind, like ours. Enough square footage for you to move your decorating stuff from your storage building. And it's discounted because Culpepper's would be subleasing it to you—at a reduced rate, because your design services would be a branch of our company."

"W-what? You're asking me to go into business with you?" Shelby's hand started shaking. Scott offered her the startup opportunity she'd dreamed of, not only for an office area, but for a shop. A shop with their own brand of rustic elegance. And more amazing, the offer meant he aimed to keep her in his life long-term. That he was so confident in their relationship he wanted her to join his family in a business venture.

"I want to keep flipping houses with you, Shelby, just like you envisioned. Only without the camera crews." Scott gave her a lopsided grin. "And my mom wants to assist you with decorating them. I know this is a lot to ask you, and you don't have to answer right this minute. But I've prayed a lot about this, and I feel peace. To me, the future … it just seems so obvious."

"Together." Shelby felt hot tears spill down her cheeks.

He smiled tenderly. "Yes, together. Are you willing to give it a try?"

She raised a hand to Scott's smooth jaw, suddenly able to see how everything that had gone before had prepared her for this moment. And now, the future that had so recently looked bleak held unspeakable promise. "More than willing."

A second later, Scott's arms around her and his warm lips on hers dissipated the autumn morning chill. Amazed at how secure, how treasured she felt close to him, Shelby snuggled in.

A throat cleared nearby. Shelby pulled away from Scott's embrace to find Betsy Lou standing at the corner of the house, watching them. "There was a lot of noise, so I came over to see what was going on."

"It's finally reveal day, Miss Betsy Lou." Scott spoke with enthusiasm to welcome the older lady, despite having to quickly drop his arms back to his sides. "The first time the Wentworths get to see their new house."

Shelby felt a nudge in her spirit. "Would you like to come inside and meet them?"

"Well." Firming her lips, Betsy Lou pushed her hands into the pockets of her cardigan. "I guess I can do that. But I should bring a gift, maybe some of my snowbank boltonia. It's past time to divide it anyway."

Scott stood, drawing Shelby up with him. He squeezed her waist, letting her know he approved of her friendly gesture. More importantly, the warmth in her spirit confirmed that God did too.

"That would be very neighborly of you, Betsy Lou, but no need to go digging right now. Come join the party."

The kitchen door swung open behind them, and Lester's voice boomed out. "There you are! Sneaking out to spark your girl, huh?"

Shelby glanced around to catch Ruby elbowing her husband. Ruby smiled. "We wondered if you could come back in for that prayer dedicating our house to the Lord. We'd like you to say it, Scott."

"I'd be honored, Ruby."

"Lester, Ruby, this is your neighbor, Betsy Lou Clark." Shelby held out a hand to the elderly woman. "She was just coming to meet you. And I have a feeling you're going to be very good friends."

"Oh wonderful." Ruby pushed the door open wider with a big smile. "I can always use another friend. Please come in."

As Scott helped a tottering, hopeful-looking Betsy Lou up the steps, he turned to smile at Shelby with a look of such love it took her breath away. Thank God for second chances. Hand-in-hand, they joined the others in their fall flip to dedicate all their futures to God.